THE LAST PETAL
Love Me or Else

To my friends,
Manon and Yvon

Sharon Eikishberger
Apr. 2009

Also by Sharon L. Eibisberger

THE WEDDING CHILL

THE LAST PETAL

Love Me or Else

A Suspense Novel

Sharon L. Eibisberger

iUniverse, Inc.
New York   Bloomington

iUniverse books may be ordered through booksellers or by contacting:

iUniverse
1663 Liberty Drive
Bloomington, IN 47403
www.iuniverse.com
1-800-Authors (1-800-288-4677)

Because of the dynamic nature of the Internet, any Web addresses or links
contained in this book may have changed since publication and may no longer be
valid. The views expressed in this work are solely those of the author and do not
necessarily reflect the views of the publisher, and the publisher hereby disclaims
any responsibility for them.

ISBN: 978-1-4401-2653-6 (sc)
ISBN: 978-1-4401-2652-9 (ebook)

Printed in the United States of America

iUniverse rev. date: 02/25/2009

I extend a special thank you to my husband Walter for always saying, "Yes, you can." His encouragement has been an inspiration throughout the writing process of my first novel, THE WEDDING CHILL and its sequel **THE LAST PETAL** - Love Me or Else. I also want to thank my many Canadian and American friends for their help in launching the first book, and for their encouraging me to write the sequel. Last, but certainly not least, a huge and very heart felt thank you to my wonderful daughter Christine. Her invaluable suggestions, guidance, and input in the developing plot and storyline enabled me to intertwine the love story and the ensuing suspense that I hope will delight readers. Thank you Christine [comma] for your patience and for reading and re-reading the early manuscripts.

With all my Love, Affection, and Gratitude

PROLOGUE

E lliot took a seat at the bar and ordered a drink. The headline of the local paper caught his eye. "Search for missing woman continues", it read in large bold letters. He reached over and pulled the paper closer so he could read the story while he waited for his drink. A cold sweat broke out on his forehead as he read. "Amanda Harrison's whereabouts are unknown. Ms. Harrison was last seen on Tuesday evening at Henry's Bar and Billiards where she is the part-time Manageress. Ms. Harrison is described as white, in her mid-twenties, standing 5' 1". She has sandy-blond shoulder length hair, and is of slight build. When last seen she was wearing a pale blue T-shirt with off-white casual slacks and white running shoes. Foul play has not been ruled out. Police are investigating the case. Anyone knowing her whereabouts or with any information about her disappearance is asked to notify the local police authorities."

Elliot folded the paper so the headline and the story on the front page were not visible before he put the paper down. He wiped the sweat off his brow with the back of his hand.

Henry, the owner, returned with Elliot's drink and placed it on the bar in front of him.

"Hey fella—are you okay?"

"Yeah, it's a bit hot in here."

"It's a bit hot everywhere these days," Henry agreed. "We haven't seen you around here for a few days."

"There was an illness in the family and I had to be away for awhile," he lied. He picked up the paper again and pretended to read. He didn't want to get into a conversation with anyone tonight. He lifted the glass to his lips and took a long swallow. The strong drink burned its way down into his belly.

It had been awhile since he'd gotten himself a part-time job and money was running low. Reluctantly, he decided that tomorrow he would seek out another meaningless job to put a few bucks in his pocket. He pulled out the last of his cash to pay Henry. His hand shook and he tried to calm himself as he forked over his last ten-dollar bill. He finished his drink and was thankful he had a full bottle of liquor stashed away at home.

While Henry retrieved his change, Elliot scooped a handful of nuts from the large dish on the bar. He thrust them into his pocket. Scotch and nuts for dinner tonight, he thought to himself. It didn't really matter because he wasn't hungry anyway. When he was on one of his booze binges, food was the last thing on his mind. Food—yeah, he would have to remember to take food along on his next visit. His mind raced as he thought about what he had done.

As he left the bar, he scanned the street and parking lot to see if anyone was watching before he slipped behind the wheel of his old, beat-up car. He fumbled as he tried to get the key into the ignition. It took three tries, but finally the motor roared to life. The car shuttered as Elliot pressed in the clutch and shifted into first gear.

His driving was erratic. He wasn't sure if that was because of the booze or his jangled nerves. Several times he heard the crunch of gravel as the right wheels of his vehicle left the pavement.

He breathed a sigh of relief as he steered the car onto his small driveway. When he removed the key, the motor continued to shake and sputter for a few seconds. "Damn, this old jalopy just can't run on that cheap shit gas. Hell, it's probably laced with f---ing water. The engine gave one final belch and then died.

Outside of town, the neighbours were few and far between. He had been living in his deceased brother's house so rent hadn't been a problem. Paying the property taxes would be another matter, but he would cross that bridge when he got there. Right now, his bottle was waiting.

Before he left Henry's he had tucked the paper under his arm. Now, it lay on the seat beside him. He grabbed it up and opened the car door. A quick glance around assured him there was nobody watching; he opened the trunk and reached in to retrieve his weathered shotgun. "Come on Betsy, it's been a long day," he mumbled.

Once inside he propped his shotgun in the corner behind the front door and headed for the kitchen. When he tossed the paper onto the kitchen table the centre pages slipped to the floor. The front page remained on the table with the headline staring up at him. He ran his trembling fingers through his hair and then rubbed his hands across his eyes wanting to make the front-page story disappear, but it remained as a glaring reminder of the last couple of days. He opened a cupboard door and reached for the bottle.

Chapter ONE

Caroline stood on the porch gazing at the teal blue water through the opening where the path led down to the shore. She stepped off the porch and walked down to the edge of the lake. She removed her shoes and cautiously dipped her toes in the clear water. It was cold, refreshingly cold not painfully cold.

This was Jason and Caroline's first vacation since the birth of their son Michael Jay who would soon turn three. Jason had worked hard to build up his thriving detective agency and getting away for an extended time wasn't easy. Caroline's parents were ecstatic at the idea of having Michael Jay all to themselves for three weeks. Caroline wasn't quite as enthusiastic about leaving their son for such a long period, but the beautiful, serene pictures of little tourist towns, miles of sandy beaches, the sparkle of the sun reflecting off the blues of the water as it tickled the bushy cedars, and tall pine treed shorelines made it impossible to pass up. The promise Jason made of them spending long leisurely hours together, walking hand in hand, fishing, and exploring quaint little towns like Wiarton, Lion's Head and at the northern most point Tobermory soon had her packing. Caroline thought about the stack of brochures she had accumulated on her kitchen table at home. She'd contacted both the Ontario and Quebec Tourist Boards and had been flooded with information about places that all looked perfect. It hadn't been an easy decision, but the pull of the Bruce Peninsula won out.

The real estate agent that rented the cabin to them mentioned an ancient Indian burial ground and the ruins of an old mansion as well as several other sites worth checking out. Caroline was anxious to see as much as possible, but the first few days would be devoted to the three R's…rest, relaxation, and romance.

Out of earshot of Caroline, the agent's assistant informed Jason of an ongoing search underway for a missing woman and suggested he keep his eyes open. "They suspect she may have been taken against her will and the police hadn't yet ruled out foul play. Amanda is a nice young woman; we sure hope nothing's happened to her. The police are checking to see if she has gone off to stay with friends or relatives. There is a domestic conundrum to boot; she and her husband were living apart. In your e-mail, you mentioned that you were a detective. I don't want you to think this has anything to do with that. We are asking everyone to keep their eyes open. Anyway, the police are still investigating," the agent told Jason.

Jason, while dealing with his own detective agency in New York was used to hearing stories such as this. He didn't pay it much heed. Right then he was anxious to obtain the keys to the cabin and get on with their vacation.

The lower, heavier branches moved gently in the early morning breeze. Caroline smiled as she thought to herself that she and Jason would be able to take a swim later in the day. Glancing around she realized that there probably wasn't another living soul for miles. Maybe they would skinny-dip.

It was a dreamy morning. Small foamy waves licked along the shoreline by the dock. Cormorants, seeking a tasty fish breakfast, dove and disappeared for overly long periods of time only to reappear a great distance from where they originally dove under the surface.

Further back from the water's edge loomed large sand dunes dotted by rugged rocks. Each rock seemed to have its own occupant, either a cormorant with wings out stretched to dry itself, or a snowy white seagull. Most gulls had their head tucked behind a wing and appeared to be sleeping soundly after an early morning fishing expedition. Each group of gulls had an alert sentry watching for any sign of danger.

When Caroline left the cabin, Jason was still sleeping peacefully. After spending three hectic years in the midst of the bustle of New York, they dreamed of getting away for a well-deserved vacation. Their good friends Tabitha and Doug Willis had suggested this trip to Canada. Both Caroline and Jason, in their single days, had visited Toronto with its tall skyscrapers, CN Tower, Ontario Place, and all the fabulous boutiques and eateries, but neither of them had ever ventured north of the city to the scenic Bruce Peninsula.

Caroline was looking forward to the quality time she'd spend with Jason. She hadn't fished since she was a young girl when her mom and dad had taken her to Lake Erie. She'd caught her first fish during that trip. She remembered the aroma of the fish cooking over the wood fire. At first, the woods had been spooky. The crackle of leaves and fallen branches in the silence of the woods made her feel uneasy, but with her dad's reassurance she had quickly learned to listen and enjoy the sounds of nature… sounds often unheard by others. Caroline remembered how long the days had been. She and her dad would rise early to go fishing. They would giggle as they tiptoed around trying not to wake her mom. After enjoying thick slices of home baked banana bread, they made their way to the little rowboat. Hours later they'd returned to find Mom relaxing in the sun. After their fish dinner they'd roasted marshmallows. The first few caught fire and became charred, blackened lumps, but soon she caught on and turned out perfectly golden, soft-centered treats for the whole family.

She stood quietly enjoying the early morning warmth of the sun when suddenly a huge Canada goose and its mate came swooping in unceremoniously. They landed with much ado, but settled quickly into a pair of dunking diners as they snacked on the lichen and other plants growing in the shallow water along the shore. She admired their grace and beauty; they accepted her as part of the landscape. She was surprised how swiftly the sun had risen. It resembled a huge yellow balloon as it rose over a small island between her and the distant shore. She thought about going back to the cabin to wake Jason, but decided that after his long drive yesterday she'd let him sleep until he awoke on his own. She plucked a wide blade of grass and stretched it between her two thumbs. Bringing it to her lips, she blew hard. When nothing happened, she laughed. As a child, she could get the blade of grass to give a shrill whistle. She tried again. This time a weak little bleat was heard. Laughing, she said aloud "I think I've still got it." She eased herself down on a nearby rock. Although the sun had only been above the horizon for a short time the rock was already warm.

A loud cracking sound made Caroline jump. She turned quickly expecting to see Jason on the lightly trodden path behind her, but nobody was there. She scanned the woods around her. The little hairs on the back of her neck stood on end and she felt uneasy, almost as though she were being watched. The two geese also startled at the unexpected sound. They stopped feeding and quickly fled into deeper water. Now, all was silent. "Must have been some of your land buddies," she said to the large geese as they returned closer to shore and were now feeding just a few feet in front of her. They certainly didn't appear to be spooked now and she chastised herself for even a moment's angst. She pulled her feet from the water and let them air dry before slipping them into her Dockers. Several other geese joined the first comers and a soft honking between them became a serenade. "Enjoy your buffet," she said to the geese as she stood and stretched. They continued to feed unconcerned by her presence. Caroline started back toward the cabin. Not far from the shore, she spotted a narrower, less travelled path leading off to the north. On her way down to the lake, she hadn't noticed the small opening. It was only while travelling the main path in this direction that the north path entrance was detectable. She looked around in all directions. The feeling of being watched lingered on and she shivered as she hurried past the spot where the path branched off in another direction.

Chapter
TWO

"Sure Henry, see you tomorrow," Amanda said to the owner of Henry's Bar and Billiards. This was one of her nights to manage the place and close up at 11:00 o'clock. Sundays were usually quiet.

Two men sat at the table in the corner beside the old-fashioned jukebox. One of them fed money into the machine. He continued to play the same song *"Just between an old memory and me."* "Hey Sweetheart," he called over to Amanda. "Bring us a couple more beers." Neither man was from around these parts, but she had seen them in the bar before tonight. One had a wrinkled photograph tucked into the band of his western style hat.

She waited as the two steins of beer filled, settled, and filled some more until their frothy heads of foam stood tall and inviting. She lifted the heavy glasses onto the round tray and with an easy jerk, lifted it to rest against her shoulder. She placed two new coasters in front of the men and grabbed up the two coasters that were now wet from condensation from their previous beers.

"There you go boys, nice and cold. Are you new around here?" She asked being friendly. They were good tippers.

"We'll be around for a couple of months. We're part of the building crew putting up the new place out on the highway."

"Yeah, that's coming along nicely. I read it's going to be a drug store or a grocery store," Amanda said keeping up the chitchat as she placed the two heavy steins on the new coasters.

One of the men pulled out a twenty from a fairly good-sized wad of bills. "I'll get this round," he said to his companion.

"Right on both counts," the other man said to Amanda. "It's going to be a super store—groceries, drugs—you name it, and they'll have it. It will turn this town on its ear. Competitions good though," he assured her. "You'll see!"

The man fingered the photograph in his hatband.

"Nice picture," Amanda commented.

Quicker than a flash he pulled the photo from behind the band and thrust it towards her. "This is my wife and kids," he beamed. "Louise, that's my wife," he said pointing out the only woman in the picture. "This is Anthony, we call him Tony, he's seven and smart as a whip; then there's Frankie, he's four and this little lady is Rebecca, she'll be two in August." There was a far-off look in his eyes. "Boy do I miss them."

"I'll bet you do," Amanda said. "You've got yourself a beautiful family; it must be hard to be away from them for so long." The other man, the younger of the two, picked up his change from the twenty and left a generous tip on her tray.

"Thank you," Amanda said sincerely. "Did you have to leave your family as well?"

"Nope, I'm a loner. Only have myself to worry about and generally speaking I don't usually give myself any grief," he laughed a pleasant laugh. "You single?" He asked. "Maybe I can buy you a burger sometime."

"Thanks for the offer, but I'm afraid I'm a married lady," she responded with a smile. She held up her left hand and pointed at her ring finger.

"Sorry," he apologized as he looked at her hand. "I didn't notice the ring on your finger. My buddy is right; it does get lonely when we are on a job for so long."

"No problem," she replied. She returned to the bar and started to tidy up the counter. Henry wasn't the neatest man and each time she reported for work he'd apologize for the mess. Amanda didn't mind cleaning up, especially on Sunday when it was so quiet. It gave her something to do. The bell over the door announced the arrival of a few more patrons.

"Hi Amanda," they called out in unison.

"Hi guys! George, tell your wife I got that recipe I asked for, but haven't had a chance to try it out yet. What can I get you guys?"

"How about a beer for me and Pete and a rum and coke for Gary." They nodded their agreement as they took a seat at the bar. Conversation was easy, often including Amanda as she got their drinks.

While she waited for the steins of beer to settle she mixed up the run and coke and slipped a small wedge of lemon into the glass. She placed it in front of Gary. "Just the way you like it."

When their beer arrived, Pete asked, "Anyone feel like a game?"

"Sure, if you want to lose your shirt," George joked.

"Amanda, can you rack us up some balls?"

"Sure thing Pete." She reached under the corner cabinet where the pool balls were stored.

The three men picked up their drinks and headed over to one of the large pool tables at the far end of the bar.

"Hey you three, keep those drinks off the pool table or Henry will have *your* balls to play with if he finds rings on his new tables," she scolded them light heartedly.

"We've already been read the riot act by the boss himself; you can bet your bottom dollar the first rings won't come from us," Gary confirmed giving Amanda a salute while clicking his heels together.

Amanda racked up the balls and delivered another unnecessary warning. "Remember I don't want to see any money on the table either."

"*Yes Mommy,*" George intoned mockingly.

The two construction men ordered yet another round. This time Amanda brought over a large order of fries and two forks with the two steins of beer. When they protested, she smiled and said, "These are on the house."

Henry often did this and encouraged her to do the same. He claimed it was a goodwill gesture. "They'll return and more than pay for a few potatoes," he'd say.

"Thanks pretty lady," the single one said.

"You know, she's right; I can feel the beer. Maybe we should order something to eat," the married one said.

"My name is Amanda. Can I get you something else?"

"How about two bacon and cheese burgers and two orders of onion rings." He turned to the younger man, "Okay with you?"

"Yeah, I guess we'll need lots of strength to walk all the way back to the motel again." He looked up at Amanda. Too bad she was married; she was quite a looker and that loose fitting waitress outfit wasn't disguising her cute little figure.

She caught him staring and he blushed. "Sorry again, but no harm in looking is there? You're very pretty." He blushed again.

"Good for you two," she complimented them ignoring the compliment paid to her. "Beer and gasoline don't mix; you'll want to get back home to that beautiful family in one piece."

Mr. Family man nodded and gave her a smile.

"Burgers and rings will be right out." She tucked her order pad back into her pocket and headed for the little kitchen out back.

They watched her walk away, especially the single one. "Damn, why are all the good ones taken?"

When she returned from the kitchen with their order there was another man sitting at the bar.

"Sorry, I didn't hear you come in."

"How's my girl tonight?" He asked.

Caroline ignored his comment. "I'll be with you in just a minute."

"No rush honey, I'm not going anywhere."

He would often come in for a drink or several drinks. She didn't much like the way he looked at her; it made her feel uncomfortable.

Usually he drank a lot, played a couple of games of pool, drank some more and then left. He was always alone, but more often than not, he found someone willing to have a game or two of pool. One of the locals told her his name was Elliot and that he lived somewhere outside of town. He kept his cards close to his chest. He was a big guy; not bad looking, but hardly ever sober enough to be anyone you'd want to get to know better. As many times as she told him her name was Amanda and pointed out her nametag he still insisted on calling her *his girl*. At first, it was annoying and then she finally resigned herself to the fact that she didn't care one way or another as long as he paid up before leaving. He flirted with her; she continued to ignore him. On a few occasions when he'd come in sober they had actually had a conversation. Well, she'd had a conversation. He hadn't told her much about himself, just that he worked odd jobs and lived somewhere outside of town.

If anyone had told her he might be the last person she would ever see on this earth—she would have said they were crazy.

Chapter THREE

Caroline filled the little kettle and placed it on the stove; she took down two clear glass mugs and a stout little teapot. The whistle had just started to sing as Jason poked his head out of the bedroom door.

"What time is it? Why didn't you wake me?" He said groggily.

"Good morning handsome; how'd you sleep?"

"Great. I didn't even hear you get up; have you been up long?" Jason ran his fingers through his tousled hair.

"I've been up about two hours. I've already been down to the shore. It's going to be a wonderful day. We can go for a swim later. I also met a few friends!"

"Friends?"

"Yeah! Some fine feathered friends. There were a couple of Canada geese down there. They accepted me and seemed to have no fear. I wish I'd had some bread with me, or something to feed them."

"It's better to just enjoy their beauty; they know how to feed themselves."

"I guess you're right," Caroline said with a shrug. "How about some eggs and Canadian bacon?"

"How about a hot passionate kiss and about two weeks under the covers…just you and me?" He countered as he wrapped his arms around her.

"So what did you have planned for week three?"

Caroline snuggled into his chest as he held her close. Since Michael Jay's birth, they hadn't had enough time to devote to each other. Their passion was strong and they planned to make the most of it during this vacation. Caroline drank in the scent of his warm skin. When she was in Jason's arms, everything was right with the world. She wrapped her arms around his waist and enjoyed the warmth that surrounded her. She felt his hand move gently through her hair. Her hair was quite long now. At home, she usually wore it severely pulled back and secured in a low pony, or twisted into an up do of some sort. This morning she let it fall softly down her back. She knew Jason preferred it loose, but being a homemaker, mother, and part-time worker didn't call for soft and flowing it called for neat and contained.

Jason let his fingers slide gently through her long, wavy hair. He smelled the faint apple blossom shampoo Caroline used. Slowly he released his hold on her. As he moved back, she lifted her chin to look into his eyes. "You are more beautiful than ever," he whispered. "I have been waiting for this vacation for so long. Just the two of us—here together." He lowered his head and softly caressed her lips. Gently he trailed tiny kisses along her lower lip and then traced a line of kisses down her throat. He raised his eyes to study her face. She had closed her eyes and tilted her head back. "Can we postpone breakfast?" He murmured into her breast.

"Breakfast; who mentioned breakfast?"

Jason found the bottom of the light track top that Caroline had pulled on before leaving the cabin earlier that morning. Slowly he worked it up over her head, and slid it down her arms. Jason felt the heat rise from within as Caroline places kisses across his body. He had to remind himself to take his time; he wanted her to be as satisfied as he knew he would be. With very little effort, he swept her into his arms and carried her to their bedroom.

Caroline ran her hands down his bare chest until she came to the waistband of his PJ bottoms. She slipped her hands inside and ran them slowly over his skin. She felt him release the clasp on the back of her lacy bra.

Jason lowered the straps from her shoulders. His eyes were transfixed on the soft swell of her full breasts under the lacy fabric. Slowly he removed the lace from her breasts and exposed their soft nipples. His fingers caressed each dark lobe and watched as they responded and came to attention. He was surprised when he realized that Caroline had somehow managed to remove his PJs. He must have helped or at least cooperated, but he didn't remember doing either. He was concentrating on what he was doing to her, how his touch was bringing her body alive.

Their bodies responded as each took care to see that the other was brought to exalting peaks of passion and gently back down to again rise and soar gloriously higher and higher.

Exhausted, and cradled in each other's arms they drifted off to sleep.

Jason's eyes fluttered open to greet the sun shining through the bedroom window. The curtains moved gently in the breeze. His stomach growled and he remembered that they hadn't eaten yet. Caroline lay nestled in the crook of his arm. She looked like an angel. Her steady breathing raised and lowered the thin sheet draped over her breasts. He studied her face for a long while. She was everything to him; his love couldn't be more complete. As he gazed at her, a small smile lifted the corners of her lips.

Without opening her eyes she quietly asked, "Think we should have breakfast now?"

Jason gave her a playful pat on the butt and in a deep, masterful voice demanded, "Eggs...wench! Eggs, toast, and lots of Canadian bacon. I'll be in charge of pouring orange juice, setting the table, and...," he hesitated, "I was going to offer to help you with the eggs, but on second thought we both know what a mess that could become." He threw back the light sheet and blanket and lowered his feet to the floor.

Caroline pulled the covers up around her and lounged comfortably in the roomy bed. "Perhaps I should be demanding breakfast in bed."

"Now we're really talking about a disaster about to happen. You can shower first if you want," Jason said after they agreed she should cook breakfast.

"I already miss Michael Jay," Caroline whined as she got out of bed.

"Me too! I'll bet Nana and Papa aren't missing us one bit though; they will have a great time. We'll probably have to get a court order to get our son back from them."

"I'm sure, and the way he loves them I'll probably have to forcefully tear him from Nana's arms."

They both laughed knowing what they said was not far from the truth. They considered themselves lucky to have such a loving family.

"What would you like to do after breakfast?" Jason asked.

"It's still a little early for a swim, but we could take the little rowboat along the shore and just enjoy the scenery, or maybe hike along one of the trails!"

"Rowboat it is! As I recall you bragged about being a pretty good oarsman, or oarswoman," he corrected.

"Oh no I didn't! I'll leave the rowing to you; I tend to go in circles." She did a dizzying turn around the bedroom. "I do know how to make perfect eggs though so I'll stick to what I know and leave the driving or in this case the rowing to you." She breezed by him on her way to the shower. Soon she emerged looking fresh and smelling wonderful. "Don't be long. Breakfast will be ready soon," she said passing him on her way to the well-equipped kitchen.

When Jason stepped out of the shower, he could already smell bacon cooking. He listened as Caroline belted out her renditions of *"He's my man"*. He smiled as he rubbed the oversized bath towel over his body, pulled on a Tee, and stepped into khaki shorts. This would be a day to remember.

Chapter
FOUR

"**L**ook—over there!" Caroline whispered excitedly pointing toward a long legged heron wadding leisurely along the shore. It stood almost motionless until it spied a delicious morsel and *bang* it struck with lightning speed to capture its prey. "It makes you realize that in a fraction of a second everything could change—turn around—take off in an unexpected direction. Life certainly is anything but predictable."

Jason laughed at her when she tried to explain things from the little prey's point of view. "You know what they say, "*every cloud has a silver lining*". God often lets things happen that are far beyond our understanding; sometimes we just have to trust he knows best," Jason said.

Tiny ripples of water followed the little boat as they continued to explore the shoreline. The surface of the lake was now virtually motionless, like a huge mirror. The oars dipped silently, in and out of the still water. They watched birds feeding, diving, and bathing themselves. Jason steered the little boat through a narrow channel that took them behind a small island near shore. Cautiously Jason eased the boat close to a beaver dam.

"Do you think beavers still live in here?" Caroline asked.

"Probably…it has the appearance of being well kept."

"Let's wait awhile; maybe we'll get a glimpse of one."

Jason tucked the oars inside the boat and they waited patiently and silently.

"Is that a beaver?" Caroline questioned pointing into the water some distance away from them.

"It could be."

As the animal approached, it became evident that this was Mr. Beaver bringing home building material. From an underwater entrance, Mrs. Beaver popped her head above the water. She accepted the large stick from her mate and proceeded to make home improvements by strategically placing it, with some effort, in the perfect designer spot. Within minutes, two more little heads broke the water's surface.

"Look Jason… they have twins."

"I wish Michael Jay could see them," Jason said as he snapped several pictures of the beaver family. Father continued to bring small logs and sticks and Mother carefully arranged them as she saw fit. The twins played and pretty much just got in the way. As silly as it sounded it made Caroline miss Michael Jay even more.

Turning the boat around, Jason manoeuvred the tiny craft back to their landing dock. He held out his hand as Caroline unbuckled the lightweight life vest. Jason's long legs allowed him to step up easily onto the dock. They both swam like fish, but Jason had insisted they wear their life jackets. There was a large storage locker on the dock to protect life jackets and other dock items from the elements. Jason placed both jackets into the box and allowed the lid to fall back in place. They both heard the bang from the locker closing and almost simultaneously, what sounded like a second unexplained bang.

"What was that?" Caroline asked.

"I'm not sure; it was probably an echo of the locker lid slamming. You know the water makes things sound different."

"That wasn't the lid banging that I heard." She was sure she had heard a second bang, a different bang almost simultaneously to the closing of the lid. "Jason, it sounded like it came more from over there," Caroline said pointing to the west.

"I'm sure it was nothing more than an echo. We're just not used to the quiet around here. The water magnifies sounds. I didn't realize how heavy the lid was and I probably let it fall sort of hard," he added as an afterthought.

"Yeah sure." For the second time in one day, the hair on the back of Caroline's neck stood on end.

The air had suddenly become silent. The birds stopped singing and unbeknownst to each other, both Jason and Caroline experienced an uneasy feeling as they surveyed their surroundings. Nothing appeared out of the ordinary although everything remained eerily silent.

Returning to the edge of the dock, Jason said, "Toss me the bowline." He securely tied the line to the cleat on the dock. He noticed that Caroline had already stowed the two oars along the inside gunwales. They worked well as a team. "Give me your hand." Carefully Caroline stepped from the seat to the side of the boat and took a giant step up to the dock. Jason pulled her into his arms and held her close to him. "You smell soooo good honey," he drawled as he buried his nose in her hair. Caroline didn't answer; she just snuggled close to him. He kissed her on the forehead. "Let's go whip up some lunch and then we can go exploring, or do whatever you want to do."

As they walked the path back up to the cabin Caroline pointed out the lesser trodden path to the north. Jason agreed you would have to have been quite observant to detect its opening, but beyond the fallen debris blocking the entrance you could discern that it had indeed been used.

"Maybe later we'll see where that path takes us," Caroline said.

"Sure, what ever you decide you want to do."

They continued toward the cabin.

Jason held back a protruding branch on the main path until Caroline passed by safely.

The sun was directly overhead now and the temperature had risen considerably since Caroline's walk down to the shore earlier that morning. She was glad for the shade the lush cedars and pines provided.

As they approached, Jason got his first good daytime look at the rustic log cabin that was to be their home for the next three weeks. A wide porch ran around three sides. Several comfortably padded chairs had been strategically placed. A large glass topped wicker table and four matching chairs sat outside the double doors off the kitchen. A futon, covered with a sturdy floral fabric stood against one wall and two brightly coloured rocking chairs sat on either side of a tile-topped coffee table. Two steps led up to the porch. Each step was flanked by large ceramic pots, home to decorative spiral cedars. They appeared out of place in the wildness of the ambient foliage. The surrounding area was polka-dotted by a large variety of wildflowers.

Jason waited for Caroline to catch up; she had slowed her ascent due to the heat. "Come on slowpoke," he teased. "Hey, don't you agree that this is a neat cabin?"

"I agree. I had a chance to look around while your sleepyhead was still in bed this morning. Did you notice the nice BBQ?"

"You bet…I checked it out while you were making breakfast. You'll be happy to hear that it has a rotisserie and it was left surprisingly clean."

"Good," said Caroline. "I'll plan a few meals on the grill. I saw some delicious looking steaks and chops when we shopped yesterday. I'm surprised how well equipped the kitchen is. I can't wait to do some real cooking for us."

"What do you mean *real* cooking?" Jason quizzed. "You always cook great things."

"You know something more lavish than the twenty minute meal. With my part-time job and our active son I usually look for nutritious and quick, but I'm looking forward to doing something a little special; maybe I'll try some new recipes."

Jason nodded, but she realized he probably wasn't paying attention to what she was saying.

"What...yeah, we'll go into town and do a more thorough shopping tomorrow or..." Again, his mind drifted away.

"I'll make us a couple of sandwiches," Jason offered. "See if you can find some small plates. Did you buy pickles?"

"Yeah, I got those kosher garlic spears you like." She opened several cupboards trying to locate the sandwich plates. Finally locating the plates, she said, "If this was my kitchen the first thing I'd do is rearrange all the stuff in the cupboards." She loaded a tray with glasses, napkins, and a small dish of dill pickle spears. "I'll mix up a pitcher of lemonade. Let's take our lunch out to the porch." She grabbed a damp cloth to wipe off the outdoor table.

"Sounds like a plan. I'll get the tray if you carry the lemonade." Jason placed the two sandwich plates on the tray and handed Caroline the large pitcher of lemonade.

Caroline gripped the lemonade pitcher and pushed open the screen door. There was a noticeable rise in temperature as they left the coolness of the cabin. "It's going to be a scorcher," Caroline commented as she quickly wiped the table.

When they finished eating, they took their lemonade and sat on the two rocking chairs. They sipped, rocked, and talked. "It's nice to be able to enjoy some adult conversations without the tug of little hands always wanting some urgent question answered, or something higher than three feet retrieved." Caroline said.

Jason stretched out his long legs.

Minutes later, Caroline giggled.

"What's so funny?"

"Don't move your feet, but check out your little buddy."

Jason glanced down and was surprised to see a small field mouse curiously playing with one of his shoelaces. Instinctly he drew his foot in and the little mouse flew across the porch and hid under Caroline's chair.

Caroline laughed aloud and again the little mouse took off. It scurried along the back wall to hide beneath the futon.

"Most women would be screaming and jumping up on a chair, but you're actually enjoying our little visitor."

"I think he's beautiful; he's just a part of country life. Moreover, he'll stay beautiful just as long as he stays outside. Did you see those big round ears?"

"He took off so fast all I caught was a glimpse of his tail," Jason chuckled.

Caroline closed her eyes. Within minutes, she had drifted off.

Jason's eyes wandered to the futon and then back to Caroline. He wondered if he should wake her. Her head was resting against the back of the rocker. She appeared to be quite comfortable, so he decided to leave her as she was. Her cheeks were pink from the sun reflecting off the water during their boat ride. She looked so beautiful—so relaxed. He walked to the stairs at the other side of the porch. All was peaceful and quiet in the surrounding forest. These were the memories that he would place in the wine cellar of his mind to be uncorked later. The only sound came from the birds flitting from bough to bough carrying their song amongst the pines. He stepped down from the porch and strolled towards the dock. His plan was to sit awhile, maybe dangle his feet in the water. He thought about grabbing a fishing pole, but decided against that idea. He knew Caroline was looking forward to going fishing with him. A smile crossed his lips as he pondered whether she would be squeamish about baiting her own hook. He'd purchased bait at the last gas station when they had tanked up. The attendant had carefully placed the big fat worms in a large can of earth and sphagnum moss. The fishing rods hadn't been unpacked, but the can of worms had been placed under a corner of the porch where it was cooler.

"From New York eh?" The attendant had asked.

"Yeah, just here for a little R & R."

"Planning on going fishing eh?"

Jason smiled and nodded his head. He was tempted to say "No, the little lady's going to cook us up a mess of fried worms," but on reflection, he kept his mouth shut. He filled the tank and made a mental note to convert Canadian litres to US gallons. He picked up a newspaper and paid the attendant. When he returned to the car, Caroline had the little map to the cabin out.

Dusk had settled in by the time they arrived and the distant sound of a loon welcomed them as they unloaded the back of the car.

The worms were safe in their shaded spot, and the fishing could wait. When he reached the obscure path leading north, he turned that way; he thought he'd go a short distance. He stepped over a fallen tree limb and pulled aside other low spreading boughs before actually reaching the path itself. The description *path* was almost a joke. He stepped over and ducked under obstacles as the path wound back and forth. He travelled further than planned. The trees were sparser here and in the distance, he could see cliffs dropping down into what looked to be a clearing, possibly a field or lake. It would be fun to discover what it was later with Caroline. He turned and started back. Just then, he heard a loud backfire, like that from a car in New York traffic. The woods were suddenly silent. He would have liked to think that the loud crack was a falling tree somewhere up ahead, but...! He stood quietly listening for a moment. Hearing nothing more he turned back toward the main path. A few paces back along the untidy path a small bird fluttered from beneath a thorny bush and something bright caught his eye. He pushed aside some of the lower branches and was surprised by what he uncovered. Lying on the ground was a large butcher knife. The dried blood on both the sharp looking blade and handle made him suck in his breath. His training as a private detective told him not to disturb it in any way. He'd have to return with a plastic bag later. There were no signs of anyone having been there recently. The knife was well protected by the heavy branches and could easily have been there for some time, or at least that's what he told himself. On his return walk to the cabin, he tried to explain away the knife as a hunter's, or an illegal poacher's careless loss, but even he was having trouble swallowing that. He decided not to mention it to Caroline; in fact, he decided not to mention that he had even ventured onto the path. When he approached the porch, Caroline met him at the top of the steps.

"Did you hear that bang? What was that? It woke me—where were you?"

Jason hesitated for a moment. "It was probably just a tree biting the dust, or a distant backfire." More cautiously, he added, "It might even be some local hunter." She gave him a sideways glance, but asked no more questions. She turned and went inside; he followed. He was almost certain there wasn't a hunting season during the summer, but it sounded an awful lot like a gunshot.

The afternoon passed quickly. "It's too early to start dinner, but we could go down to the lake for a swim," Jason suggested.

"Okay, your suit is in the bottom drawer of the bedroom dresser. I'll get the towels from the bathroom cupboard, and then I'll change." As she passed him, she planted a quick kiss on his cheek. "Jason," she called out, "grab the sun lotion off the dresser on your way out. The worst of the afternoon sun has passed, but we city slickers don't need a burn on our first day."

Jason stripped down and pulled on his swim shorts. He thought about the knife in the woods. There didn't appear to be any blood on the ground and the blood on the blade and handle was dried… and in all probability old. He wished he could have examined it more closely. Maybe it was from a poacher who killed an out-of-season deer somewhere far away and just ditched the knife before coming out into the open. When he got the chance, he would return, bag the knife, and give it to the authorities in town. He would have to find a way of retrieving it without Caroline's knowledge. There was no reason to worry her about what would surely turn out to be nothing.

Chapter
FIVE

Jason plunged in headfirst. The water was deep and clear alongside the dock. He stayed underwater for a long time. Finally, he surfaced and called for Caroline to join him. "The water's fine," he sang out shaking the water from his ears.

"Don't you dare," she shrieked as Jason cupped his hands to scoop water to splash her. Caroline took the inch-by-inch approach to getting wet and it drove Jason crazy. Gradually she got deeper into the water; she took a deep breath and submerged her body. "Wow, this is wonderful," she exclaimed as her head broke above the surface. She noticed that Jason had already moved a fair distance from shore; she kicked off to join him. Effortlessly, she swam toward him while he treaded water waiting for her.

From the corner of his eye, Jason thought he saw something move onshore. It was a dark shadow behind some bushes only a few feet back from the waterline. It was just a split second glimpse, but it left him with an unsettled feeling he couldn't explain. He wasn't sure what he had seen. His eyes darted back to Caroline as she quickly closed the gap between them.

They swam together a good piece from shore, dunking each other, laughing, and sharing kisses.

"Bet I can beat you back to shore!" Caroline called over her shoulder already giving herself a good healthy head start.

"You're on." Jason dug deep into the water. He poured on the speed and soon caught up. As he swam past her, she grabbed at his ankles. She didn't get a good hold and he easily escaped her grasp. "I'll have dinner ready before you reach shore," he teased.

Caroline laughed and wound up swallowing a big gulp of lake water. She sputtered and called after him—"I think I swallowed a fish."

"Well… then you won't need dinner," he yelled over his shoulder just as he reached water shallow enough to stand up in and wade to shore. Jason picked up one of the big towels and vigorously dried himself.

She was only slightly out of breath when she reached the shore moments after him. "Hand me the other towel Honey."

Jason picked up the other towel and tossed it to her.

Caroline dried her face and wrapped the towel around her body.

"Here, let me help," Jason said as he approached her. Gently he rubbed the towel up and down over her arms, shoulders, and back. He bent and gave her a long intimate kiss. Her skin felt cool from the water, but her kiss ignited a fire within him. He thought how wonderful it was for an old married man to be so very much in love. He and Caroline had discussed the idea of perhaps returning home with a very special souvenir of their vacation in Canada. Their pregnancy and birth with Michael Jay had been an easy one. He remembered how he would tell Caroline that his feet were swollen just like hers; she'd laugh and tell him his head was swollen and then they'd both laugh.

"Let's go up and have a drink before dinner," Jason suggested. "After dinner maybe we'll bring a glass of wine down here to the dock and watch the sunset." There wasn't a cloud in the sky and a spectacular sunset was a certainty.

"Do you plan to get me drunk and take advantage of me?" she coyly asked.

"Oh good—you've done this before."

Caroline picked up the bright orange pool-noodle that she had brought down to the dock and gave him a whack before tossing it into the life jacket locker.

As they headed up the main path, Jason scanned the woods; all was as it should be although he couldn't shake the feeling that they were being watched.

"Give me your swimsuit and I'll hang it out to dry," Jason said as he gathered his own suit and the two wet towels. He glanced through the bathroom door and caught sight of Caroline daintily stepping out of her clinging one-piece suit. Earlier she had shown him a new string bikini that she had bought; he couldn't wait to see her in the tiny suit. Her body was well toned and beautifully proportioned. You would have never guessed that she had given birth to a bouncing nine-pound boy. After the birth, she had struggled with a few lingering post pregnancy pounds, but time and endurance had paid off. His heart warmed when he remembered the times he would watch her lying on her back on the living room floor lifting their cooing and sometimes drooling son high over her body. *"He put it on me,"* she'd say, *"now he's helping to take it off."* By the time Michael Jay had cut his first tooth Caroline was looking hot. Now, she was looking better than ever.

Caroline blushed demurely when she caught Jason staring from the bathroom door. "Okay Tom, hang up the suits they're dripping all over the floor," Caroline whispered in a husky voice.

"Tom—who's Tom?"

"Peeping Tom," she said with a little laugh as she tossed her wet suit towards him and gave the door a gently shove.

Last night she had heard him say something about a raccoon and the garbage, but she was already too close to sleep to answer. Tonight would be different!

After pulling on a pair of Capri's and a print top Caroline entered the kitchen. She watched Jason through the window as he hung the swimsuits and towels on the line stretched beneath two gnarly old apple trees.

Jason stepped inside and let the screen door close behind him with a bang. "What can I do? Assign me a task; I will obey," he said as he bowed low in her direction removing an imaginary hat and sweeping it before him like a gallant knight.

"I thought you'd never ask!"

"Well, you know I'm more than willing and able."

She knew he wasn't referring to the task at hand. Taking Jason by the shoulders, she turned him around, opened the screen door, and gently guided him toward the porch. "Your job gallant Sir is to test out that futon. I'm in charge of dinner and with an unfamiliar kitchen I sure don't need you under foot." She gave him a pat on the back and gently guided him in the direction of the porch futon. "Besides, you'd better rest while you can. You might need your strength later."

"Yes my dear. Let me know if you need help; I excel at can and jar opening."

"There won't be any cans or jars involved in this meal," she assured him.

Caroline removed the beef from the fridge along with the other ingredients she needed for her delicious beef stroganoff. Mounted on the back of the kitchen counter was an array of kitchen knives on a magnetic bar. It held everything from a large, very dangerous looking meat cleaver to a tiny paring knife decreasing in size from left to right. Caroline passed over the cleaver. She selected the large butcher knife to cut thin slices of beef for her dish. After several cuts, she rated the knife as just too large to handle. The next size down was missing so she tried the next in line. It was perfect and soon she had skillfully sliced the beef into perfectly proportioned strips of red meat. Progressing down the line, she found just the right size knife to do each job. Soon onions, peppers, and mushrooms, all chopped, sliced, and diced awaited their turn to join the beef strips. When she was ready to start cooking, she had used almost every knife, except a mid-sized one that she deemed either too large or too small and the dangerous looking meat cleaver. While the meat browned, she went to the door to see if Jason wanted anything. She smiled as she watched his chest rise and fall in a peaceful sleep. The futon must have been very comfortable. Between the two of them, there had been a few short catnaps throughout the day attesting to the fact that this vacation was long overdue.

It wasn't long before everything was simmering gently and giving off wonderful aromas. Caroline rummaged through a small duffle bag and found a Taste of Home magazine she had been saving for just such an occasion. She took her magazine out to the porch being extra careful to close the screen door quietly so it wouldn't bang and wake Jason. He had changed position, but the serene look on his face was still evident. Caroline took a seat on one of the large padded chairs and leafed through her magazine. Page after page delicious recipes presented themselves. Maybe she'd try them all during their stay. Jason's rhythmic breathing had changed to light snores. Caroline was glad he was getting some well-deserved rest. After reading awhile, she placed her magazine face down on one of the little tiled tables and went to check on her dinner preparations.

"Just in time," she called out when she saw Jason stand and stretch. "Dinner will be ready in about five minutes."

"Everything smells great. Can I set the table, or do anything to help?"

"I've chosen a nice Merlot to go with dinner. You can open it and let it breath." She gestured toward the tall bottle of red wine on the counter. "I've already set the table; we'll eat outside—okay?"

"Sure, that's a good idea. Sorry I wasn't any help." He examined the wine label.

There was no dead air time during dinner. They laughed, chatted, and reminisced. They talked about their best friends back in Dallas—Doug and Tabitha Willis and their beautiful little daughter Caroline-Jay. Caroline and Jason felt honoured when they were asked to be her Godparents. She was not only beautiful, but she was extremely bright for her age. They talked about how the investigation to clear Doug of a murder charge on his wedding day had brought them to the realization of their true feelings for each other. A time of turmoil for their friends that was thankfully behind them now.

"I can't eat another bite," Jason said as he pushed his chair away from the table. "That was delicious."

"I should have told you to save room for dessert."

"Are you serious; I just couldn't?"

Caroline laughed at the pained expression on his face. "Don't worry… it will keep."

One thing the cabin didn't have was a dishwasher, but with the two of them working together it didn't take long before the kitchen was shipshape with the dishes washed and stacked in the drying rack.

"You didn't touch your wine," Jason said as he picked up the dishtowel and began to dry.

"You can have it; I think I'll have a soft drink. A Sprite with lemon in a nice tall glass would be nice. The sunset won't wait for us much longer. Let the dishes air dry."

"Sounds like a much better idea to me." He was glad to leave the sizeable stack of dishes and pots to dry on their own.

"I'll carry our drinks if you bring the two folding chairs," Caroline said.

"By the time we reach the shore our glasses will be empty," Jason teased.

"I thought about that… I'll cover them with Saran wrap, they'll be okay."

As they left the cabin, they again experienced the heat of the day. Once the sun dropped below the horizon it would cool down quite a bit but right now it was damn hot.

The sunset was not a disappointment. The entire sky glowed a flaming orange/red. If you had viewed a painting with such vivid hues you would probably have declared it *un-natural*. Before the sun disappeared, Jason started a small bonfire down on the beach. As darkness crept over them, they moved their chairs from the dock and sat down on the beach beside the fire.

"Jason, before you get too comfortable and it gets too dark, would you mind going up to the cabin to get us a flashlight? I meant to bring it down, but I had my hands full with our drinks. It's on that little shelf by the front door."

"Sure, I'll pour myself another glass of wine. Is there anything I can bring you?"

"Yeah, there's a bag of marshmallows in one of the upper cupboards…if you're not too full from dinner. It's been ages since I roasted the perfect marshmallow."

Jason thought he'd listened to exactly where Caroline told him the flashlight was, but still it took him longer than expected to locate the item. With flashlight, wine, and marshmallows in hand Jason pushed open the screened door. He was surprised how quickly night had descended upon them. The air was very warm, and he dismissed the idea of going back for sweaters.

Caroline sat by the crackling fire listening to the late calls of the loons before they settled down for the night. She heard the odd buzz of a mosquito and silently congratulated herself for insisting they both spray on a little bug repellent before heading to the dock. She remembered the days when her dad would say the mosquitoes were so big and ferocious that they could carry off a small child. You can believe she stayed close to her dad back then. On more than one occasion, the annoying, biting little monsters had chased them inside. She and her mom would watch through the window as her dad doused the remains of their campfire all the while waving a cedar bough all about his head and body as protection, and then he'd make a mad dash for the safety of the indoors. No matter how careful you were, there was always one bloodthirsty mosquito that managed to slip in and hide until you were lying vulnerably in the dark. Then, there he was—buzzing right beside your ear—hungry and searching for any patch of skin that wasn't protected by the covers.

Caroline wondered what was taking Jason so long. She looked up the dark path several times but there was still no sign of Jason. She was about to look again when a splash attracted her attention. A fish jumped directly in front of the dock. She watched as the barely visible circles fanned out. A small breeze came from nowhere and although she wasn't cold a little shivers ran up her back. She took a step toward the path, and then she noticed the small bobbing orb of light coming toward her. She sighed with relief. She wouldn't have wanted to negotiate the path in the dark.

"What took you so long? I was about to come looking for you."

Jason handed her the marshmallows and balanced his wine glass on a nearby rock. "It took me a few minutes to find the flashlight."

"I told you it was…"

"I know." Jason interrupted her, "I guess I wasn't paying enough attention." Jason shone the light around and found two long sticks on which to roast their marshmallows.

The uneasy feeling was quickly forgotten once Jason returned.

The loons quieted down and their calls were replaced with the soft hoots of an owl. The odd fish jumped leaving the familiar widening rings glistening in the light from the moon.

Jason and Caroline sat side-by-side holding hands. Conversation waned as they enjoyed the stillness of the summer evening. Several minutes passed in peaceful silence. Caroline shivered and Jason reached out and placed his arm around her shoulder. He leaned over and kissed her cheek. "Think we should head on up?"

"I guess so," she answered reluctantly.

They were about to stand when a rustle from the bushes by the dock stopped them in their tracks. They sat dead still staring blindly into the area where they heard the sound. Two bright piercing eyes looked back at them.

Jason squeezed Caroline's hand and whispered, "Shh—don't move—just watch."

A large raccoon gave them the once over and determining them harmless lumbered down to the water's edge. Seconds later two smaller coons bounded down to join their mother. Before long several clams had been washed, expertly shucked and devoured. The empty shells were quickly discarded. Bandit, as Caroline aptly named her, and her children continued to move slowly down the beach turning over rocks in the water until they found unsuspecting clams and crayfish to add to their dinner menu. When they had moved far enough down shore that it was difficult for Caroline and Jason to watch them feed, Jason took hold of Caroline's hand and helped her to her feet. "Stay here by the fire; I'll put the chairs away." He folded both chairs and leaned them against the dock locker. Soon he returned with a large pail of water to douse the remaining embers. The smell of the wet ashes permeated the air. Holding hands, they picked their way up the path following the little beam of light.

Caroline's eyes darted to the right as they passed the north-leading path; she was certain Jason's pace quicken as they passed by the opening.

Jason thought about the bloodied knife. Why would it be in such an unlikely place and whose blood was it? His mind kept coming back to the idea that maybe it was discarded by an out of season hunter or a poacher after deer. There were questions Jason would have liked to have answers to, but he didn't, at least not yet.

Jason turned the flashlight off as they covered the last twenty to thirty feet so it wouldn't attract any night bugs. He opened the screen door and gestured for Caroline to enter ahead of him. Once inside with the door closed Jason flipped the switch by the door. Lamps on various tables around the room came on spreading a soft golden glow over the log walls. The small clock above the TV showed it was already 10:30 p.m.

"I'm going to put these dishes away before we turn in."

Jason joined her in the kitchen. "I'll give you a hand. Where do I put these?" Jason asked with a fistful of cutlery.

"There, in the top drawer," she said pointing out a drawer close to the sink. "Those big weapons go up on that magnetic bar over by the cutting block," she added.

After Jason had sorted the table knives, forks, and spoons to the drawer by the sink, he carefully removed the sharper members of the cutlery family. "Hey, this magnetic bar is neat. Can we get one of these?"

"Sure, it will keep our edges from getting dull."

"I didn't think *we* had any dull edges."

"I'm talking about our knives. You will always be as sharp as a tack, or in this case a blade."

When Jason had all the knives back on the rack, Caroline, without thinking, shifted them to reflect the space where the one had been missing when she began cooking.

"Why did you do that?"

"There was a place for another knife here." She pointed to the open space. "It's probably in one of the drawers; I'll put it back in place when it turns up."

Jason knew exactly where the missing knife was and knowing only magnified his curiosity and his apprehension. He would be sure to lock the doors tonight.

After they finished up in the kitchen, they returned to the living room. "I didn't get a TV listing yesterday, but I'm sure if you flip through you can catch the news at eleven."

"Okay," Jason responded. "I'd love a coffee, but don't want to risk being awake half the night. Do we have any orange or tomato juice?"

"Both. Which would you like?"

"Tomato," he said heading back into the kitchen. "I'll get it. Are you going to join me?"

"Maybe just half a glass." She would have looked at her magazine but it was still on the outside table where she left it before dinner. She wasn't going to chance letting in that one hungry mosquito just waiting for a chance to sneak through an open door. Instead, she picked up the remote. Almost instantly, the picture jumped to the screen. "Reception isn't great but without cable or satellite it's not bad," she called out to Jason. The TV was an older model and took up a large amount of space compared to the newer flat screen models. "I packed everything but the kitchen sink; I wasn't expecting a log cabin to be so completely equipped, or so charming. I thought our little portable radio was going to be our only way of keeping abreast with world affairs."

The real estate agent had informed them that the cabin had everything they would need for a three-week stay, or a three-month stay. Caroline had taken that with a grain of salt. Now, she found herself watching the last half of *Law & Order*. She didn't bother to change the channel. Caroline looked forward to what would in essence be their first night together in the woods. Last night they had both been tired from the long drive and were asleep almost as soon as their heads hit the big plump pillows. The king-sized bed had a plush feather comforter on top of a crisp sheet and lightweight blanket. Because of the warmth of the evening, they had pushed aside the comforter but by morning, it was pulled up snug under their chins. Here by the lake the cooler night air made for perfect sleeping weather.

Jason entered the living room carrying two glasses of juice. He sat down on the large couch beside Caroline. "Here's to a wonderful holiday—eh!" He said in his best Canadian accent as he clinked his glass against hers. "How many channels do we get out here?"

Caroline grabbed the remote from the coffee table and placed it in Jason's free hand. "Knock yourself out!" She took a large gulp of her juice. "Hey! This tastes different," she said with surprise.

"It's not tomato juice. It's Clamato. I guess you grabbed the wrong one at the store yesterday. It's good though. I thought it would be even better with a jigger or two of Vodka. I put in some of that Creole seasoning you brought with us, a little celery salt, and a dash of Tabasco."

"I guess *dash* wasn't the operative word," she said fanning her outstretched tongue.

"Yours is a virgin Caesar. I left out the Vodka; I know you don't care for it much. If it's too spicy I'll make you another."

"No—it's okay. You should have warned me though, or a least stood by with a fire extinguisher," she laughed as she took a more cautious sip.

Jason put the remote down and took her drink from her hand. He placed both glasses on the coffee table. Gently, he took her in his arms and tenderly kissed her lips. He tasted the spiciness of the virgin Caesar he'd concocted. He explored the warmth of her mouth with his tongue. His hand caressed her back and he heard a little gasp of air as his hand possessively cupped her breast through her thin jersey.

Caroline melted at his touch. "If you keep this up I might still need that fire extinguisher," she whispered. She slipped her hand under his shirt and felt the hard ripple of muscles. His body was warm to her touch. It had been awhile since they had the freedom, or privacy to make out in the living room. It was exciting, somewhat titillating. She soon found herself aroused. The urgency Jason demonstrated by his heavy breathing served to electrify the moment.

Jason felt the fire rising in his groin. He slipped his shirt over his head. He gazed into the greenest eyes he had ever seen. A small moan slipped over his lips as if it had to escape or he would explode. With a flowing movement, he released her breasts from the clinging jersey. He didn't hurry to remove the lacy bra. He held her close feeling the warmth between them rise. Slowly, he traced her profile with tiny hot kisses. Although she'd only had a small amount of her drink, he could still taste the spiciness on her lips. He kissed and caressed his way down to the top of her Capri pants. With the mastery of a surgeon, he undid the top clasp and slid the fabric down the length of her long legs. He admired their shapely form. He felt her fingers as they played through his hair. The Capri's were soon nothing more than a pool of fabric on the floor. Long, lean legs draped themselves over his knees making it difficult for him to remove his cargo shorts. A small tattoo of a red rose adorned her right ankle; a thin gold anklet hung delicately around a shapely left ankle. She helped him remove the bikini panties that matched the lacy bra. Easing her back against the large, overstuffed throw pillows, he drank in her beauty—it overwhelmed him.

Her eyes were partially closed. She waited while he removed his remaining clothing. Her bra was the last item to join the other clothing on the floor.

Jason was a wonderful lover. He moved slowly allowing her to peak, teasing her and himself to the brink over and over before allowing the world to explode around them. Their bodies melded together as one.

The TV program continued, the ice in their Caesars melted, somewhere along the shore the fat raccoon and her babies fed, as they did every night while Jason and Caroline loved each other as if for the first time.

Later they headed into the bedroom leaving the pile of discarded clothing beside the couch. Just before drifting off Jason remembered he hadn't locked the front door. He pulled himself from the bed and padded barefoot to the door; he turned the lock. He jumped when an owl called out in the darkness. He thought about the uneasy feeling he had when they came out of the water, a feeling of being watched from afar. "Give yourself a shake," he whispered to himself, "There's nobody around here for miles. I'll bet nobody in these parts even locks their doors," he reasoned aloud. Last night he had also forgotten to lock the door. He had dragged his tired body out of bed and locked up. When he returned to the bedroom, he'd commented to Caroline... something about their biggest problem for the next three weeks being to keep the raccoons out of the garbage. As hard as he tried, he still couldn't put the knife under the bush out of his mind. "I sure hope the raccoons will be our only problem," he whispered to the darkness.

Chapter
SIX

J ason awoke before Caroline; today he would let her sleep in.
Her hair was tousled and a large curl rested against her cheek.
Life would be worth nothing without her. Last night they had
agreed that breakfast would be something simple — toast, cereal,
or maybe just coffee. Caroline had picked up a box of Kellogg's
Just Right cereal; it was one they hadn't tried. She also bought a
package of Craisins, dried cranberries that looked like red raisins.
Jason quietly removed a bowl from the cupboard. He struggled to
open the box of cereal and then the waxy bag on the inside. "Almost
child proof," he mumbled to himself. Finally, the cereal spilled out
into the bowl. After adding half a sliced banana, some Craisins,
and milk he carefully wrapped the remaining half of the banana in
plastic wrap. He then took his bowl out to the porch. The sun was
just barely above the horizon. The rays, as they played through the
branches of the pines, seemed to beckon to him. He settled into
one of the padded chairs and ate his breakfast. When he finished
eating, he took his bowl back into the kitchen, rinsed it, and laid
it upside down in the sink. He searched through several drawers
before locating a plastic shopping bag in the pantry. He planned

to retrieve the knife from the woods before Caroline awoke. What his next step would be was still undecided.

After peeking into the bedroom and finding Caroline still sound asleep, he left the cabin. Already he could feel the early morning temperatures rising around him; it was going to be very hot again. He removed the scrunched up bag from his pocket. He was a visitor in this country—did he want to get involved—could he resist getting involved? Jason's long strides took him quickly to the north path. He again stepped over the fallen log and over the various other obstructions at the entrance of the path. He walked what he thought was about the same distance he'd covered yesterday. He opened the plastic bag and pulled back the bough that held the mystery of the knife. Jason stood up not quite believing his eyes when the knife was nowhere to be found. He looked around thinking perhaps he'd misjudged the distance and was searching in the wrong place. He walked a few feet further and searched for a similar ground-hugging bough. He was sure he had looked in the correct place. He turned back on the path and once again, just to assure himself, lifted the low-lying branch almost expecting to find the knife had reappeared. There was nothing there but dried debris and a few blades of thin grass trying their best to reach up for what little sun managed to penetrate through the overhead branches and low hanging boughs. Jason tucked the empty plastic bag back into his pocket. He wasn't one to doubt himself and he wasn't about to start now. The question now changed from *why was the knife there in the first place* to *who removed it and when?* As Jason retraced his footsteps, he had no answers to the haunting questions. While Caroline shopped later in the day, he would ask a few questions around town. Exiting the north path, he glanced in the direction of the cabin, but turned left towards the lake. He had pulled on his swim trunks under his shorts with the thought that he might take a refreshing morning dip. Now, what he really needed was a few minutes to think.

The water felt cold until his body adjusted. He hadn't been in long when Caroline emerged through the trees at the end of the path.

"Good morning early bird," she called out. "I thought I'd find you down here. I noticed your swimsuit was missing. You should know better than to swim by yourself," she scolded.

She had on the string bikini.

"You'll freeze to death in that."

She ignored his remark. Tossing the towels she'd brought with her onto the dock she stepped into the chilly water. "I admit this would be less torturous about 4:00 o'clock this afternoon, but you know it's dangerous to swim alone and I sure can't let you drown."

"By the time you get wet I'll be a prune."

"Well, I can't let that happen either." She waded to the edge of the boat channel and took a deep breath before plunging into the deep water headfirst. Without taking a second breath, she swam underwater until she surfaced mere inches from Jason.

"You're right; I would have frozen getting wet in my usual fashion. Speaking of fashion, how do you like my new suit?" She wiped the water from her eyes.

"What suit?"

She placed both hands on the top of his head and pushed him under the clear water. He in turn grabbed her by the ankles and pulled her under with him. Their cold lips met and the heat between them was immediately evident to both. For several minutes they frolicked like children. Caroline's hair floated around her head like a wispy veil. Caroline finally suggested they should head to shore. "Can't have you turning into a prune."

As they slowly made their way towards shore Jason asked, "Have you eaten anything yet?"

"No, I wasn't hungry but I am now. How about you?"

"I had cereal with those cranberry things and sliced banana. I could use a slice of toast. Maybe a stack of blueberry pancakes, some Canadian Maple Syrup, and about half a dozen sausages," he added with a smirk. "Maybe some fresh berries on those pancakes."

"Sounds great honey; I think I saw a restaurant in town that specializes in breakfast."

As they emerged from the cool water, Jason took in her magnificent figure in the tiny suit. He also noticed how the cold water had hardened her nipples. Funny how cold water has different effects on males and females, he thought. The way she looked this was going to be a very sexy vacation, or holiday as the Canadians would say. Caroline grabbed one of the fluffy towels and wrapped it tightly around her. She shivered.

Jason wiped the water droplets from his face and then used his towel to blot the water from Caroline's hair.

"Save yourself kind Sir," she said through chattering teeth.

"Save myself indeed," he replied. "And who is going to cook, clean, and please her master? Let's get you into something warm and dry." Jason rolled his eyes. "Who would ever believe I just suggested getting you into clothes?"

They grasped hands and attacked the path at a good-paced run. As they advanced their way up the path, the extra exertion left them both breathless. This path wasn't a cakewalk. About three quarters of the way up they stopped to rest and exchange a small kiss. The tall pines protected them from the morning breezes. Caroline felt warm enough to remove the towel.

Removing the towel was all it took to make the heat rise within Jason. He hoped the three weeks would pass slowly, very slowly.

They listened as a small wren sang its melodious song. The notes were carried on the morning breeze to be answered by the little wren's mate. Their song, a rapid, liquid, bubbling chatter drifted through the air. Wild daisies swayed rhythmically to the floating notes. With a gentle hand, Caroline picked one of the most wondrous of all the blooms. She plucked one petal at a time from the golden face of the daisy. "He loves me, he loves me not, he loves me, he loves me not," she chanted as each petal drifted like softly falling snow to the ground below.

"I think you have that all wrong. May I show you how it's supposed to go?"

Caroline handed him the flower.

Slowly he removed a petal never taking his eyes off her face. "He loves you," he spoke softly. The second petal floated gently downward. With the third, fourth, and fifth petals he continued to repeat, "He loves you, he loves you, he loves you." When only one single petal remained clinging to the bright yellow face of the chosen bloom he returned it to Caroline. "You try it now," he said. "The last petal never lies."

She held her hand out and accepted the sunny face with its last outstretched promise. Carefully she removed the last white petal from the daisy and kissed its velvety softness. Gently she blew the little petal into the air. She watched as it drifted slowly, as if on the wings of a dove, to join the others scattered on the ground. She turned her face up to his and said, "She loves him too!"

After changing into dry clothes, Caroline returned to the kitchen. Jason stood by the double doors enjoying the view.

"So, what's your desire for breakfast?" She asked.

"I think I'll pass." He picked up the other half of his banana, "I'll finish this. You'd better eat something though."

"I'll make some toast. I bought a jar of cherry jam from a vendor in one of the little towns we came through. The lady makes all her own jams and I'm anxious to try it."

Jason didn't ask Caroline what she would like to do. Instead, he said, "I'd like to take a trip into town. We can explore around… maybe check out some of those little shops on the main street."

"That sounds like fun. Give me a few minutes to eat and get ready."

While she readied herself and prepared a shopping list, Jason picked up the newspaper. The news would be yesterdays but he didn't care. It was something to wile away a few minutes. Jason perused the front page. There was a large picture of a European cruise ship that was scheduled to make a stop in a nearby port on its tour of the Great Lakes. A smaller article caught his eye. It was the story about the mysterious disappearance of a young woman. When he examined her picture, a cold shiver ran up his back. He turned the page and tried to focus his attention on other articles, but he couldn't put her image out of his mind. Imagine what her family must be going through, he thought. The article reported her missing for three days. Again, a shiver made the hair on his arms stand on end. He closed the paper and studied the picture of the beautiful young woman. His mind wandered back to the discovery of the bloodied knife. Tragedies happen every day, he thought, we just have to hope and pray they aren't played out in our own backyard.

After several minutes, he tossed the paper on the table and went to look for Caroline. He found her in the bedroom making the bed. He moved to one side to help. When she was ready, they locked up and headed to town.

Caroline jumped at the chance to shop. On their way to the cabin, it had taken only a few minutes to drive through the nearest town, but Caroline possessed the inherent female ability to record the location of several quaint little shops that she would be obliged to call into as an act of courtesy. She probably had a list as long as her arm of things she wanted to buy today. There would be another list of the names of people she'd take a little gift to back home. As with any tourist town, the locals flourished off the things that parents just had to have for their kids or themselves. The tourist season was short and here the winters would be long.

The ride to town was pleasant. They talked and sang along with the radio. Caroline opened her window all the way and let the wind blow through her hair. They travelled approximately sixteen miles without passing another car until they reached the outskirts of town.

Along the main street there was a two hour parking limit and very few empty spaces. Jason knew, from firsthand experience, that this wouldn't be enough time. Luckily, he spotted an off-street parking lot with no time restrictions. He could see the excitement in Caroline's eyes; she would enjoy exploring the town.

"Tell you what," Jason said as he parked the car and they took a shortcut through a small park to get to the main street, "you enjoy yourself; pick up something extra special for Michael Jay, something for Nana and Papa, and I'll meet you here at say… twelve noon. I'll spring for lunch."

"What are you going to do until then?" Caroline asked giving only a part of her attention to his answer.

"I'll take a walk around town. Maybe I'll go down to the marina to watch the boats. You know me; I'll poke my nose into something that's none of my business," he laughed. "I'll be fine… unless you think you need my help."

It didn't take Caroline a nanosecond to assure Jason that she'd do just fine without his help. "You have a great time," she added quickly.

As they walked through the park, Jason noticed that her pace had quickened and the goodbye kiss she gave him barely skimmed his cheek. He couldn't help but laugh.

"What's so funny?" She asked crinkling her nose and looking over her sunglasses.

"Nothing."

"Okay then, I'll see you later."

"Have fun," he called after her as she hurried away.

Now, where to start! Jason thought. He wandered the town for awhile and looked in a fishing tackle shop. He bought a new lure that the owner of the shop guaranteed would catch fish the first time he used it, or he'd get his money back. It was more expensive than he would have liked, but the guarantee was a deal maker. After leaving the tackle shop, he headed down to the marina. The view of Colpoy Bay was spectacular. Beautiful white cliffs peaked through tall trees along one side of the bay. You could see for miles. Numerous boats, both motor and sail came and went as he soaked up the ambiance of his surroundings. He found a bench close to the water and sat down to people watch. Several people stopped to talk. The more leisurely pace of life was appealing and first impressions of the town were good. After awhile he headed back to the main part of town. The real estate office would be his next stop. A small bell on the door announced his arrival. A young woman was talking on the phone. Jason indicated that he'd be glad to wait. While he waited, he studied the large wall of listed properties. Prices were high, but if the many number of SOLD banners was any indication it appeared that sales were brisk.

"Thanks Mr. Stanley. We always like to hear that people are happy with the service. I knew that particular house was just what you and your wife were looking for. When you're around town drop in and say hi to Keith. He'll be pleased to hear how happy you are." She paused a moment listening to the person on the other end of the call. Then she completed the call with…"Hope to see you both soon." She stood and moved around from behind her large, busy looking desk. "Good morning Sir. How can I help you?"

"Hello. Is Chris Collins in the office?"

"Yes, I'm Christine Collins," she replied.

Jason hesitated a moment. He had expected Chris to be a man. "Nice to meet you Ms. Collins. I'm Jason White." He didn't expect her to recognize his name.

"Hi Mr. White," she said as she approached him hand outstretched. "I hope my assistant was able to accommodate your rental requests as per your e-mail."

"Thank you Ms. Collins."

"Please call me Chris. So—what can I help you with today?"

"No help needed. We love the cabin and I just wanted to let you know personally that we were very happy with the accommodations."

"Well Mr. White we're pleased to hear that. It was nice of you to stop in personally."

Jason waited for an opening. "Please call me Jason and my wife's name is Caroline—she's shopping."

"We're pleased to hear that too," she said with a wide grin. "There are some lovely shops here in town and several just outside that are worth a visit."

"I'm sure my wife will find them all. She has a homing instinct when it comes to stores."

"We welcome the tourists and their dollars around here. Did Keith mention that the cottage you're renting is for sale—fully furnished and equipped?"

"Yes, I believe he did, but I think we're happy with the present arrangements. I just wanted to stop in to say thank you." After exchanging a few more niceties, Jason turned to leave the office. "Oh, just as a matter of interest, is there any kind of hunting season right now?"

"No, sorry Mr. Wh…" she corrected herself, "Jason, you can fish to your hearts content, with a license of course, but no hunting allowed until October."

"That's what I thought. We have the fishing licenses and with my luck, my wife will out fish me every day. I did buy a new lure—guaranteed to catch fish," he laughed as he held up the small bag with his purchase. He opened the office door and stepped out onto the main street. Great thing about small towns everything you need is usually found on the main street, or nearby. He looked both left and right. On the other side of the street, he spied Caroline as she exited one store and entered the next. She was carrying several bags. He smiled to himself knowing what a great time she was having and realizing how completely miserable he'd be if he'd had to tag along. Men truly were from a different planet when it came to shopping, he thought.

Next to the real estate office was a small restaurant and next to that the local newspaper office. That would be his next stop.

A young woman greeted Jason as he entered the front door. "Can I help you?" She inquired looking up from her paper-strewn desk.

The by-line at the top of the missing woman article named Bill Blakley as the writer.

"Is Bill Blakley available?"

"Sure," she said too quickly. Then, "I'll see if he's in. Can I tell him what this is about?"

Jason got the impression that if she weren't able to give Bill a reason for his visit it would be highly possible that he wouldn't be available right now.

"I'm an American visitor to this area; I just wanted to let him know how beautiful we think it is and how much my wife and I are enjoying our stay and his articles in the paper," Jason said diplomatically.

She barely cleared Blakley's door before he came out smiling ear to ear. He must have heard every word, Jason thought.

"Bill Blakley," he said extending his hand.

They shook hands and Jason introduced himself. He played it cool. If he'd started out with questions he surmised that Blakley would have clammed up so tight that the raccoon we watched last night skillfully open up her shells wouldn't have stood a chance in hell of getting this guy to open up. They chatted about the beautiful scenery, the town, the weather, and the fishing. Blakley's eyes sparkled when they reached fishing—a good time to slip in hunting, Jason thought.

"No hunting at this time of year," Blakley adamantly insisted. "Big fines these days. They confiscate your hunting equipment and make life pretty wretched. A costly proposition," he shared with Jason.

"So, what's the big story around these parts?" Jason ventured to ask.

"Well, lets see... the local elections are always front and centre, the airport happenings are of interest, and we can't forget the environment."

Jason mentioned the article from a couple of days ago... the one about the missing woman.

"Oh that," Blakley lowered his voice. "Probably some sort of domestic thing. A nice couple though. Supposedly high school sweethearts, but they were having problems."

Jason was glad he'd taken the bait and talked about the missing woman article.

"She probably took off on her own. I think they came from somewhere in Saskatchewan. Anyway, they have no reason to suspect the husband. He was tutoring some kid the night she left. They lived apart, but the husband said things had been going better lately. Then she up and disappeared."

"My wife's shopping here in town. She'll probably be gone for another half hour or so. Can I buy you a coffee or something?" Jason offered.

"Can't see why not," Blakley said with a toothy grin. "It's always nice to talk with our cousins to the south."

They entered the little café next door. "The décor's not much, but they've got the best coffee in town." Blakley led them to a corner booth. When the waitress came to the table he ordered two coffees.

"Would you like anything else…a donut or something?" Jason asked.

"No thanks, coffee's fine. Call me Bill. Most of this town is on a first name basis."

"Sure, Bill it is. As I mentioned back in your office, I'm Jason."

Bill extended his hand again. "Pleased to meet new comers to town. How long are you going to be around this part of the country?"

"We're here for three weeks; if I can keep my wife away from our son that long."

"I can understand that." He nodded of his head. "We have four kids, three girls and a boy. I can't get my wife to take a holiday."

"So how's the hunting in this area?"

"Good, in season. If you're only going to be here for three weeks you won't get any hunting in, but the fish are biting."

Jason tried to steer the conversation back to the missing person article in the paper. Each time he brought it up, Blakley would change the subject. Jason guessed he didn't want his little town too closely linked to a scandal. Jason was glad when they finished their coffee. He signalled the waitress to bring the check.

Bill rose, "Thanks for the coffee. You have a wonderful holiday."

They left the café together. Bill headed back to his office. Jason started out in the opposite direction. He hoped he'd run into Caroline. He mulled over the superficial conversation he and Bill had. A waste of time, but at least the coffee was good.

After walking almost the full length of town Jason sat on a bench to people watch again. He had just nicely settled and was enjoying the warm sun when he spotted Caroline coming down the street. Many small bags and one huge one dangled from her hands. He sprang from the bench and with several long strides relieved her of her load. "Wow, did you buy out the stores?"

"No, I left lots for another day." She beamed with the glow of a woman on a shopping spree. "I found a fantastic straw hat for Mom; it will be perfect for her to wear when she's gardening, and for Dad, a super BBQ apron. Wait until you see it. He always claims to be *King of the Q,* and now he really will be. It even came with a matching chef's hat."

"Sounds like you had a good time." Jason shifted the bags in his hands.

"Oh, and wait until you see the wonderful book I found. It's an original 1952 printing of *Charlotte's Web,* by E. B. White. I've always loved that story and the diagrams are fantastic. Michael Jay and I are both going to enjoy reading it at bedtime. When you're home we'll let you listen in, or maybe you can read a few chapters and I'll listen."

"That sounds great. Don't you just love reading to him? The way he looks at the pictures… it's as if he believes we are making up the stories ourselves. I guess we can declare this trip a success then." They proceeded down the street enjoying the beautiful day. "So, what did you buy me?" Jason teased not actually expecting anything.

"Could I forget my favourite *big boy?*"

"Really...you bought something for me? What did you buy?" Before she could answer, he continued. "Is this gigantic bag my surprise?"

"Well, I imagine you'll enjoy it as much as anyone, but no that one isn't for you. It's a huge red fire engine for Michael Jay. It has ladders and hoses and actually pumps water. We might not tell him that though," she said with a laugh. "It comes with a whole crew of firemen and its own Dalmatian. He'll be delighted with the battery operated siren."

Jason thought about the siren. "Maybe we shouldn't tell him about the siren either."

"Maybe your surprise is ear plugs."

"Don't keep me waiting. What did you buy for me?"

"Clogs!"

"What on earth is a Clog and do I need more than one?" He shook his head and made a sour face.

"Yes, you definitely need more than one." Caroline laughed. "I have no idea which of these bags your Clogs are in so you'll have to wait until we get back to the cabin to see your surprise."

"What if my Clog, no Clogs," he corrected, "go bad in this heat?" He asked trying to get her to give him a clue what the hell a Clog was.

She shrugged her shoulders. "We'll just have to take our chances. Speaking of heat, let's get our groceries; I'm anxious to get back home for a swim." Grocery shopping with Jason was a challenge at best. He wanted everything he saw. "We're only here three weeks and only have one fridge," she reminded him more than once. "I have meals planned and I assure you that you won't go hungry."

"With your delicious cooking my only worry will be to not gain ten pounds," he gave her a broad smile.

"I'll just have to make sure you swim and hike to work it off."

"I can think of better ways to work it off," a smile turning up the corners of his mouth.

With the groceries loaded Jason manoeuvred the car out of the crowded parking lot. "I promised you lunch. Would you like to stop at a local restaurant, or maybe pick up a pizza to take home?"

"After buying all those cold cuts I think we'd better save the pizza for another day."

"Ah, you're no fun, but I guess you're right," he reached over and squeezing her hand. "I just don't want you working your whole vacation."

"Preparing meals for my favourite man isn't work, its pleasure; besides, I'm looking forward to trying a few new recipes."

"So I'll be your guinea pig?"

"As I recall… the dictionary says something like: a *guinea pig is a small stocky, nearly tailless South American rodent, often kept as a pet.* Let's analyze that—you're not small, nor stocky, hardly tailless," she blushed, "and you're not from South America. As for being a pet… let's not go there. It's probably best if we just say that I'll cook and you eat, or even better you eat what I cook," she laughed. Their hands were still joined and she returned his earlier little love squeeze.

It took them less time to arrive back at the cabin now that they knew the route and didn't have to navigate from a small map in the dusk. Traffic was almost nonexistent. They passed one car travelling in the opposite direction and a couple, dressed in black leather riding a motorcycle.

"They must be hot." Caroline and Jason said in unison as the bike roared past them.

When they arrived back at the cabin, Jason said, "Tell you what; I'll help put the groceries away, and then after a swim I'll make sandwiches on those crusty rolls."

"Thanks Jason, that sounds great."

After a refreshing swim in the clear, cool water, they enjoyed lunch out on the porch. Jason was wearing his lime green Clogs. He hadn't put up any resistance and even seemed to like them.

Caroline sipped her lemonade as Jason took the luncheon plates back into the kitchen. She left the table and returned to what had become her favourite padded chair. She picked up her magazine and leisurely leafed through the colourful pages. A small bird landed on the porch railing. It sang a harmonious song for Caroline and then flew off again.

Jason returned to the porch with a peeled tangerine. "Would you like a few sections?"

"No thanks."

Jason ate his tangerine and stretched out on the futon without removing his Clogs. He watched the gulls fly over seemingly with no other purpose than the pure joy of flight. His eyes were heavy. He tried to fight off sleep, but finally gave in to the urge to doze.

Caroline smiled as she watched his eyes flutter a few times and then remain closed. It was good that he was relaxing and getting some well-deserved rest. The last few years he had worked hard on case after case building his detective agency to the success it was today.

After finishing her lemonade Caroline decided to walk down to the shore. She stopped at the place where the north path began. Her original plan was to wait for Jason, but she couldn't resist the temptation to venture just a little ways into the unknown.

She stepped over the fallen tree trunk at the entrance and pulled aside the low boughs hiding the path. When she let go of an unruly branch it snapped back and scraped the back of her leg. Once past the obstructions she surveyed the damage. A trickle of blood ran down her right leg. "Damn," she muttered. She removed a tissue from her shorts pocket and wet it with her tongue. She dabbed at the wound and declared aloud, "The wounded will live to see another day." It was only a small surface wound, but she was surprised at how much it bled.

The path ahead had not been frequently travelled. The tall pines formed a canopy overhead and provided cooling shade from the hot sun. As she got deeper into the woods, she couldn't help but notice the eerie silence. Again, she had to navigate her way over another fallen tree, this one somewhat larger than the one at the entrance. She contemplated going around the obstacle, but didn't want to leave the barely discernible path. She found a patch of tiny violets and stooped to admire their beauty. Noticing her shoelace had loosened, she dropped to one knee to refasten the lace. Her eyes drifted to something white and almost hidden from sight by low crawling bushes. It was only from this low advantage point that the item would be visible. Caroline's jaw dropped when she discovered what she thought might be a flower was a woman's shoe. She kicked at it with her toe and gasped when she saw what looked like large drops of blood on the side of the sneaker. The sneaker was clean and in good shape except for the bloodstains. It couldn't have been there for long. Caroline didn't further disturb it, but she no longer had the desire to continue along the path. She was close to a steep wall of rock. At its base, she could see the sun sparkling off the surface of a body of water. As much as she would have liked to explore further, the shoe had spooked her and she turned to backtrack along the path. She wondered what Jason would say when she mentioned the shoe to him. There could be any number of reasons for it being there. A hiker could have lost it from a backpack, or maybe even discarded it on purpose after accidently getting it bloodied from a cut, or... She didn't want to speculate any further, she just wanted to get back to the cabin. She and Jason would have plenty of time to check out the body of water and the cliff.

Chapter SEVEN

Caroline's pace quickened on the return trip and by the time she reached the porch she was short of breath. She noticed that Jason was still asleep on the futon. As she took the steps, her toe caught on the edge of the bottom step. She came down hard on both hands creating a loud slapping sound. Her hands saved her from further injury as she nearly fell flat on her face. Her loud, involuntary grunt brought Jason bolt upright at the alarming sound.

"Are you okay?" He jumped up and anxiously rushed to her side.

"Yes," she replied breathlessly. "I just tripped."

"You've cut your leg."

She had totally forgotten about the little run in with the unruly branch.

With Jason's help, she stood and examined the back of her leg. It had started to bleed again. A red line of blood reached all the way down to the back of her shoe and stained the heel of her sock. "A branch attacked me," she offered with a weak smile. "It will be fine." She held out her hands palms up and examined them. The sudden slap on the top step had left them red and burning, but no real damage done.

Jason led her inside and tenderly attended to her little cut. It was nothing more than one of those nasty little cuts that bleed more than expected. He unlaced and removed her sneaker and sock. The stain tinted the top edge of the sock band.

Caroline didn't mention the north path, or the shoe. "Thanks Jason, if you weren't already a brilliant detective you would have made a great doctor. I'll soak this sock in some cold water before the stain sets."

"I'll get us something cold to drink."

Caroline positioned the plug in the little bathroom sink and ran some cold water. When it was full enough she submerged the sock. Almost instantly, the water around the stain pinkened. She left the sock to soak. She retrieved another pair and pulled them on. The little cut had not bled anymore. She healed quickly; in a couple of days, it would totally disappear. When she came out of the bedroom, she spotted Jason on the porch with their drinks. He was reading the newspaper.

Caroline had an uneasy feeling in the pit of her stomach, but decided not to mention the shoe. It was probably as innocent as her sock. The screen door squeaked as she pushed it open.

Jason passed her a tall cool glass. "It's Sprite with a good healthy squirt of lemon juice…it's quite refreshing."

She took the drink from his hand. The condensation on the outside of the glass made it difficult to hold and it almost slipped from her hand. She realized her hand was trembling slightly; she hoped Jason hadn't noticed. She placed the glass on the little table and sank into the nearby chair.

Jason continued reading the paper. She watched as a concerned look appeared on his face.

"Why the worried frown?"

"Am I frowning? I guess it's the same all over the world. There's never much in the way of good news to read about, not even in a small town." He turned to the crossword puzzle and picked up the pen from the table.

Caroline sipped her drink and leafed through her already read magazine. She thought again of telling Jason about finding the shoe, but quickly pushed it from her mind. They were here to enjoy themselves and that's exactly what they were going to do.

The next two days passed leisurely. They slept, they relaxed, and they enjoyed wonderful gourmet meals prepared by Caroline with Jason's assistance. They washed dishes together, swam, took long walks, and even longer boat rides. For their own reasons they had not ventured onto the north path.

One morning they got up so early that they were out on the lake with their rods and can of wiggly worms before the sun rose. Jason had checked the rods the night before and they had set the little alarm clock for 5:00 a.m., but they were both wide-awake and eager to go before the alarm went off.

The birds hadn't awoken yet and Caroline and Jason enjoyed the quietness of the morning. The only sound was the gentle dipping of the oars into the glassy surface of the lake. Though there probably wasn't another soul for miles, they kept their voices to a whisper. Even their whispers sounded louder than they were as their voices drifted effortlessly across the water. This morning they ventured further up the shore and came to a lovely protected inlet.

"That would be a great place to fish," Jason whispered.

"Okay with me. I hope the fish are plentiful; I didn't take anything out of the freezer for dinner tonight."

Jason thought back to the gas station attendant. "If we don't catch any fish we can roast up some of these big, juicy worms."

"Yuck!" Caroline scooped a hand full of water and splashed him.

Jason sucked in his breath when the cold water hit him. "You'll pay for that," he said as he stretched the cold wet fabric of his shirt away from his body. They both laughed and the sound echoed across the water.

Once inside the protection of the inlet they marvelled at the huge cliffs at the north end.

Caroline knew exactly where they were. She felt uneasy. She knew they had arrived at the end of the north path. She scanned the opposite shoreline for any telltale sign of a path, but saw nothing that resembled an opening.

Jason also realized that these were the cliffs he had seen in the distance on the day he discovered the knife. Not wanting to spoil the moment, he said nothing to Caroline. He stopped rowing and the boat drifted slowly toward the cliff's craggy rocks before coming to a stop.

"Should I drop the anchor here?" Caroline asked, slightly distracted.

"This looks like as good a spot as any."

Caroline hoisted the five-pound anchor over the bow and let it drop. It made a loud *kerplop* sound as it hit the water sending a little splash up to meet Caroline square in the face. She giggled. "That was cold."

"You didn't seem to worry about the temperature when you splashed me."

Caroline peered over the bow of the boat ignoring his comment. She followed the yellow anchor line down through the water until it disappeared. "How deep do you think it is here?"

"Well—only a guess, but the anchor is definitely on the bottom since the line is stretched out in front of us and not going straight down; I estimate about twenty feet of anchor rope and there's still about three or four feet in the boat so let's say it's probably around fifteen feet deep," he proudly intoned.

"Spoken like a true detective." She watched as the remaining few feet of rope played over the gunwale. She was impressed by the way Jason had calculated the anchor depth.

The boat swung on the anchor line as they got closer to the cliff's edge. "See those rock platforms jutting out above the water's surface—they would be great to dive off. Lets start fishing and maybe later we'll take a swim." They couldn't see the sun yet, but the noticeable lightening of the sky indicated that somewhere the sun had risen above the horizon.

Caroline picked up her rod with one hand and shoved the other down into the can of worms. Seconds later, she passed Jason a large wiggly worm. She thrust her hand back into the can to get one for herself.

Jason didn't ask if she needed help baiting her hook. It was obvious she had matters in hand, literally. He smiled as he watched her masterfully position the worm on the hook so it could wiggle to attract fish, but wouldn't be able to get free, nor would a fish be able to get a free meal without having to deal with the sharp barb of the hook. A much smaller kerplop was heard as she expertly cast her bait a good distance from the boat. Jason also cast his line and then readied the keeper chain.

The first half-hour was quiet. The odd nibble kept them interested. The beauty of the rising sun was enough to keep them fully diverted. With the increasing light, they had progressed from whispers to quiet voices. The sun quickly warmed the morning and before long Caroline reached into her bag and grabbed the suntan lotion. She poured a generous amount into the palm of her hand and had just started to rub it into her arms when it struck. Zzzzzzz the line sang out as the fish took off in an attempt to escape. Caroline grabbed her rod and set the hook. The fish put up a good fight, but in the end Caroline was the victor.

"You could have given me a hand," she scolded Jason. "Do you have any idea how difficult that was with all this suntan lotion on my hands?"

"You were having a ball, I wasn't going to deny you one minute of fun."

She laughed as she posed proudly to allow Jason to take her picture with the first catch of the day.

Jason helped her remove the hook from its mouth although he was sure she was more than capable of doing it herself. He placed the fish on the keeper chain and lowered it back into the cool water to await the return trip home. Several more fish were soon added to the keeper chain. By 10:30 a.m., the score was Caroline-three, Jason-two.

"How about we take that swim now?" Jason suggested.

"We don't have suits; I thought we'd go later in the afternoon."

"I don't think we need suits here; are you game?"

After taking a quick glance around, she answered, "Okay but you first."

Jason peeled off his shirt and let his shorts drop to the bottom of the boat.

Caroline puckered her lips and gave Jason a low wolf whistle.

"Flattery will get you everywhere," Jason said. In one smooth motion, he dove into the clear water leaving the boat rocking back and forth.

Caroline scanned the coastline and agreed with Jason's assessment of not needing swimsuits out here. She removed her sleeveless blouse and her shorts. She contemplated swimming in her bra and panties. She noticed that Jason was already climbing out of the water onto one of the jutting rocks at the bottom of the cliffs. In just a few short days he had already picked up a nice tan. The white of his bum was in stark contrast to his tanned back and legs. Caroline removed her watch and slipped it into the pocket of her shorts. She could clearly see the visible white band around her wrist where the watch usually rested. She watched as Jason executed a perfect dive. She released the clasp on her bra and slipped out of the scanty panties. She would have preferred to carefully lower herself over the side of the boat, but found it necessary to plunge in as Jason had. She swam towards Jason.

Chapter
EIGHT

Caroline found Jason on the porch. She stood quietly and watched as he went through his morning exercise regime. She admired the ripple of muscles as he lifted the weights high into the air. On more than one occasion it had been necessary for her to shift his weights out of the way and she found them extremely heavy.

"Hi Mr. America, or perhaps I should be calling you Mr. Canada while we're here?"

He assumed the muscleman pose. "Well, what do you think?"

"I think you should be using more suntan lotion, that's what I think. Those pecs look a little red," she said as she moved away from the door.

Jason was unsure whether she was serious or was teasing him. He followed her inside. The kettle whistled and he watched as she poured the scalding water over a tea bag in her cup. She had taken to having a cup of tea in the morning instead of her usual coffee. "Are you alright?"

"I'll be fine; it's just a headache."

"I thought we'd go into town today. Maybe we could have lunch and pick up a few things," Jason said.

"I don't think I feel up to that. She took a sip of the hot tea. "I'd rather just laze around this morning. Why don't you drive into town; there are a few things we could use."

"We can go in later or even tomorrow when you're feeling better."

"No honey, you go ahead. I'll just take it easy until this headache lets up; it's probably from a little too much sun." She forced a smile. "Today might be a good time to pick up a pizza for lunch and bring it back."

Caroline didn't get headaches often, but when she did a couple of aspirin and a little downtime usually did wonders.

Jason grabbed a piece of paper and a pen and began writing: newspaper, milk, bread, O.J., butter tarts, white wine, beer, and pizza. He pushed the list toward Caroline. "Anything else we need?"

She half-heartedly read the list and shook her head in agreement. "That's about all. We'll go in midweek; I'll pick up a few more things then." She walked out to the porch with him. "Maybe you can add a dozen eggs to your list and some fruit."

He didn't answer, but gave her the thumbs-up sign to indicate that he'd heard. As he pulled away he opened the driver's window and waved, calling back, "Take care of your headache. I'll see you soon."

Caroline stood on the porch and watched as the car disappeared down the road. Once back inside she went into the bathroom and took out a clean facecloth. She soaked the cloth under the cold-water tap, then wrung it out and pressed it against her forehead. She chose the futon to rest on. When she sat down on the futon the newspaper Jason had been reading fluttered to the porch floor. She reached down to retrieve it and noticed that Jason had finished the crossword puzzle. She also noticed the article about the missing woman. She folded the paper in half and began to read. Her hands were shaking. Immediately she thought of the bloodstained shoe. The blood drained from her face; her headache pounded harder than ever. It had been days since she was on the north path. She'd pushed the whole incident so far from her mind that she wasn't sure it had actually happened. She would wait until Jason returned and they could check it out together. As she tried to rest, her mind raced. This is silly, she thought. The missing woman and the discarded shoe had nothing to do with each other.

Caroline put the damp facecloth on the table. The sky was overcast and the radio had forecast rain for today. She thought about the shoe and decided to retrieve it before Jason returned and before it rained. She didn't want to read anything into the shoe, but Jason would know what to do. When she reached the entrance to the north path, a shiver ran up her back and she almost turned back. "Give yourself a shake girl," she said aloud. "You're acting like a ninny." She stepped over the fallen log. This time she was careful not to let the unruly branch snap back and get her. The path seemed dark and gloomy. Again, she scolded herself. Of course it was dark and gloomy since there was no sunshine today. She looked up through the tall pines; their tops swayed back and forth whispering in the light breeze. If you listened hard, it sounded like they were talking. It was like watching big fluffy clouds turn into sheep, hearts, trees, puppies, or whatever your imagination could conjure up. She listened closely to the trees.

It was definitely going to rain, but not for awhile. She quickened her pace and continued toward the cliff. She cursed softly when she realized she hadn't brought a bag for the shoe—if she could even find the shoe. She hoped she would be able to locate the right area of the path. That day she had stooped to tie her shoelace and she remembered catching a glimpse of the cliffs and the sun sparking off the water in the distance. The water was still not in sight so she kept moving along the path.

A large, noisy blue jay sounded a loud whee-oodle and oolink call as it swooped from one tree to another right in front of her. She jumped and nearly turned and ran. Again, she reminded herself not to be so foolish. A few minutes later, she spotted the water through the trees. There was no sparkle today; in fact, it looked ominous. Stopping to orient herself, she scanned the low bushes on the side of the path. They all looked the same; she would never find the right spot. She lifted one bough—nothing! She lifted another a few steps further along the path—again nothing! She actually felt relief that she hadn't found the shoe. She lifted another and yet another until one bough revealed the hidden shoe. She let the branch settle back down. "So now what?" she asked aloud. Her own voice sounded hollow, somehow strange to her ears.

She left the shoe where it was. She picked up a couple of nearby sticks and worked them into the ground making a small cross at the side of the pathway to mark the location. Jason would know what to do. It would be more than an hour before he returned. Now that her headache had subsided, she'd continue further along the path towards the water. The path became harder to follow as she approached the shore. Again, she was forced to pull tangled boughs away and to step over fallen tree trunks. Once out in the open she looked around. If the sun were to come out it would be breathtakingly beautiful.

The cliffs were further from the shore than she had expected. Distances had been deceiving from the boat. She thought she saw the jutting rocks where she and Jason dove and swam after fishing. Then she realized there were many such rocks and they all looked remarkably the same.

She bent and picked up an open clamshell. Its pearly inside was iridescent and beautifully coloured. She put it in her pocket. There were others—probably left by Bandit and her babies or their relatives. She picked up several to take home to Michael Jay. The sun peeked through a hole in the darkening clouds. Immediately the sparkle returned to the surface of the water and the temperature seemed to rise almost instantaneously. She remembered her headache and was thankful that it was going away. There were several varieties of wild flowers along the shore and she wandered along admiring their beauty. She lost track of time as she discovered one little surprise after another.

Then she heard a different sound. She worked her way back from the shore a short distance following the sound of the waterfall before she actually saw the beautiful cascade of shimmering water as it fell and danced into a small pool before finding its way somewhere underground down into the lake. This cliff was not as high as the one on the other shore, but was just as rugged. She would bring Jason here; they could swim in its pristine water. She returned to the shoreline and ventured further down the beach. Now she was anxious to see what else she might discover. The clouds continued to move swiftly across the sky as the sun played hide-and-seek. She had travelled quite a distance down the rugged shore and by now the wind had grown in strength; she decided it was time to head back home. When she checked the time, she realized she had wandered aimlessly for close to an hour. Changing direction, she attempted to backtrack toward the path. Everything was unrecognizable. She remembered when they were fishing how she had scanned this shoreline looking for the entrance to the north path without success. She was confident that on foot and this close up she would be able to find the opening without difficulty. After several minutes, a feeling of apprehension spread over her.

"Damn," she said, "everything here looks exactly like everything else." She felt her heart beating rapidly and realized that she had picked up her pace. Her headache had returned and she was thirsty. The wind had strengthened.

Finally, she stumbled across the opening and entered the cooling shade. After a time, she said aloud, "I should have reached the crossed sticks by now." She turned to orient herself to the cliffs and noticed that this path hadn't taken her in a straight line from the cliffs, as the north path would have. Her head was pounding now and she rubbed her temple. She wanted to rest; she needed a minute to think.

A small bird landed on a branch near her. It chirped loudly and somewhere nearby another returned the same musical tones. There was a large boulder off to one side; she left the path to sit down and rest. The sun again slipped behind heavy clouds, but the heat did not subside; in fact, the humidity rose substantially. She walked for another half hour. If she had been on the north path, she would have been more than halfway back to the main trail leading up to the cabin. The clouds were looking increasingly ominous and the winds had picked up considerably, even here in the shelter of the trees. She told herself that if she continued she was sure this would come out on the road somewhere nearby. After all, they were only a few miles from town—not on another planet—and someone had made and used these paths. If she returned to the shore, she would still have to locate the north path entrance and her confidence in accomplishing that had waned. She decided to continue along this path. Ten minutes later the first drops of rain hit her arm. "I must be almost there," she said aloud, "but where is *there?*" There was nothing to indicate which direction she was travelling. The path seemed to peter out and she found herself at the edge of a large clearing. "Now what?" She asked. "Coming here by myself was a stupid idea. Oh great…now I'm talking to myself." The wind seemed to steal her words from her mouth.

The rain, thus far, was holding off, but it was coming and soon. The sky had darkened and the clouds had turned angry looking. She could hear thunder rolling in the distance. When it did start, it was going to be a real downpour.

She scanned the perimeter of the clearing and saw what looked like an old shed on the opposite side. Trying to outrun the approaching storm, she hurried in that direction. It would be a place for her to take shelter until the storm passed. She was rushing now, but it still took her about fifteen minutes to cross the clearing. Before she reached the old shed, she turned to look back across the clearing. Her heart sank as she realized that she had no idea where the path entered the clearing. She resigned herself to the fact that, like it or not, she would have to backtrack to the shore to locate the correct path that would take her back to the cabin. Jason would be back by now and he would be worried about her. After the storm she would cross the clearing again and search for the illusive entrance. The tall pines around the clearing waved wildly in the increasing wind gusts. She looked in what she thought should be the direction of the cliffs, but she couldn't see any sign of them.

The wind was now grabbing large raindrops and slamming them into her as she raced the last few feet toward the shed.

Chapter
NINE

Jason sang along with the radio as he drove back from town. A delicious aroma from the hot pizza filled the car. He had ordered anchovies on half for Caroline. He could handle almost anything on a pizza, even pineapple, but never anchovies. He glanced over to the passenger seat. He wished Caroline were sitting there and hoped her headache was better. He'd carefully placed the big bouquet of cut flowers on her seat. Caroline loved flowers. He didn't surprise her often enough with them.

Dark clouds had begun to build on his way to town and now it was just a matter of time before the sky let loose. He hoped he'd get back before the heavens opened up. If it rained this afternoon, he'd offer to play scrabble with Caroline. Scrabble was not his favourite way to pass time, but Caroline enjoyed playing. She usually won and when she didn't, he suspected that she might have let him win just so he wouldn't get discouraged. He had watched her pull that little trick on Michael Jay. She was not only beautiful—she was smart too, he thought to himself as a smile curled his lips.

Just minutes from the cabin, Jason rounded a curve to see two deer grazing at the side of the road. He brought the car to a full stop and enjoyed the magic of their beauty. Slowly they moved off into the woods seemingly unfazed by the close proximity of the car. Jason hoped that Caroline would have a chance to witness a similar scene before returning home; she would be awestruck. He wished he had brought the camera along. "Note to self," he said aloud, "always take the camera with you." After the last white tail disappeared through the trees, he resumed his drive. While in town he debated whether to talk to the police about the knife, but realistically he knew they would tell him exactly what he would have told anyone in similar circumstances. Without the knife there wasn't much to investigate. Although it went against everything he would have advised anyone else he thought the best course of action was to forget he had ever seen a knife.

When he reached the cabin, he pulled the car into a spot that had offered shade from the sun before the clouds moved in. He was sure the sun would be out before he needed the car again. He jumped out and retrieved his packages from the trunk. He didn't call out in case Caroline was still lying down. He hoped she had gotten over her headache. Halfway to the porch he remembered the flowers on the passenger seat. Juggling the packages and the pizza, he returned to the car, managed to open the passenger door, and scooped up the flowers. Burying his nose in the bouquet, he inhaled deeply. They smelt almost as good as Caroline. He felt the first raindrops as he took the porch steps in one stride. Quietly, he opened and closed the screen door then headed to the kitchen. After placing the bags on the counter, he removed those things that needed to go into the fridge. He would leave the rest for Caroline to put away, that way she would be able to find things when she needed them. He put the pizza, still in its box, inside the microwave. When they were ready to eat, it could be zapped. The rain had started; he could hear it striking the roof. This wasn't going to be a sun shower; they were going to get a good soaking. He could hear thunder rumbling in the distance.

Jason quietly approached the bedroom expecting to find Caroline asleep. He was puzzled when he discovered the bed untouched. She must have lain down on the futon, he thought, although he couldn't image how he hadn't noticed her there. He returned to the porch.

The rain was coming down hard now and a gust of wind grabbed at the screen door. The futon was empty. The old newspaper lay on the floor. He assumed the wind must have blown it off the futon where he had left it. He picked it up before it could be scattered further. The damp pages of the paper were open to the article about the missing woman; he didn't give it a second thought. Perhaps Caroline had gone down to the dock! Surely, she would return when she saw the sky getting so black. He tried to remember if there was a place down there where she could take shelter. He was worried now. Lightning flashed and thunder crashed all around the cabin. If she had turned an ankle or something else like that had happened maybe she wasn't able to get back on her own. He considered looking for an umbrella, but decided that could be more dangerous with the extreme intensity of the jagged lightning.

He again took the steps in one stride. In seconds, he was soaked. He had only one thing on his mind, and that was to find Caroline.

"Caroline, where are you? Can you hear me?" He shouted her name. He knew it was in vain as the thunder and wind drowned out his words as if he hadn't spoken them. The path was now quite slippery and a couple of times he stepped wrong and had to catch himself. After the second slip, he slowed down. It wouldn't do if he were to break an ankle. Thunderstorms normally didn't make Jason nervous, but this one had his skin jumping and the hair on his arms standing on end. It felt like the air all around him was charged. The cracks of thunder and flashes of lightning were so close together and so frequent that he could no longer tell which came first, the booming thunder or the blinding flashes of light. He knew that nobody should be out in this, but… he had to check down by the lake.

When he reached the shore, he searched for any sign of Caroline. It was as dark as night. Each flash of lightning exposed the shapes of the tall pines as their tops whipped violently in the high winds. A wind of this force could tear the shirt off your back, but Jason's shirt was so soaked that it clung to him like a second skin. He had to press his body into the wind to stay upright on his feet. "Caroline," he shouted repeatedly at the top of his lungs. There was no answer. Jason spied the large dock locker. There were no life jackets on the dock. Caroline was petite enough that perhaps she'd managed to climb in on top of them. He leaped up onto the dock. It was slippery, but he managed to reach the locker in three long strides. He flung open the lid and stared down onto lifejackets and Caroline's pool noodle. The wind tugged at the lid and it took both hands and a fair amount of strength to close the locker. A terrifying flash and simultaneous crack of thunder made Jason twist around toward the cabin. He stood in awe as a huge pine folded itself in half. He watched as the upper half of the tree moved downward, almost in slow motion. The tree had sustained a direct hit and had snapped like a toothpick. Scanning once again and seeing no sign of Caroline, he reluctantly headed back to the cabin. Several more shattering claps of thunder quickened his steps. Caroline will be safely undercover somewhere, he thought. He would wait until the storm passed and then she would return. She would explain to him that she had been safe and dry, and they would have a good laugh at how things turned out. At least that is how he prayed it would play out.

Back on the porch, Jason peeled off his sopping wet shirt and tossed it onto the outdoor table. He kicked off his wet sneakers and went inside. In the bathroom, he grabbed a towel and dried himself. Just as he was coming out of the bathroom the phone rang. "Hello," he said as he flipped open the cover and tried to wipe some of the water off his cell. The ringing continued. He whirled around to locate the sound. He traced the ringing to the sofa. Caroline's cell was wedged down the side of the couch. He had questioned why she would carry it every day on a vacation and she had explained that she would feel better if she were reachable. "You know," she'd said, "Just in case Nana and Papa tried to get hold of us." She usually carried it clipped to her pocket or waistband.

"Caroline?" He said into the little phone. He hoped she was calling her own number to locate the missing phone. He didn't think about where she could be calling from since he had her cell. By the time he had located and answered the ringing cell the caller had hung up. He was about to check the last caller ID record when it rang again. This time he answered quickly.

"Caroline," he blurted out.

"Down here in Dallas we usually say *Hello*," Tabitha said cheerily into his ear.

"Oh, sorry Tabitha, I was hoping it was Caroline."

"Why would Caroline be calling her own phone? I thought I'd check and see how your vacation is going. Where is she? Why do you have her phone?" She continued.

"I wish I knew the answer...to all your questions. Caroline woke up with a headache this morning so I went into town on my own to pick up a few things we needed. When I came back, she wasn't here. I just now found her cell down the side of the couch. She probably doesn't even realize she's misplaced it. Usually she carries it everywhere."

"Did she leave you a note?" Tabitha asked. "Or did she sneak away to do some shopping?"

"I haven't come across a note." Jason felt foolish that he hadn't thought to look for a note on his own. At home, Caroline would put notes on the fridge with little magnets. He headed into the kitchen to check the fridge.

"Hey, how are you guys?" Jason asked trying to make his voice sound lighter than he was feeling.

"We're great. Hold on a moment Caroline-Jay wants to talk with you."

"Hi Uncle Jason. Can I talk to my namesake?" The little girl asked excitedly.

"Sure, but you'll have to ask Mommy to call him at his Nana and Papa's back in New York."

"Where are you and Aunty Caroline?"

"We're in Canada on a vacation."

"You went away without Michael Jay?" She made it sound as if they had committed a dubious crime.

"I'm sure he's having a wonderful time with his Grandma and Grandpa." Jason assured her.

"Can I talk to Aunty Caroline?"

"She's not here right now Sweetie."

"Where is she?"

"She's out for a little while," Jason said hoping he was telling the truth.

"Okay. Mommy wants the phone again. Love you Uncle Jason." Without another word, she was gone.

A loud crack of thunder shook the air.

"Hi Jason. Wow, was that thunder I just heard?"

"There's one hell of a storm going on here," Jason said. "I wish I knew where Caroline was."

"Maybe she's visiting with a neighbour and got stuck there because of the storm."

"Yeah except there aren't any neighbours for miles. She probably went for a walk and had to take shelter. I'm sure she'll be back as soon as the storm passes over. Storms like this don't usually last long."

"Jason, I won't keep you on the phone—you know phones, storms, and old wives tales. I'm not sure if those tales pertain to cell phones, but I'll let you go anyway."

"Okay Tabitha. Give our best to Doug and a big kiss to our favourite little girl. I'll tell Caroline you called…she can call you back later."

"Talk to you later. Bye Jason."

There wasn't a note on the fridge. Jason looked at today's newspaper on the counter. The missing woman story was back on the front page today. "*Missing several days…,*" he read on, "*asking for the public's help.*" He sank onto one of the kitchen chairs. God, how must her husband be feeling? He thought back to Bill Blakley's comment about the missing woman. "*Some sort of domestic thing,*" he'd said. There was an Ontario Provincial Police (OPP) magnet on the fridge door. He removed it from the door, ran his finger over it, and then returned the magnet to the door. "Come on Jason get a grip on yourself," he spoke aloud. "A storm of this velocity couldn't possibly last long. When it's over Caroline will head back here. She'll walk through the door and probably scold me for being so worried. I'll realize how foolish I was and we'll both have a good laugh."

Chapter TEN

There were several wallboards missing, but it had a roof, probably a roof that leaked, but a roof nonetheless. There was a door that hadn't been closed for a very long time. It hung precariously from its top hinge. Caroline slipped inside. "I'm home dear," she sang out. "I may be temporarily, helplessly lost, but I haven't lost my sense of humour," She could barely hear her own words with the crashing thunder, torrential rains, and wind. Although it was early afternoon it was as dark as night. Each flash of lightning allowed her to look around her temporary shelter. There were a few large bales of hay stacked against one wall. An oxen yolk hung on the only wall that was still intact. A very rusty old Massey Ferguson tractor was parked just inside the door. It had probably been years since anyone set foot in the place.

Lightning flashed followed shortly by a deafening crack of thunder. The ground shook—so did Caroline. "What was the old rule of thumb to tell how far away the eye of the storm was by counting the time between a flash of lightning and the next clap of thunder?" She spoke aloud. The sound of a human voice comforted her, even if it was her own voice. Memory failed her, but she guessed the storm couldn't get much closer than it was right now.

However, it did get worse. The lightning came fast and furious. The thunder was ear splitting. The shed shook and the old boards creaked under the pummelling of the wind and rain. Caroline prayed the shed would continue to hold together. The pounding of the rain on the roof was merciless; it did nothing to help her pounding head. She huddled down close to the huge bales of hay for what little protection they afforded. There were more places in the roof that leaked than places that didn't. Luckily, the hay bales were in a reasonably dry area. One board, held by not more than one or two rusty old nails miraculously managed to hang on as the winds tore through the shed. When the storm grabbed hold of the board Caroline was sure the next gust of wind would rip it free. She wondered how many storms, such as this one, the old shed had withstood. She prayed that this would be just one more. It was so dark that she was unable to see the time on her watch. She waited for the next flash of lightning... it was almost two o'clock. Jason would be frantic. She hoped he would wait until the storm subsided before coming out to look for her. She allowed her mind to wander; their cabin could be just through the trees. This old shed could even turn out to be one of the cabins outbuildings. Not likely, but right now it made her feel better to think that a possibility.

Just when it seemed that the storm would never give up, the winds began to calm down. It had been a few minutes since a clap of thunder shook the ground, but the rain continued to pour down. To Caroline the hard rain hitting the ground sounded like a steak sizzling on a hot grill. "There goes my imagination," she whispered to herself. She was hungry. It was starting to get lighter. The worst seemed to be over. She would wait awhile longer until the relentless downpour let up some and she was sure there wasn't going to be another wave of thunder and lightning, and then she'd try to backtrack to the shore.

Caroline felt something touch her leg. She glanced down prepared to brush away a piece of hay. A small field mouse, the kind with the big Mickey Mouse ears, poked its head out from the hay bale. "It's a good thing I'm not afraid of mice," she said to her unexpected company. "My Michael Jay has a pet white mouse that he adores. There were times I wished I could have crawled inside one of these bales with you," she continued talking to the mouse. His little black nose twitched, but he didn't run away. She speculated that he had probably never seen a person therefore showed no fear. He scurried to the top of the bale and began washing his whiskers. The rain was finally showing signs of letting up. She stood and went to the door to have a look outside. Large drops of water hit the top of her head as she passed under some of the gaping holes in the old roof. The door, hanging from its hinge was still in place, so was the tortured wallboard. The sky had lightened considerably and the rain had eased to heavy showers. It was hot and humid. She didn't mind a little rain, but was glad she hadn't been out in the open during the lightning. Hunger pangs picked at her stomach. She reached into her pocket and took out a Werther's candy. It would fool her stomach into thinking it was fed. She unwrapped the candy and put its gold foil wrapper back in her pocket. She bit off a tiny corner of the hard candy and returned to where Mickey still meticulously cleaned his whiskers. She placed the tiny piece of candy on top of the bale. "Would you like a piece Mickey?" Before she could even pull her hand back, Mickey's curiosity got the best of him. Jason always teased her about her habit of carrying a Werthers or two in one pocket and her lipstick in the other. "*Have lipstick—will travel*," that was her motto. Today she hadn't put her lipstick in her pocket, but was glad she had the little candies. Now she'd have to revise her motto to "*Have Werthers—will travel*".

Within minutes her hunger subsided. She returned to the doorway to check out the rain situation. It was barely a drizzle now and rays of sun played on the far side of the field. Arched across the clearing was a beautiful rainbow. Even if she got a little rained on she knew the coming sun would soon dry her.

"Bye Mickey. It was nice meeting you. I'll say hello to your cousin when I get back to my porch. I hope you enjoyed your candy."

Caroline started toward the door. The sound of a muffled moan stopped her in her tracks. "I've got to find a way to control my imagination," she whispered. The storm had heightened her nerve endings. She stood still and listened. All was silent. Again, she headed toward the door. Again, she heard the questionable sound. This time the muffled moan was accompanied by a *clomp* sound. This sound was definitely not a figment of her imagination. Caroline took a deep shaky breath, "Is anyone there?" Again, she heard *clomp, clomp*. It sounded like it came from the bales of hay. It sure couldn't be Mickey, she thought. She returned to stand beside the hay. Mickey continued to lick his piece of candy. He turned it over and over in his tiny paws. The clomp, clomp sound must have been a sound he was used to since he showed no fright. Her heartbeat quickened. "Who's there?" She asked hesitantly. Now the *clomp, clomp* sound grew stronger. She grabbed hold of one of the large bales of hay and with all her might she tugged; it moved to one side. She tugged again and again until she had moved it several feet. Mickey didn't move from the top of his hay bale. He continued to enjoy his piece of candy. Beneath the hay bale, Caroline saw what looked like part of a trapdoor. She had to drag a second bale away to expose the entire door. Now her quickened heartbeat almost stopped; the banging sounds continued. There was no handle or knob on the trapdoor, but she managed to get her fingers under one ill-fitting edge. She pulled up on the heavy door not knowing what to expect. She managed to lift and slide the door out of position. She let it fall back to the floor with a loud thump. Loose pieces of hay scattered from the force of its fall. Mickey didn't take this in stride; he disappeared quicker than the blink of an eye taking his candy with him.

"Oh my God," Caroline groaned as she peered into the dark hole. What was left of her candy slipped down her throat and she sputtered a little cough.

A woman lay on her back on the earthen floor. Her hands and feet were bound and her mouth was covered with a wide strip of duct tape. A scarf was tied over her eyes. She emitted another muffled whimper. Caroline froze. The hole appeared to be about four feet deep. Caroline spoke softly so as not to frighten the blindfolded woman as she eased herself down into the hole being careful not to step on the distraught woman. She noticed that one of the woman's shoes was missing from her bound feet. As warm as it was Caroline couldn't suppress the cold shivers that ran through her. She continued to speak softy and urged the woman to try to stand. When Caroline grasped her elbow, she noticed that the woman's skin was cool and damp. First, she removed the blindfold. Frantic eyes searched Caroline's face.

"It's okay," Caroline said softly. "I'm going to release your hands first so you can help me remove the tape from across your mouth." The woman nodded her understanding.

There were marks around her wrists where the tightly tied ropes had cut into her as she struggled to free herself. When the woman's hands were free, she almost collapsed into Caroline's arms.

"Help me get this tape off," Caroline said. The woman's hands shook as she pulled at the edge of the sticky tape. Even in the semidarkness, Caroline could see sticky residue at other places on her face indicating that the tape had been removed and replaced on more than one occasion. As soon as the woman's mouth was free, she started to speak.

"Help me get away," she sobbed. "I'm terrified he'll kill me."

"Who is *he*?" Caroline asked as she stooped to release the ropes from around the woman's ankles. There wasn't much room for two women in the small space.

The woman didn't answer Caroline's question. "Get us out of here. I'll tell you everything—but first get us away from here—fast. If he returns he's liable to kill us both."

The woman was panicking and Caroline didn't blame her one bit. Caroline was also teetering on the brink of an anxiety attack. "Keep calm," Caroline whispered, not sure whether her words were for the woman or for herself. "My name is Caroline."

"I'm Amanda…Amanda Harrison." She was frantically trying to free her feet from the tangle of rope.

Caroline immediately recognized the name from the newspaper. "Of course you are; they're looking for you." She realized how foolish that must have sounded.

"Please hurry," Amanda begged.

Caroline nodded as she pulled herself out of the hole. She turned and took hold of Amanda's out stretched hands. "Ready?" She gave a huge tug and was surprised how easily she was able to pull the woman from the hole. Caroline was petite at 5' 4", but when Amanda stood beside Caroline, Amanda was at least a couple of inches shorter.

"God bless you," Amanda breathed in a whisper.

Once out of the darkness of the hole Caroline could see crusted blood under Amanda's nose. She grabbed the woman's hand and they hurried toward the door.

"Which way do we go?"

"Straight across!" Caroline didn't confess that she had no idea where they were.

Caroline took a firm grasp of Amanda's hand and started out for the other side of the open field.

"No—no," Amanda cried pulling back. "We can't go straight across. I don't know how he gets here. If we're out in the open, he'll see us for sure. If he catches us…well…there's no telling what he might do. No, he can't catch us. He'd probably kill us both. You don't know him." There was shear terror in the woman's eyes.

"Okay, we'll skirt the outside edge of the clearing. We'll be okay. Just keep your eyes open."

Amanda nodded.

The ground was wet under foot. Caroline could feel her shoes sinking into the soft earth. She glanced down at Amanda's bare foot. Although Amanda grimaced in pain once or twice, she never complained; in fact, she almost pulled Caroline along behind her. They were both out of breath by the time they reached the area Caroline judged to be almost directly across from the old shed.

"Where to now?" Amanda managed to get out between laboured breaths.

Caroline looked at Amanda with the eyes of a deer caught in the headlights. She hesitated… "I don't know!" She stuttered. "I took a wrong path and wound up here. I would have backtracked to the shore, but the storm forced me to seek shelter. Help me look for an opening; there's a path here somewhere."

The two women searched the dense tree line looking for anything that might be a path. The sun shone down intensely now and the humidity was almost unbearable.

Caroline was about to suggest that they take a breather when she felt something hard prod her back. She whirled around to see a tall, unshaven man with a shotgun aimed directly at her.

"Hold it right there little lady," the man shouted, "or you're both dead meat."

At the sound of his voice, Amanda spun around in their direction. He had appeared as if from thin air and neither woman had seen or heard his approach. Amanda was as pale as a ghost. "Oh God," she groaned as she sank to her knees.

"Going for a walk—were you? And I see you have a new friend." He again poked Caroline with the long barrel of the shotgun.

"Elliot, please stop this before it's too late," Amanda begged. Tears spilled from her eyes.

My head flew around to meet Amanda's plea. "You know each other?" Caroline managed to gasp out.

"Yes… we know each other," Amanda replied in a whisper.

"Oh, I know the bitch all right. She had it all but that wasn't enough…" He motioned Amanda to her feet. "She couldn't be happy until she took my heart and chopped it into tiny pieces." He pulled a flask from somewhere and took a drink. "She was *my girl*, but that wasn't enough for her. She liked all the attention those men at the bar paid her. I just wasn't enough. But, I showed you— didn't I honey?" He poked the shotgun into Amanda's ribs.

"I'm not your girl. You knew I wasn't interested in you. You're making that up," she shouted. "There was never anything between us. Not now... not ever." Her voice dropped to a barely discernible volume.

"Well honey," he slurred, "you won't need a man where you're going."

Caroline realized the man was very drunk.

He herded the two women back toward the shed continually prodding one or the other with the barrel of the shotgun.

Several times Amanda begged to rest. "I haven't eaten much," she tried to tell him. "I'm weak."

"After a stunt like this you won't need anything to eat," he slurred.

This time they headed directly across the open clearing toward the shed. The ground was saturated. Caroline was having a hard time with shoes on. She couldn't imagine the difficulty Amanda must be having with one bare foot. Skirting the perimeter had been hard enough, but the giant pines either had protected the ground around the edge, or had quickly soaked up the excess rainwater. Caroline reached over to take Amanda's arm to assist her as she stumbled along.

"Don't touch her you bitch," the man yelled at Caroline and jabbed her with the end of the gun. "I don't need you two pulling any more funny stuff. She'd better be able to make it on her own... or maybe I'll just put a shell through that beautiful head right now." He stopped and raised the barrel of the gun. "I don't need her now that I've got you...now do I?" He directed his comment at Caroline.

Caroline was no hero, but instinct took over. She stepped between Amanda and the end of the shotgun. "Come on…" Caroline searched for his name. What was it Amanda had called him when he first came upon them? "Elliot." she said. "You don't want to hurt her; you don't want to hurt anybody… you're just angry."

"You're bloody right I'm angry. She screwed with me. Nobody screws with me and gets away with it; get to your feet you little bitch or I'll leave you right here—you'll be food for the turkey vultures."

Amanda attempted to stand. Caroline reached out to assist her. This time Elliot didn't try to stop her.

"Get moving," was all he said as he lowered the gun.

Chapter
ELEVEN

Elliot was a large man and with his heavy work boots, he was finding it difficult to walk across the soft surface. Thankfully, he slowed his pace. It took them as long to go straight across as it had taken Caroline and Amanda to skirt the perimeter.

When they reached the shed, Elliot started laughing. "Well ladies... does anyone want to take a piss before I tuck you in for the afternoon?"

Amanda turned and spit at him. "You pig," she snarled. "Give us some privacy; we can't go anywhere way out here."

"No way sweetheart; I've discovered it's a turn on to watch a lovely lady squat and pee. So either you do it my way or piss your pants—your choice."

"It doesn't matter," Caroline whispered to Amanda.

"Hear that sweet thing; your friend doesn't mind giving me a little turn on."

Neither woman said anything more. Amanda led Caroline to the area where she had been relieving herself behind the shed and Elliot followed close behind.

"You're a pervert," Amanda growled as she stumbled behind some low bushes that offered very little cover.

"Feisty little broad—ain't she?" Elliot chuckled. "I like them feisty. Cute little ass too."

Amanda opened her mouth to censure him.

"Shh," Caroline said giving Amanda's hand a squeeze. "He'll pay for this," she assured Amanda in a quiet whisper.

Under different circumstances Caroline would have been thoroughly embarrassed, but this creep wasn't worth a moment's anguish. She squatted and relieved herself. It had been a long time since she had considered her bodily functions. It must have been a long time for Amanda as well. When they finished Elliot motioned them back to the shed and herded them inside with the prodding of the shotgun.

"Now ladies, what the hell did you do with my ropes?"

Neither woman answered him.

"Well then Betsy," he said, as he patted the butt of the shotgun, "I guess we'll have to shoot out their pretty little guts since I don't have my ropes."

Caroline stepped forward. "The ropes are in the hole." She tried to sound calm and in control; what she really wanted to do was crack Betsy's butt over his drunken head.

"Now that's a smart girlie." Addressing his gun, he said, "We'll save our fun for later Betsy. Now Sweetie, get that beautiful body down into that little hole and bring me up those ropes you so disrespectfully removed from my property." He ran his finger down the side of Caroline's cheek.

Instinctly she pulled away.

"What's the matter Sweetheart? You treat me right and maybe I won't blow your pretty little brains out your pretty little ears."

"Let her go Elliot," Amanda shouted. "This has nothing to do with her."

"You shut your pie hole... bitch. You had your chance to be with me, now maybe I'll show you what you missed. I'm quite the ladies man... you know good between the sheets."

Caroline wanted to run, but she knew she wouldn't get past the door. If she made a break for it, he might shoot her, or Amanda, or both of them. Instead, she took a deep breath and keeping her voice as steady as she could she repeated, "Elliot, you don't want to hurt anyone. Listen to Amanda. Stop all of this before it's too late."

Elliot laughed. "So I just let you both go and we let bygones be bygones—right?" He didn't wait for an answer from either woman. He grabbed Caroline roughly by the arm and shoved her toward the hole. "You do as you're told. Get your ass down there and get those ropes."

Caroline quickly slipped into the opening and retrieved the ropes from the ground. Her mind was racing. She wondered what she could do. Maybe she could grab the gun. If she did the wrong thing that fool could shoot them both, probably without a moment's hesitation. With Amanda, it would be two against one, but he was a big brute, and drunk to boot; that made him very unpredictable. She decided to play it minute by minute. She heaved herself out of the hole and handed him the ropes.

"Now, I want you to tie up your little friend. Do a good job, or you won't have to worry about being excess baggage," he snarled as he held the dangling ropes in his extended hand.

She took back the ropes she had removed from Amanda's wrists and ankles.

"Now tie up my little angel the way you found her." He was attacked by a bout of hiccupping.

"I'm not your little angel... you creep. Somehow, I'll make God damn sure your ass is grass. You can't do this to me."

"You bet I can. You wanted me."

"You're insane... I never even gave you a second glance," Amanda said.

"You'll love me; I'll make you love me, or you'll pay the price."

Caroline gave Amanda a nudge and shook her head to indicate that Amanda shouldn't talk to him.

Amanda clenched her teeth together to stop herself from giving him a reply. She was drained. She didn't resist when Caroline began to tie her hands together.

The two women stood eye to eye. Caroline moved her eyes in quick succession between Amanda's eyes and her wrists. She hoped Amanda would look down and that Elliot wouldn't notice the eye contact, but Amanda stared straight ahead. A look of surrender glazed her eyes.

"Hurry it up bitch," the man yelled between hiccups.

"I'm doing the best I can," Caroline snapped back sarcastically.

"You should watch your lip beautiful lady. I only have enough rope to tie up one of you," he retorted equally as sarcastically.

She turned and glared at him.

"Keep your eyes on your job," he said poking her shoulder with the barrel of the gun.

With a calmness that belied the panic Caroline was feeling she wound the rope around Amanda's wrists and without a seconds hesitation made a small loop in the rope and forced it between Amanda's clenched fists.

Amanda's eyes immediately went to her hands and back up to meet Caroline's wide-eyed expression.

Caroline blinked slowly and deliberately. At that moment, communication between the two women was more than words could ever have conveyed. They needed to escape from this lunatic.

"What's taking you so long?" He came closer to examine the ropes Caroline had fastened around Amanda's wrist. He was close enough that Caroline could smell his disgusting breath. She said a silent prayer that he wouldn't make her re-tie Amanda's hands behind her back or wouldn't notice the small loop she had forced into Amanda's hands. Amanda was clenching her hands so tightly together that her knuckles were white.

"I'm doing what you asked; give me a chance I'm not used to doing this." Caroline continued to do as she was ordered. She wrapped the remaining rope around Amanda's ankles being sure to secure the knot at the front of her legs. Amanda was wearing lightweight chino slacks and as Caroline placed the ropes just above Amanda's ankles she was careful to entrap the bottom of the fabric. She pulled the fabric tight against the inside of Amanda's calves and folded it to the outside. Hopefully, this maniac wouldn't notice what she was trying to do. This would give Amanda wiggle room once she freed the trapped fabric from under the ropes. If he hadn't killed her yet chances are he would continue to keep her tied up, a prisoner—his prisoner. Her own fate was more uncertain. She thought about Jason and Michael Jay and a tear slid down her cheek. Quickly she wiped it away with the back of her hand.

When the ropes were tied, she stood face to face with Amanda. "Keep your faith," she whispered so quietly that Elliot didn't hear a word. She stepped back and faced the scumbag.

He reached somewhere behind him and pulled out his flask. He took a long swig. As he drank the barrel of the long gun dipped toward the floor. Caroline considered jumping for it, but she knew he would be able to easily overpower her and there were two lives at stake should she cross the wrong line. Heaven knows what he might do if she angered him further. He lowered the flask from his mouth and surprised her by shoving it towards her and saying, "Want a drink?"

She hesitated. "Sure." She allowed only a small amount of the liquor to pass her lips. She wanted the telltale smell of liquor on her breath so he'd think she drank willingly from the vile flask. The strong alcohol tasted horrible. She did everything in her power not to spit it out or gag. As she swallowed the despicable liquid, she forced a smile. "Thanks."

"I don't want to kill anyone else, but if I have to I will," he slurred. "Why couldn't you love me? You could have given me a chance. That's all I ever asked—just for you to love me," he pleaded turning toward Amanda.

She hung her head, but didn't answer him.

His eyes were glazed and Caroline envisioned a number of ways this could go. If she could gain his confidence she thought maybe he'd take her back to town, or to his place, or wherever. Almost anywhere would be better than way out here. She thought she might have a better chance of running into someone, or Amanda could escape and find help to rescue her.

"I'm hungry," Caroline said.

At first, Amanda couldn't believe that Caroline was actually talking to him and treating him normally, even friendly. She quickly realized that Caroline must have a plan and she didn't do or say anything that might rock the boat.

"Me too Elliot," Amanda whispered instinctively playing along with Caroline.

"Yeah, I brought you food." He had a small backpack hanging from his shoulder. He pulled out a sandwich. It was scrunched up from the way he had it crammed into the backpack. He also had a previously opened bottle of water. It was pee warm.

"You broads will have to share this. I didn't know we were going to have company," he laughed and hiccupped at the same time.

Again, Caroline noticed the barrel of the gun droop downwards. He tossed the sandwich to her. She removed the wrapping and passed half to Amanda.

Amanda took it with both bound hands and raised it to her mouth; she devoured it quickly. "The least you could have done, you bastard, is to feed me," Amanda spat out angrily as soon as she had swallowed.

Caroline passed her the other half of the sandwich. Elliot didn't notice. Amanda wasn't going to take it, but Caroline pressed it into her hands in a not to be misunderstood manner. It disappeared as quickly as the first half. Amanda must have been starving. Caroline wondered how much Elliot had given her to eat since he'd kidnapped her. The multiple tape marks on her face showed that the duct tape had been removed and replaced at least a few times. Caroline hadn't eaten anything since breakfast, except for her Werthers, but she was sure Amanda was much hungrier than she was. She hoped she'd get answers to all her questions, and the sooner the better. Caroline was encouraged by his lack of attention to what was happening around him.

"Got another drink?" She asked him with a fake smile.

He hesitated a moment, and then passed her the flask.

She feigned a long drink and then returned the flask to him. He took another long drag on the half-empty container.

"I ain't never seen a little lady take to this stuff," he said with a grin.

"It's stronger than what I usually drink, but it's okay," she pretended. Just when she thought things might be going a little her way, he did a flip-flop.

"Okay Honey... time to get you back under cover." He unceremoniously shoved Amanda toward the hole. "Back into the root cellar," he said. "You'll keep better in there," he roared at his little joke.

"Please Elliot," she pleaded, "don't do this. Maybe we can talk."

"You and me are done talkin. Get down there yourself, or I'll help you and you won't like it my way."

Amanda plunked down on the edge of the opening and lowered herself, as best she could, down into what for her had become hell.

Caroline tried to move behind him.

"No—No, pretty lady you stay where I can see you," he raised the barrel of the gun and aimed it directly at her at point-blank range.

Caroline was mystified by the fact that he could bounce between being completely aware of his surroundings one minute and in another realm the next. "Come on Elliot, you don't have to worry a damn about me." She tried to sound friendly. "Maybe we can go somewhere nicer," she said looking around the shed as if disgusted. "We could have a few drinks together. I'm always looking for a little fun." Caroline was literally shaking in her boots, but she had no choice but to try to win him over. "You and Amanda have to work this out between yourselves." She shrugged her shoulders and continued, "I'm not going to spill any beans. I'm a visitor to this Country and I don't need a boat load of trouble."

"Yeah, I noticed your Yankee plates. New York eh! I ain't never been to New York myself. Hey, I know a great place to get hot wings," he said. For a minute, he forgot himself and it looked like she might be winning his trust. Then he suddenly flipped again. "Hey, wait a minute—you can't piss on my head and tell me it's raining. I know what you're trying to do," he sputtered taking another swig from the flask. "I ain't got no more rope, but you ain't goin nowhere Sweetheart."

Caroline could feel the blood drain from her face. She thought he was going to kill her.

Without taking his eyes off Caroline, he cautiously moved behind one of the straw bales and returned with a large roll of duct tape. "Sorry babe, but I can't take you with me—not this time." Roughly, he pulled Caroline towards the hole. She tried to resist. "You better behave yourself pretty lady or I'll have to go visit that husband of yours up at the cottage. You probably don't want him to die so young—now do you?"

"My husband?" She was now on the very edge of panic. "Oh, that guy is just a friend," she tried to sound casual. She didn't want Elliot to attach any importance to Jason. "My old man's back in the States. We're split, but I've got a beautiful little boy who needs me. You're an okay guy... you shared your drink with me... didn't you?" She falsely flattered him. "I'm sure you don't want to hurt an innocent bystander. I'm also sure you won't hurt Amanda. If that were your intention, she wouldn't be here now. You're just in a bit of a bind. You'll get it all figured out." She tried to humour him. "It's got nothing to do with me... you'll figure it out."

"Hey, if you're a mother, what you doin up here with your *friend*, if that's what he is?

"I'm just like you Elliot my friend; I like a little fun. Let's go back to town and maybe we can have some fun together." Caroline could hear the quiver in her voice. She hoped Elliot wouldn't notice.

He nodded his head and for a moment she thought he was going to agree. Then he stared at her as if she wasn't quite in focus.

"Don't tell me what I'll do." His voice got louder and much uglier. "Get those hands behind your back girlie." He quickly secured her wrists with layer after layer of duct tape. She tried to space her hands as far apart as possible, but he did a more than competent job. Caroline couldn't even wiggle her wrists.

"How do you know where my friend is?" Caroline asked hesitantly.

"I know a lot of things. Like I know that you look damn good in that little bikini. You're a bloody sexy broad. And, that day you stripped down in the boat, I nearly died. My hard-on practically blew the zipper out of pants," he said rubbing his hand over the crotch of his jeans. Hey, and I know you can cook. The smells coming from that kitchen almost drove me up a tree. Man… I would have loved to just walk right in there and join you for dinner. I can't remember smells like that coming out of any kitchen."

"You spied on us?"

"Call it whatever you wanna. Yeah! I watched the two of you more than once. You two screwed up my plans. I was in the cottage when you first got here. You near scared the shit out of me. I needed a drink so I looked around. Found me a full bottle of Brandy. I was plannin to stay the night when I saw your car lights coming up the road. If you had come an hour later, you would have found a nice rabbit stewing." He laughed a sinister laugh. "I took my rabbit and the Brandy and got the hell out of there. I watched the way you two were acting in the lake and I'm guessin that good-lookin bastard is more than a friend. Watching the two of you in the water got me damn horny. Maybe you and me should get it on babe," he said running his hand down the side of her cheek and down her arm.

Caroline clamped her teeth together to try to calm herself. "I'm usually open to ideas, but certainly not this way and not way out here."

"Nice try babe, but I told you I ain't buyin it for one minute; you ain't goin nowhere. You just sit yourself down there and I'll see if I can keep you from takin another walk with your little friend." He shoved her down onto one of the hay bales.

As he secured the duct tape about her ankles she realized he was right…she wasn't going anywhere. Caroline prayed that Amanda would be able to escape and could return the favour by rescuing her. Only this time they couldn't get caught. In the meantime, she continued with great difficulty to keep her voice even. She tried to assure him that he could trust her. She kept up a steady stream of talk until he roughly secured a large piece of tape over her mouth.

"You better not forget what I said pretty lady. You behave, or I'll take care of that good-lookin friend of yours. I've done it before and got away with it; I can do it again. It would be easy, maybe even fun. Maybe I'll let you watch." He laughed.

Caroline's heart pounded faster when she realized that he was talking about having murdered someone and gotten away with it. She swallowed hard.

"Maybe before I take care of your friend I'll tie him up and let him watch you and me having some fun." He bent down and kissed the tape he'd placed across her mouth. "You could model that little bikini for me. Doesn't that sound like fun? Sure wouldn't take me long to get that suit off your sweet little body. Maybe I'll let your friend take it off for me. That way we could both enjoy that cute little ass and those perky tits."

This time he had overlooked covering Amanda's mouth. Probably another lapse in judgement due to his alcohol consumption. Caroline was glad Amanda remained quiet and didn't try to talk with him. He nudged the side of Caroline's leg with the barrel of the gun. "Time to join your new friend," he said with a sinister chuckle.

Caroline unceremoniously tumbled into the hole beside Amanda.

Amanda sat slumped against the earthen wall with her face buried in her arms. Caroline remained reclined on her back where she'd landed.

The darkness was sudden. The slam of the trapdoor created a strong earthy smell as the swoosh of air fanned the old sides of the root cellar.

Caroline listened for the sound of him dragging the straw bales over the door.

"Now, my little angels, you behave yourselves. I'll be back," they heard him say. Then silence.

Chapter TWELVE

Neither woman dared move for several minutes. Amanda took the first step. "Try to sit up Caroline; I'll need a little elbow room to get out of these ropes." When Caroline tied Amanda's hands in the front Elliot hadn't noticed—his first slip. Amanda helped Caroline to a sitting position. She could faintly make out Caroline's features in a tiny ray of light slipping through the edge of the ill-fitting door. Raising both hands, Amanda gently pulled the duct tape from Caroline's mouth. Caroline struggled to free her hands to no avail. "Wait," was all Amanda said.

Caroline could see the shadow of Amanda's body moving and could feel her brushing up against her as she worked on the ropes.

"You're a genius," Amanda whispered. "That little loop you thrust into my hand gave me just enough leeway to wriggle out of these ropes. I was afraid to try before Elliot left in case he checked them again," she added. "I know him; he'll go into town and tie one on, like he's not already feeling the booze, and then he'll either sleep it off, or he'll return here. He's come back here so drunk he could hardly stand. I don't know how he made it. God help us both if he returns; he's a mean drunk."

"Free your feet and then help me," Caroline instructed her.

Amanda tugged at her pant legs. Once she had wriggled the fabric free from beneath the ropes, the ropes hung quite loosely. She was able to untie the knots within a minute or two.

Caroline waited impatiently; the few minutes felt like a lifetime. She had to keep telling herself that somehow they would get out of here. Jason and Michael Jay never left her thoughts.

Once free of her bindings Amanda turned to Caroline. She picked at the tape on Caroline's wrists, but quickly realized she wasn't making any headway in the darkness. "Let me see if I can open the trapdoor first." The hole was not deep and Amanda could quite easily reach the door. "Please don't let the hay bundles be on top," she said to the darkness. She pushed straight up and the door gave and then settled back down again. At least now she was sure the hay wasn't going to be an additional problem. Elliot's second slip. Again, she pushed up on the edge of the door's frame. She removed her remaining shoe and wedged it under the side of the heavy door. She could push her arm through the opening now. She thought if she could get her shoulder under the door maybe she could shove it aside. It wasn't a hinged door; it just rested in the opening under its own weight.

Caroline twisted around until she was on her knees. "Step on my shoulders; that will give you extra leverage."

Amanda climbed on Caroline's shoulders and placing her back and shoulders against the door; she shoved with all her might. For a small woman she was strong as an ox. The creaky old wooden door raised and moved to one side. "I've got it Caroline. Just one more shove and we can wiggle out." She repeated the process, but still the opening wasn't enough to allow a person passage. "Sorry Caroline, but we need to do this one more time."

"If you must…but try to remember that I have a dinner date." Caroline's sense of humour broke through the surface of the dire situation in which they found themselves. Even Amanda let a small laugh escape.

"I'll be joining you if you don't mind."

Two more shoves and the trapdoor was opened far enough to allow them to get through. The extra light the opening provided would make it easier to free Caroline of her tape bindings. Amanda returned to the next job at hand. She clawed at the duct tape, but got nowhere. The many layers of tape that Elliot had wrapped around Caroline's wrists and ankles might as well have been chains. There was no way Amanda could loosen them.

"I can't help you," Amanda moaned.

"Amanda, you have to find something up in the shed that will cut the tape," Caroline ordered. Caroline tried to maintain a steady voice, but she sensed that Amanda, at least right now, needed someone to take charge. Caroline was just as frightened as Amanda, in fact, she was scared shitless, but if Amanda knew the truth she might fall apart and be of no help to either of them.

Amanda's reaction was instantaneous. She scrambled over Caroline and pulled herself up into the shed. She apologized as her cold, bare feet slid up Caroline's arm. Amanda sat down on the shed floor and pulled on her shoe. Feverishly she searched for something that would cut. She ripped the old oxen yolk from the wall and examined it for any parts that were sharp. She flung it away in disappointment. The nail... The nail was just out of her reach and so she retrieved the oxen yolk to give her a little boost; it provided her that little extra height she needed to reach the nail. She pulled, pushed, and pried. She tried everything in her power to remove the nail, but it held fast. A stream of cuss words flew around the shed. All the while, she kept urgently repeating, "We've got to get out of here." Stumbling over to the old tractor she tried every part that she thought might pry away, but despite all the rust, or perhaps because of it the tractor was in one solid piece and was going to stay that way until Mother Nature decided otherwise. Finally, finding nothing she slumped to her knees beside the hole. "I can't find anything," she groaned in despair.

"It's okay," Caroline consoled her. "We'll think of something."
Caroline had managed to get to her feet. They were quiet for a
moment. "Amanda, if you come back down here maybe you can
boost me enough so I can get out," she suggested. "With your help
I can get outside; I'll hide in the woods until you get someone to
help us."

"I don't know where we are; I don't know where to go," she said
downhearted. Her face was dirty and streaked with tears.

"Amanda, you can have a breakdown as soon as we're safe, but
for now—suck it up!" Caroline said rather harshly.

Amanda stared unbelievingly at Caroline for a moment.
Then Caroline watched as her strength and determination return.
"Okay Caroline move over; I'm coming in." She tried several times
to hoist Caroline high enough to get her to the floor of the shed. "I
think if I grab you around your calves I'll be able to shove you up
above the floor level. It won't be pretty," she said, "but if you can get
your upper body on the floor; I can pull you out."

"Pretty's not my target." Caroline doubted that Amanda would
be able to lift her high enough, but Amanda had the strength of a
bulldozer. Either she had a cargo load of guts, or she was running
on adrenalin—probably both.

Caroline felt like a fish out of water as she lay on the edge of
the opening. She thought she was going to slip back into the hole.

As Amanda climbed out of the hole, she kept hold of the
back of Caroline's shorts preventing her from slipping back down.
Amanda apologized as she grabbed Caroline under the arms.
"This might hurt."

Jason would be beside himself by now. Caroline knew that
Jason would come searching for her, but she also knew he had
absolutely no idea where or which way she might have gone.
Others would be searching for Amanda, but also there was the
huge unanswered question of "where"? Today it would be a
search and rescue mission—if Elliot returned it might turn into

a body recovery mission. The thought did nothing to help the situation and shivers ran up her back.

Amanda sat silently on the earthen floor to catch her breath.

"Amanda, our only chance to get out of here," Caroline left off the word *alive*, "is for you to find help. My husband will have people scouring these woods," she lied. Jason would probably search himself before involving others. "You will run into someone. Whatever you do, don't call out for help; Elliot might be the one to hear you. Cross the clearing, search for a path, any path, the woods are laced with paths." Caroline was panicking and she tried to calm herself. "You'll find someone to help us."

"So, the man Elliot was referring to is your husband?" Amanda asked.

"Yes, I'm here with my husband; you'll meet him soon," she promised.

"First we have to get out of this shed," Amanda said with determination.

Caroline wasn't used to being dragged around by her underarms; Amanda had been right, it did hurt. Once she was away from the hole Amanda helped her to her feet.

"I can't carry you," she said. "If I help can you hop?"

"I excelled at cut, paste, and hop in preschool," Caroline replied. "Just get us out of here."

The rain had completely stopped and once again the sun made an appearance. Now they knew which direction was west as the sun sank lower in the sky. Not that it would do them any good, but it was one positive piece of information. Anything that was a sure bet was a comfort.

Amanda took hold of Caroline's arm. "Okay, let's go."

With her ankles so tightly bound together, Caroline found hopping wasn't easy. Several times, she would have fallen if Amanda hadn't steadied her. Slowly they made their way across the shed to the doorway. With Amanda's help, Caroline managed to get a fair distance into the woods. Caroline was exhausted; she leaned against a tree to recoup her strength.

Amanda tried again to loosen the duct tape. She broke branches from trees and gouged at the bindings with little effect. Elliot had done a thorough job ensnaring his prisoner with the unyielding tape. "Who could ever image tape being such a strong barrier?" Amanda sighed.

"What do you expect? They use this damn stuff on space shuttles," Caroline said. "Listen Amanda, I'm okay here, you've got to go before Elliot reappears. He'll never find me."

Amanda stared at her—unhearing.

"Amanda, listen to me. Go! Get help."

Amanda snapped back to the present. She knew Caroline spoke the truth, but she still didn't want to start out on her own. "It will be dark soon," she said. "The mosquitoes will be ferocious. I'll be right back." She went deeper into the woods.

Caroline could hear Amanda grunting and cussing as she moved around; she could no longer see her. Caroline called out, but Amanda didn't answer her. In a few minutes, Amanda returned with an arm full of cedar boughs.

"This will have to protect you; it's the best I can do right now." She settled Caroline down onto some ground cover and placed the boughs over her paying particular attention to the area around her head. "Don't make any noise. If Elliot comes back and finds us gone, he'll be livid. Chances are he's not coming back tonight, but you have to keep yourself hidden," she said. "You'll see that son of yours again—don't worry. As an afterthought she asked, "There really is a son...right?"

"Oh yeah... there really is a son; he's not yet three and he needs his Mommy."

Amanda reached her hand in through the boughs and removed a tear from Caroline's cheek.

"Amanda, after you reach the other side of the clearing, look for a path. When you find it stay to your left. That should take you back down to the shore. You'll need about half an hour or probably twice that once it's dark. When you reach the shoreline, go to the right; follow the shoreline all the way until you reach a boat dock. That's where our cabin is." She did not mention the north path. It would have only complicated matters. She remembered the day Jason had rowed to the cliffs; it hadn't seemed all that far. She wished she had paid more attention, but she and Jason were enjoying the wonder of watching the sunrise over the water. She could have never imagined she'd find herself in such a desperate situation.

"I have to go now."

"Don't go yet," Caroline said urgently. "Take my shoes. I won't need them here."

Amanda hesitated a moment; she wiped the back of her hand across her eyes. She plunked herself down to unlace Caroline's sneakers. Sometimes Caroline wore socks in her sneakers, unfortunately today wasn't one of those times.

"Thanks Caroline, these will make it much easier for me to cover some ground." She placed her sneaker on Caroline's foot. Amanda had stuffed the ropes from her wrists and ankles into her pockets. She removed one and wrapped it around Caroline's bare foot, turban style. "It's not the latest style, but it should help with the bugs and the cool night air. I'm so sorry to have gotten you mixed up in this," she said sincerely.

"You couldn't help that I showed up here. Besides, even if I'd known where I was going... if I knew you were here needing help I would have come. Only difference is that I would have brought help...now that's your job."

Amanda moved a few feet away. She turned and scanned to see if Caroline was sufficiently camouflaged. The woods looked normal; it would be hard to spot anyone unless you knew exactly where to look. She called back..."Don't worry Caroline; I'll get help." Before moving out into the clearing, she hesitated and then returned to where Caroline lay. "What's your husband's name?"

"Jason. Jason White." That's all Caroline said and Amanda was gone. She disappeared within seconds. The woods were thick here. Elliot wouldn't be able to find her, she hoped. A jumble of different thoughts ran through Caroline's mind. If Elliot were to recapture

Amanda and God forbid, he should kill her... She tried to force the thought from her mind. Cold shivers coursed along Caroline's spine. Nobody would find her here under her camouflage and if she dared to call out it would probably be Elliot that would find her first. She estimated that Amanda had probably less than an hour of daylight left. The sun had almost disappeared and clouds had begun to move in again. She huddled quietly under the cedar boughs. She wondered if Elliot would return tonight. The darker it got, the less chance there was that he would come out into the woods again today. He was probably sleeping it off. There was also a good chance that once darkness set in there would be no rescuers for Amanda to run into. Caroline reluctantly admitted that Amanda was probably on her own. It would be a long time before Amanda could find help and for them to return here to rescue her. She questioned whether Amanda would have the strength to return all this way without first taking in some proper nourishment and a well-needed rest. Maybe when she mentioned the clearing and the shed to some locals, they would know exactly where to go and Amanda wouldn't be required to return herself. With these and other thoughts running rampant through her mind, the minutes slipped by agonizingly slow. Soon darkness settled in around her.

Chapter THIRTEEN

After the storm passed, Jason again searched for Caroline. Something drew him toward the north path. He followed it to the shore. When he returned to the cabin he took down the fridge magnet. This time he dialed the OPP number.

Officer Randy Barnard answered and Jason quickly explained the situation. "Hold for a minute; I want to refer your call to another officer," he said.

After what seemed like a long time, Officer Bruce had taken the call. "Hello Mr. White. I'm Officer Bruce. Please repeat what you said to the other Officer?"

"Yes, yes of course."

"We require that a person be missing for a minimum of twenty-four hours before we investigate, but…" Officer Bruce chose not to mention that they were already searching for a missing woman. "I'd like to come out and have a look around."

"I'll be waiting." Jason explained where they were staying.

"Yeah, the old Miller place; I know where it is. I'll see you as soon as I can get there."

Jason decided to walk down to the shore again while he waited for the police to arrive. He half expected to meet Caroline on her way up the path, or down at the dock or... On his way out the door, he grabbed the flashlight. The shore area was just as it had always been. There was no sign of Caroline. Jason blinked the tears from his eyes and said a silent prayer. "Please let her be okay," he whispered. When he returned to the cabin, he flipped the light switch inside the front door. The room was bathed in a soft glow. It was hard to believe it could get dark so quickly.

A car pulled up the driveway. Jason was surprised that the police had arrived so quickly. The cop must have driven like a bat out of hell to get all the way out here from town this quickly.

"Hello Mr. White. I'm Officer Bruce," he said as he removed a small book from his pocket. "Mind if I ask you a few questions before we take a look around?"

"No, of course not. I don't know if I can tell you much. I'm worried sick. It's not like my wife to just up and disappear."

"Why don't you tell me what you know, and I'll take it from there."

Jason repeated the events of his earlier return from town.

The OPP listened intently, jotting things in his book. He reminded Jason of an older version of himself. He asked more questions, and then returned to the cruiser. His flashlight was somewhat larger than Jason's, but still only provided a normal beam of light. He removed his police cap and pulled a strappy contraption over his head. "Night goggles," he explained. Jason was familiar with night goggles; he had used them himself during his investigations.

"Let's have a look around. Watch your step," he called back to Jason. "The rocks around here can get pretty slippery after a rain."

When they reached the shore, he shone the beam of light into the water alongside the dock. "Can Mrs. White swim?"

"Yes, like a fish, but she'd never swim alone. She's always on my case about that. Besides, she certainly wouldn't swim with a storm brewing."

"Do you have two vehicles?"

"No. We have just the one car and I had it in town."

"Do you know anyone around here?"

"No, as far as we know there aren't any neighbours for quite a distance—like miles."

"Did you notice anything missing up at the cottage? Your wife's purse, an umbrella, anything she might have taken with her?"

"I didn't look for her purse," Jason said.

"Sorry Mr. White, but there are certain questions I have to ask."

"I didn't look for anything missing," Jason replied. He raked himself over the coals for not checking on such things. If he had been dealing with a client looking for a missing person this would have been one of the first things he would have done. The mind is a complicated thing. When something like this hits home, you react differently. Jason was the husband, not the detective. He took a deep breath.

"Just asking. Maybe she had a visitor." The officer continued, "Any booze, cigarettes, anything else someone might be looking for?"

"We don't smoke. There is some Vodka, wine, and a few beers. I didn't think about a break in." Jason did think about the uneasy feeling he'd experienced on more than one occasion since their arrival.

"What did you think?"

Jason was not surprised by this question. It was one he himself would have asked. "I just don't understand why my wife isn't here."

When they reached the dock, Officer Bruce turned off his flashlight and asked Jason to do the same. He waited a minute for his eyes to adjust to the darkness, and then he pulled the night goggles into place. He stood on the end of the dock and slowly scanned 360 degrees. Shoving the goggles to the top of his head, he again flipped on the flashlight. "I don't see anything out of the ordinary," he said as he automatically swept the tree line with his beam of light. "Let's go check on Mrs. White's purse and see if anything else is missing."

The beams of light from their flashlights scanned side to side as they made their way up the path. They were almost even with the entrance to the north path when Officer Bruce stopped. He shone his light into the blackness of the obscured path. "Where does this go?"

"It travels north for maybe two or three miles and meets the shore of an inlet. We fished there one day. There aren't any cabins or anything back there. I traced all the way back to the shoreline before it got dark looking for Caroline, but I didn't see any sign of her having been there. As far as I know, she has never taken that path. I was just checking to make sure, I didn't know where else to look. There is one thing though," Jason took a deep breath, "the day after we arrived, I was out walking on my own, and I took this path. Partway in something caught my eye. I noticed something shiny under a bush; it turned out to be a large butcher knife…" He hesitated… "It was stained with blood," he added.

Officer Bruce whirled around and shone his light in Jason's face.

Jason held his hand in front of his eyes.

"Why didn't you tell me this before? Where is the knife now?"

"I don't know. When I went back to retrieve it the next day, it was gone without a trace." Jason thought about the missing knife from the magnetic rack in the kitchen. "I believe it came from the cabin." His mind raced. "It could have been in the woods for sometime. I thought maybe a poacher, or… I didn't touch it. There was no evidence of blood on the ground, only the stained knife."

"What makes you think it came from your cottage?"

"My wife; she's a bit of a perfectionist. When I put the dishes and cutlery away—you know helping out, she straightened the knife rack to accommodate a missing knife."

"How did she know there was a knife missing?"

"I don't know… I think she said there was a vacant space on the rack when she started cooking. She thought the missing knife would show up in a drawer somewhere."

"Do you know we are looking for a missing woman, another missing woman?" He corrected himself. He studied Jason's face for a change in expression.

"Yes," was all Jason could get out.

"You should have notified the police right away," Officer Bruce said. Jason's expression offered nothing.

"Yes, I guess so, but we are here on vacation." Jason knew his answer was hopelessly inadequate, just a weak excuse.

"What proof do you have that your wife was here with you?" He was still holding the light on Jason's face.

Jason contemplated the question and the intent it inferred. "Are you kidding? Naturally, my wife is—was with me. I told you, we are here on vacation."

"Has anyone else seen you or your wife since your arrival?"

"Of course, we went shopping in town." Jason felt flustered.

"Did you talk to anyone in town?"

"Yes, I talked to Chris Collins at the real estate office and to that reporter Blakley, Bill Blakley. We had coffee at the little diner next to the newspaper office."

"Good," he said. "So both Bill and Chris can vouch that you and your wife were here together."

"Of course." After a moment Jason added, "Well, actually they didn't meet Caroline, she was shopping. I can show you the stuff she bought."

"Did she use a charge card? You know where she had to sign her name."

"No, she paid with cash. We converted our US money to Canadian at the border."

"That's too bad," he said. "Let's go have a look around the cottage."

This time he motioned for Jason to walk in front of him. Jason was beside himself. What did this guy think he was going to do…

whack him over the head? With stunned disbelief, Jason realized that was probably exactly what he was thinking.

Inside the cabin, Officer Bruce asked Jason to sit down while he looked around. He soon returned with Caroline's purse. "Please empty the contents onto the coffee table."

There was the usual purse junk: wallet, hairbrush, lipstick, a key ring with a small photo of Michael Jay in a Tweety Bird costume, a few candies, and other miscellaneous small items.

"You mentioned on the phone that you are from the US. Did you have a passport to cross the border?"

"Yes, of course—we both did."

"Wouldn't Mrs. White carry her passport in her purse?"

"She had both our passports; I guess she removed them for safekeeping."

"Where would she have put them?"

Jason was starting to get the idea that Officer Bruce doubted his every word. "I don't know."

"Did you and your wife have a recent argument?"

"No, we get along great."

"Do you and your wife carry cell phones?"

"Yes, all the time."

"Have you tried to call her cell?"

Jason knew his answer wasn't going to make things look any better. "I have her cell phone here." He answered taking it out of his pocket.

Officer Bruce didn't ask Jason why he had his wife's phone; he just waited for an explanation.

"I found it down the side of the couch; she must have lost it there." His hands were shaking. "I need a soda," Jason said heading to the kitchen. Officer Bruce followed. Jason didn't offer him a can of soda. Jason wasn't happy with the line of questioning or what the cop was deducing. Jason took a glass from the cupboard and opened the soda. It foamed up out of the can forming a sticky puddle on the counter. He grabbed a handful of paper towels and mopped up the spill. He poured what was left of the soda into the tall glass. It again bubbled up, almost to the point of overflowing the sides of the glass. He opened the freezer to get ice cubes. When he lifted the ice tray, he spotted their passports. They were securely locked into a sturdy zip-lock bag and hidden under the ice trays. This was Caroline's idea of safekeeping. Without a word, Jason handed them to Officer Bruce. The Buffalo border guard had stamped both passports, attesting to the fact that both he and Caroline had entered Canada. Officer Bruce examined the two documents.

"I can't tell you how happy I am to see these," he said tapping the two documents against the palm of his hand. "In a missing person's case, nobody is beyond suspicion. Nothing personal of course; I hope you didn't take offence to my questioning?" He appeared to be truly sincere.

Jason nodded his understanding. He dropped a couple of ice cubes into the soda and swirled them around. Not waiting for the ice to cool the drink, he downed it in one long swallow. "Would you like a soda?" He asked.

"No thanks."

"Can we go now and look for Caroline?" Jason asked impatiently.

"I realize you're under a lot of stress Mr. White, but thrashing around in the pitch-black won't help anyone. Try to get some rest and you'll be of more use to everyone in the morning," Officer Bruce told him.

"I guess your right, but I just think that I should be doing something." Jason said dejectedly.

Officer Bruce placed his hand on Jason's shoulder. "We'll find her," he said confidently. "We'll be here before sunrise. If you hear anything before then…call me at home." He pressed a small card into Jason's hand on which he had written his home phone number.

Jason lifted his glass to take another drink and was surprised to find it empty. He didn't remember drinking it; his mind was in a fog. This all seemed surreal. Jason watched from the porch as the lights of the cruiser disappeared down the road. He put his hand into his pocket and pulled out the OPP fridge magnet. He returned to the kitchen. In the silence, he heard the little clicking sound as the magnet reattached itself to the fridge door. Except for the groceries on the counter, everything seemed to be in place— everything that is except Caroline.

Chapter
FOURTEEN

The darkness closed in around Caroline like a dark heavy cloak. Her eyes widened as the darkness crept over her. No matter how she concentrated and stared, she couldn't see a thing. The expression *"Couldn't see my hand in front of my face,"* came to mind. Thankfully, the mosquitoes, for the most part, were leaving her alone. Because of her headache that morning, she had opted to skip her shower, and hadn't slathered on her great smelling after shower skin conditioner. The cedar boughs Amanda had placed around her moved gently in the night breeze. They tickled and made her itchy, but she was thankful for them. Her side was getting sore, but she hesitated to roll over in case she lost her protective covering. "If I could just shift a little," she said in a quiet whisper. An owl hooted, and the hair on the back of her neck stood on end.

She wondered how far Amanda had gotten. With luck, she could be on the shore by now, or without luck, she could still be searching for the path opening. It would be considerably more difficult once the darkness had settled around her, if not impossible. She blocked out the thought that Amanda might have run into Elliot.

Caroline's shoulder was aching; she would have to risk changing position. Slowly and cautiously, she rolled over onto her tummy. She figured from this position she could pull herself back onto her side if necessary. It was going to be a long and uncomfortable wait. The cedar boughs came with her as she rolled over. Amanda had done a thorough job of stacking and intertwining the boughs to afford her the best possible protection.

Caroline shivered in the damp night air. As she lay quietly, she felt something sharp poke her in the hip. It was the shells she had picked up along the beach. Her adrenaline flowed as she reasoned the edge of the shell might be sharp enough to cut through her duct tape bindings. Her joy quickly turned to anger as she criticized herself for not remembering the shells before Amanda set out. If she were free, she would have been able to help find their way back to the cabin. With her hands lashed behind her back there was probably no way for her to reach the shells, but she had to try. She tugged on the back of her shorts in an attempt to twist them around to bring the side pocket closer to her hands. She could feel the boughs above her slipping and had to admit she was getting nowhere fast. A tear slid down her cheek as she realized her fate rested in Amanda's hands.

She and Jason didn't attend church every Sunday, but they did have strong religious beliefs. Caroline prayed, prayed hard. She couldn't even imagine what Jason must be going through. "He might think I've drowned, or..." She thought about the missing woman story in the paper. "He might think I've been kidnapped." She moaned, her voice sounding loud in the silence of the night woods. After speaking the words aloud, it hit her like a bomb going off. "Oh my God—I have been kidnapped." The reality sank her deeper into her dark little world. She knew it could get worse if Elliot came back. He'd probably kill both her and Amanda if he recaptured them for a second time. Up until now, she had only thought of Amanda as being the victim. She wasn't sure if her shivers were from being cold, or from being scared.

The woods were anything but silent and she listened as small creatures scurried nearby. On their drive here, Jason had vaguely mentioned wild turkey, deer, and bears. Turkey and deer she could deal with, but bears! Now she had something else to worry her. She could hear the owls softly communicating with each other. A large bird went whooshing through the trees, perhaps a turkey or pheasant. She could only guess that it was something other than an owl as she had read that owls travel on silent wings. Caroline wished she could somehow tune out the sounds around her. Close by she could hear a soft rustling sound as something moved through the ground cover. Something touched the back of her leg in the darkness. She shuddered when she thought it could be a snake. Quickly she forced herself to think of something else, anything else... the little mouse perhaps. Yes, that's it, she thought, the rustling she heard was probably one of Mickey's pals, maybe even Mickey himself coming to see if she had more candy to share. Whatever it was, it was now moving away from her.

The most disturbing sounds came from the trees themselves. They creaked, cracked, and rustled as they moved back and forth in the stronger upper winds. The pines whispered their secrets to one another. In the dark it was downright eerie. Caroline closed her eyes and almost immediately fell into a remarkably deep, exhausted sleep.

The sounds of something or someone awoke her with a start. She could see nothing. She held her breath, and could feel her heart beating against her chest. Caroline wondered if she was dreaming. She whispered, so silently that even she barely heard her own words, "Please let this be a dream." Now alert, she listened to the unmistakable sounds of something or someone moving in her direction. The sound of branches snapping and ground cover rustling got closer and closer. She visualized Elliot and his gun. She dared not move.

"Caroline, don't be afraid—it's me—Amanda."

It was so dark, that even when Amanda had almost reached her she still couldn't make out Amanda's features. From her position on her tummy, it was difficult to look upward. "Amanda, are you alone, did you find help?" Caroline listened for sounds of others coming, but behind Amanda there was nothing but blackness and silence.

"I couldn't find the path that led to the shore," she groaned as she stooped and began moving aside the protective barrier. "I found one path that led me to a sheer wall of rock, and another that led nowhere...it just stopped. It was so dark. Once I almost walked right into a deer on the path. I'm not sure which one of us was more frightened; we both took off running in opposite directions." She sank down beside Caroline and helped her to a sitting position.

This close up Caroline could make out Amanda's features. Her face was strained; she looked exhausted.

"I tried to chip off pieces of the rock wall to cut through your tape. I didn't have much success, but managed to get a couple of small pieces."

Caroline sat silently. In the disappointment of Amanda's return, she had completely forgotten the shells in her pocket. Suddenly she remembered. "Amanda, in my pocket you'll find some clam shells, they might be sharp enough to cut through the layers of duct tape," she said in short raspy gasps.

"I'll try anything." She eased Caroline over sideways to get her hand into Caroline's pocket. "Why didn't we try this before?" It was a stupid question, and she knew it, almost before the words hit the air. "Sorry," she sputtered. "I guess neither of us is firing on all cylinders right now. Let's get you free and then we can hide out until first light. With the two of us looking it will be a piece of cake to find the right path."

Amanda's words were strong and confident, but Caroline could detect a slight tremor in her voice.

"Help me to stand up," Caroline whispered.

"I'll try to free your ankles first, at least then we can move if we have to."

Caroline braced her back against the base of a pine tree and Amanda began sawing away at the bindings. The mosquitoes were more annoying now that she was out from under the protective cedar boughs. Periodically Amanda had to stop sawing at the tape to swat at some of the more determined pests.

"It's working," she reported after a few minutes.

After several more minutes Caroline felt the restraints let loose.

Amanda grabbed the loosened end of the layers of tape and pulled it free of one ankle. Upon being released, Caroline's instinct was to run, but where? Instead, she waited patiently while Amanda peeled the other ankle free.

"I'll never need a wax job again," Caroline said. Amanda began to hack away at Caroline's still bound wrists.

This took longer as Amanda explained, "In the dark, I don't want to cut you and there's no room between your wrists and this damn tape. If I could just slide this shell under the tape it would go faster, but once I get it started..." She stopped talking and concentrated on the job at hand.

After what seemed like an eternity, Caroline felt her hands come free. "Thank you Amanda," she said as she gave her a hug. "Being in that position really took its toll on my shoulders."

"Yeah, I remember all too well."

Caroline nodded to the darkness. She tried to see what time it was on her watch, but it was too dark to read the little hands.

Caroline and Amanda sank to the ground at the base of the huge pine and pulled Caroline's protective boughs in around them.

"How did you know I was in the shed?" Caroline asked.

"Even though the storm was loud, I could hear you talking to someone—Mickey, I thought you called him. Up until now, I totally forgot that you weren't alone. Who is Mickey and where did he go? Can he help us?"

Caroline laughed quietly. "Oh yes, Mickey. Well he didn't join me until after the worst of the storm," she said. She could see by the puzzled look on Amanda face that she was still in the dark, literally. "Mickey is not a person, he's a mouse!"

"A what?" Without waiting for an answer, she said, "So you were taking to Disney's Mickey Mouse?"

"Not exactly—I was talking to Mickey, the shed mouse."

There was a long pause before she continued. "You're serious... you were talking to a mouse, a real live mouse? Good thing he didn't come visit me in the root cellar; I would have had a heart attack. Oh great, my rescuer is a nut," Amanda said light-heartedly.

"Hey, what are you inferring? What have you got against mice?"

They remained silent for a moment and organized their thoughts.

"Well, as I look back at this whole situation, I guess my rescue occurred because of that damn mouse. If you hadn't talked to that damn rodent—excuse me—Mickey, I would have never known you were up above me in the shed. I'd given up hope of being rescued. Once a day Elliot would bring me a sandwich. Before he'd take the tape off my mouth, he'd warn me not to start screaming. He told me there was nobody around for miles, and then he would shoot off that damn shotgun. He'd shoot right through the roof of the shed just to prove to me that nobody was within hearing distance. 'Save your breath,' he would tell me. I'm afraid of guns and he'd threaten to shoot me if I didn't do as he told me." Again, she fell silent.

Now Caroline had an explanation for the bangs she and Jason had heard. They weren't backfires or trees falling, but that Bozo shooting his shotgun. This probably explained some of the gaping holes in the roof as well. The hair on the back of her neck bristled.

She reasoned that the cabin must be quite a distance away as the shots weren't close enough to be able to say with certainty where the bangs came from or what they were. They were only distant noises.

"What's your connection to Elliot?"

"My husband and I were having some in-law problems. He had temporarily moved out at my request. I knew he wanted to come back home, but I was so stubborn. We'd been in contact, and were sure we could work things out, but I wasn't ready to have him come home yet. I work part-time at Henrys. Do you know Henrys?" When Caroline shook her head, Amanda went on. Henry's is a local bar/restaurant and pool hall. One night after I got off early I hung around talking to some people. I was hoping to run into my husband. Sometimes he'd hang out there and have a few beers with the guys. We were both working part-time jobs to save up to buy our own house. My husband was tutoring math students and I got the job at the pool hall. He's a good man, just listens to his parents too much. Anyway, I was ready to tell him he could come home. We love each other and I knew we could work out our differences. We want to have a baby, but his parents convinced him we are too young." She paused to collect her thoughts.

"I'm confused, is Elliot your husband?"

"Hell no... I told you I work part-time in the pool hall." Elliot was there most nights. One day he asked me if I wanted to play a game of pool. I'd seen him plenty of times there and around town. I agreed to play. We played a couple of games. There were a few other nights after that when we'd have a game of pool, nothing more. He drank a lot, but he seemed harmless. When he drank, he would call me *his girl*. Many of the people used little names like that—you know—Honey, Sweetheart, nothing was meant by it, it was just being friendly. I didn't think anything of it. The job beat sitting home alone feeling sorry for myself. He was a customer, certainly not a close friend, just a customer. Then one day, everything went wrong. He had been drinking a lot and he asked me to drive him home. I suggested he call a cab, but he insisted that he had to have his car first thing in the morning to go on a job interview. He could have killed himself or someone else if he had driven in that state. I couldn't very well refuse. I finally gave in and agreed to drive him home. He said he'd pay for a cab to take me back to my place." Amanda paused.

Caroline didn't rush her; she allowed her time to collect her thoughts before she urged her to continue.

"Anyway, when we got to his place on the outskirts of town, he needed help to get inside. Once inside, he blocked the door and tried to get fresh with me. I tried to leave, but he continued to block my way. When I rejected his advances, he got nasty. He backhanded me across the face; I fell and I must have struck my head on something. I guess I knocked myself out. The next thing I knew I was in a car, my hands were tied, and my mouth was taped. He tied something around my eyes so I had absolutely no idea where he was taking me. A couple of times I heard the tires hit the gravel on the shoulder of the road and I knew he was swaying. I kicked at the back of the front seat and he just laughed at me. We drove for what seemed like a long time. I prayed a cop would catch him and pull him over. I don't know how long I was out, but he sounded even drunker than before. He was babbling that he loved me and he'd make me love him back. I was shocked and scared silly. He kept referring to someone named Gloria. "*I fixed her wagon, and I can do the same to you,*" he said repeatedly. He yanked me out of the car and shoved me ahead of him. I knew we were in a wooded area because limbs of trees and bushes scrapped my arms as I stumbled along. Once we stopped, I could hear him peeing. I yanked my arm free of his grasp. He knew I couldn't go anywhere with the blindfold, but that just made him angry and he slapped me again. My nose was bleeding; I could feel it trickling down over my lip. I sank down on the ground, and he grabbed my hair and pulled me up. That's when I lost one of my shoes." Amanda let out a big sigh. "At one time I could hear water. First, it seemed to be on my right side, and then later on my left side; I couldn't imagine where I was. Then he kept me in the root cellar. I couldn't tell day from night. I knew from my hunger I had been there several days. In total, I think I had four sandwiches and he would take me outside to do my thing a couple of times a day. That was the only time he removed the blindfold. It was embarrassing as hell. He wouldn't even release my hands.

"Did that bastard rape you?" Caroline quietly asked. She was surprised that she had used the word *bastard*. Caroline's use of cuss words was *extremely* limited.

"No, he never touched me, in fact, he never even tried." Amanda answered. I knew he was watching me as I relieved myself. That was one of the worst parts… knowing that he was looking at my body as he pulled my pants up and down. Every time he came I could smell booze on his breath."

"Didn't he give you anything to drink?"

"Yeah, my sandwiches came with a bottle of water. I was so thirsty that even though it was really warm it tasted like wine from the Gods. When he took the tape off my mouth, I begged him to let me go. I asked him to free my hands so I could eat, but he refused. My hands were tied behind my back so he fed me and held the water bottle so I could drink. God knows how long he would have kept me there. There were times I wished he would just kill me and get it over. Every time he returned, he threatened me. It was just a matter of time I thought!"

Caroline placed her arm around Amanda's shoulder. "You're okay now; we'll get out of here, I promise. Let's try to get a little rest before daylight."

Before Caroline slept, she thought about Mickey and his candy. She reached into her pocket and pulled out the two remaining shells, and a single, gold wrapped Werthers. Amanda's slow rhythmic breathing indicated she was asleep. Caroline was hungry, but she tucked the candy and the shells back into her pocket. They would share the candy in the morning.

A few mosquitoes made pests of themselves, but other than that it remained fairly peaceful.

Just before Caroline fell asleep she wondered what they would do if they met Elliot on the trail. She wondered if they should separate by maybe twenty minutes to a half-hour so if he was to catch one of them, the other could still get help. Little goose bumps formed on her arms at the very thought of him catching either of them a second time. She hoped that he'd gotten so drunk he'd sleep a long, long time. She finally closed her eyes and drifted into an unsettled sleep.

Chapter
FIFTEEN

When Amanda awoke awhile later, she placed her hand on Caroline's arm. "Caroline, wake up. Do you think you can walk a little?"

Caroline was amazed at Amanda's fortitude. She was the one that had been running around and exerting energy half the night, but she was concerned about Caroline's ability to walk.

Amanda began to remove Caroline's sneakers from her feet. "You put these on and I'll take my shoe back. I can fashion a rope binding to protect my other foot."

When Caroline protested, Amanda shook her head.

"I insist," was all she said.

Caroline watched as Amanda slipped her foot into her one remaining shoe. She then took the rope that had been wrapped around Caroline's bare foot, and using the second rope from her pocket, she made some knots and some loops and within minutes had created a not too shabby sandal. "Where'd you learn to do that?"

Amanda giggled, "I learned macramé when I was a kid."

Jason and Caroline had this little thing going where when they wanted to remember to do something they would say aloud "Note to self…" Caroline added, "Note to self…learn macramé" to her list.

"What?" Amanda asked looking puzzled.

"Nothing. I think you'd better rest awhile longer; we can start out just before sun up. We'll make better time if we can see where we're going. We already know it's next to impossible to find the path in the darkness."

"Just for a few minutes longer, and then I have to make a stop at the shed." Amanda sighed.

"What's at the shed?"

"You'll see. I have an idea. Earlier I was thinking if we mentally mark off the clearing like a clock, and we're here on six, if we walk to three and find another place to hide until sunrise, we'd be safer just in case Elliot shows up here really early. I just think we should put some distance between us and this shed," Amanda said with conviction.

"Sounds good to me, but let's stay close together."

"Don't worry about that, I'll be on you like poop on a baby blanket," Amanda giggled.

Several minutes passed as they huddled together to share each other's warmth. It wasn't cold, but with them both being tired, hungry and damp, not to mention scared, the surroundings were anything but comfortable.

Amanda decided it was time to start moving. "Come on lazybones," she said giving Caroline a little nudge.

Caroline had her eyes closed, but she wasn't asleep. "Are you sure you're ready?"

"I'm ready for any number of things—like—a shower, a toothbrush, and twelve hours in my own bed snuggled up close to Ron," she replied. "But, he's not here right now, so I guess a walk in the dark with my new friend is all that's on my agenda. First I'm gong to need you at the shed."

"You still haven't told me what's at the shed that you want," Caroline said. "If you're planning on taking that old rusty tractor back as a souvenir… I'll have to draw the line."

Amanda laughed. "I like your sense of humour; you sound a lot like me. Actually, I need you as a go-between."

"A go-between?" Caroline looked puzzled.

"Yes. Between me and your friend Mickey. You have to ask him if I can borrow a couple of handfuls of his house. There's no way on earth that I'm going anywhere near that rodent's hay bale, and in the dark to boot." Amanda shivered and Caroline realized that she really was afraid of the little mouse.

"If standing up to a mouse is all you're asking of me, it's a deal," Caroline said trying to focus on Amanda's face in the darkness.

In short notice Amanda was on her feet. She grabbed Caroline's hand and assisted her to stand.

When they reached the edge of the clearing, they stopped and peered around. It was a useless gesture since they could barely see a few feet ahead of them. Quickly they traversed the distance between the edge of the woods and the old shed. Amanda froze when they reached the door. "Caroline, I can't go in there. That mouse is probably just waiting for us to return."

Under different circumstances, Caroline would have burst out laughing, but the tone in Amanda's voice was terror. Caroline took hold of her hand, "You wait here and keep watch. How much of Mickey's home do you want?" She still didn't have any idea why Amanda wanted the hay.

"Just a few good handfuls," she said squeezing Caroline's hand before releasing her hold.

Caroline entered through the sagging door. All was quiet. It was pitch-black inside. She felt her way across the shed in the direction of the hay bales. She bumped into the first bale before actually seeing it in front of her. At first, it was difficult to get a handful of hay; it was so tightly packed together. Once she was able to loosen a corner, it became easier. The hay on the outside of the bale was dry and crumbly, but once she managed to get some of the dry stuff pulled away the under layers were soft and pliable. Soon she had several handfuls of fragrant hay tucked into the pouch she made by pulling up the front hem of her top. She made her way back to the door. "Here's your hay," she said in a whisper. Caroline was surprised at how much lighter it was once she was outside of the shed.

"Thanks Caroline," Amanda plopped down on the ground. "Just dump it here beside me."

Caroline emptied her shirt.

Without hesitation, Amanda started weaving the pieces of hay into a dense little mat. When it was the right size, she slipped it between the sole of her foot and the rope sandal she had made earlier. She wove the remaining hay in and out of the ropes on her upper foot. "There," she said. "Not a fashion statement, but it will make walking easier and may even provide a little protection from the damp ground."

"And you called me a genius," Caroline remarked shaking her head in disbelief.

"So let's go, the next stop is 3:00 o'clock on the imaginary field clock." Amanda held her hand out to Caroline for a hand up.

There was no sign of a moon, but once in the clearing Amanda and Caroline could make out the shapes of large clouds sliding across the still darkened sky. They crept along close to the tree line. As they walked along each carried their own silent thoughts. Caroline tried to think where she had last seen her cell phone. She thought about her key ring. Besides her house and car keys, there was a little oval frame with a picture of Michael Jay and a small flashlight. Right now though she wished she had the little Dallas Cowboy figure that was the flashlight. It had been a Christmas gift from Caroline-Jay when she was six years old. She had been so proud when she told me she not only picked it out and wrapped it all by herself, but she had earned the money to buy it by helping her mommy with the vacuuming. A smile crossed Caroline's lips as she thought about her Godchild and how quickly Caroline-Jay had grown from a baby to a little girl. She tried not to think of Jason and Michael Jay. It was hard enough picking her way through the dark without adding the blurriness of tear filled eyes. She wondered what Amanda was thinking. She didn't know diddlie-squat about Amanda, but somehow she knew if they got the chance to get to know each other they could become good friends.

Amanda stopped to adjust her rope sandal. "What do you think Caroline? We should be about a quarter of the way around by now. I don't know about you, but I sure could use a rest."

"Let's see if we can get out of the open." Caroline said nodding her head in agreement.

They lifted and pulled on boughs until they found a spot they could slip into that was sparse enough. There wasn't a path, but there was enough room for them to comfortably, or as comfortably as possible, sit down side by side. They sat close together receiving some solace from each other just by having their arms touch. Minutes passed in silence. Both needed time to recoup. Travelling through the darkness wasn't easy, but at least they received some comfort in knowing that if Elliot were to return before daylight, he most certainly would be carrying a flashlight. A beam of light in the darkness would be visible a great distance. They would have time to hide before he came upon them. They kept their eyes peeled for even a flicker of light.

Chapter SIXTEEN

N ot knowing what else to do, Jason went back inside. A night miller flew haphazardly around one of the small table lamps.

Caroline's cell phone assaulted the silence.

Jason had left her phone on the kitchen counter. He made it across the living room and into the kitchen in time to grab it on the second ring.

"Hello."

"Now don't tell me Caroline still hasn't come home," Tabitha said jokingly.

Jason froze on the spot, not knowing what to say.

"Tabitha, things aren't going great here. I have no idea where Caroline is and I'm worried sick," Jason said in a barely audible voice.

"Jason, are you saying she's not back yet?"

"I was sure she'd return after the storm, but she hasn't come back. I don't know where she is."

Now it was Tabitha's turn to be uncertain about what to say. "Hold on Jason, I have to speak to Doug." The line went silent.

"Jason…Doug here. What the hell is going on up there?"

"The police will be here at sunrise to help search for Caroline. I want to think there's a good reason she's not here…maybe due to the storm, or a sprained or broken ankle, or something like that, but…"

"But what?" Doug asked.

"Never mind, I should have never left Caroline here alone, that's all. This is my fault." Jason couldn't allow himself to think that his Caroline could be a second disappearance victim.

"I'm sure it will be okay," Doug said encouragingly. "You have to stay in control."

"Is there anyone around there she might have made friends with… a neighbour or someone?"

"No. We're pretty isolated here Doug."

"I'll grab a plane and be there tomorrow"

"Thanks Doug, but there isn't anything you can do. I'll be out there searching tomorrow with the cops."

"Okay Jason, you know we are only a call away. Keep us posted."

"You know I will," Jason disconnected the call.

The silence was enough to kill him. He returned to the living room. The miller continued its dizzying courtship with the light bulb. Jason paced the floor. He poured himself a stiff drink, and took a big swig; it almost choked him. He added more tonic and took another drink. Jason couldn't imagine where Caroline could have gone. He downed his drink in one mouthful. He shuddered. There are many things I could become, he thought, but an alcoholic isn't one of them. He put the top back on the Vodka bottle and returned it to the cupboard. When he opened the door, a post-it-note hung from the upper shelf. There was a heart drawn on it with a marker and inside the heart, it said *"Luv ya!"* He swallowed hard and his throat closed. Caroline often left him little notes and other surprises. She'd leave a heart shaped doily in his briefcase with nothing more than a question mark in the centre. Once she had a bouquet of coloured marshmallows delivered to his office. The card read, *"I'm sweet on you."* "God Caroline, where are you?"

It was after midnight. He turned off the lamp and went into the bedroom; he lay down on top of the covers. After what seemed like an eternity, he dozed off in a fretful sleep.

She turned the water on and let it stream down over her shoulders. It felt good after her strenuous workout. She reached for the shower gel. After shaking it several times, she declared it a dead soldier. "Jason," she called.

Jason opened the door partway and poked his head into the bathroom. "What can I do for you?" He asked. He could see the curves of her body through the opaque shower curtain.

"Can you bring me a new bottle of shower gel, this is empty," she said holding up the empty container.

"Sure, where do I find a new one?"

"There's one in that mesh bin in the linen closet." She started to wash her hair.

Jason watched as Caroline piled her natural curls on top of her head and worked up a generous lather with the shampoo that smelled like green apples.

"Okay." He reluctantly tore himself away from the door. "Hey, there are two bottles of shower gel—one's blue and the other's green, which one do you want?" Jason called out as he stood in front of the linen closet. With the shower running and the door closed Caroline couldn't hear him. He grabbed both bottles and headed back to the bathroom. He was about to ask which bottle she wanted when she pulled the curtain aside and stuck her head out.

"What's taking so long? At this rate, I'll have used all the hot water and you'll have to take a cold shower."

He held out both bottles. Seeing her standing there stirred the fires in his mind and his body.

She took the blue bottle and thanked him by flicking water at him.

"You'll pay for that."

"You'll be the one paying for taking so long; there won't be much hot water left." Caroline closed the shower curtain.

"Maybe I should join you now to be sure I get some hot water."

"Maybe you should," she laughed.

Jason stepped out of his pyjama bottoms and rapped on the shower curtain.

"Knock, knock, is anyone home?"

"Come in…if you dare," she giggled.

"Oh, so now you're daring me." He pulled the curtain aside with a flourish.

"Hurry, come in before we flood the whole bathroom," she said mischievously. "As long as you're here, I might as well put you to work."

She turned her back to him and handed him the new bottle of shower gel. Her hands, still soapy from the shampoo made the bottle slippery and he struggled to open the top.

"Two strikes against you: slow delivery, and lack of action," she continued to tease as she rinsed the shampoo from her hair.

"Keep it up and you'll see some action." Jason rubbed a generous amount of the gel over her shoulders and down her back. Her skin was smooth as silk. The steam from the hot water carried the exotic fragrance throughout the bath. "Wow, you smell good enough to eat." He whispered into her wet hair.

She leaned back against him and pulled his arms tight around her. They stood so close they became one body under the pulse of the shower. She turned and took his face in her hands. "You smell pretty good yourself," she whispered as their lips met.

Jason added more gel to the palm of his hand and sensuously caressed her body.

Her breasts were full and firm; he let his fingers slide around their firmness. He fingered the dark orbs, and although the water was hot, they responded to his touch. A little moan escaped her lips. As her small hands explored his body, he also responded.

They stayed in the shower a long time, exploring, caressing, and loving being together. The temperature of the water cooled and Jason turned it off. "The last thing I want right now is a cold shower." His voice was deep and erotic. He offered Caroline his hand as she stepped from the shower.

Jason pulled a towel from the rack and wrapped it around her. In one smooth movement, he lifted her into his arms and carried her to their bed. The towel fell away as he tasted the sweet droplets that lingered on her cheek. The bed wasn't yet made and he pushed the rumpled sheets aside. They made love as if for the first time.

Jason sat bolt upright, sweat soaking his shirt. "Caroline," he moaned.

When he wasn't thinking about the dream, he passed what was left of the night worrying, dozing, pacing, and praying. Would daybreak ever come?"

Chapter
SEVENTEEN

Caroline stood and stretched; she and Amanda had been awake for a long time, but it had been too dark to start out on the next leg around the clearing. Caroline watched as Amanda adjusted her rope sandal.

"Well I guess it's now or never," Amanda said as she got to her feet. "I'm looking forward to sleeping in my own bed. I'm also looking forward to turning Elliot in to the police; I hope they nail him to the wall."

"Do you think Elliot meant it when he insinuated that he'd killed before?"

Amanda didn't answer right away. "After the past few days, I guess he could be capable of anything. All I know for sure is I don't want him to catch us again. I think it might be enough to push him over the edge. I'm afraid. I don't think either of us will be safe until he's arrested and thrown in jail." Amanda fell silent for several minutes, and then she turned to face Caroline. "Caroline, I'd like to tell you something, but you must promise not to say anything to anyone."

Caroline studied Amanda's face for a clue to what she was about to say. "You can tell me anything you want and I promise it stays between you and me." The first thing that popped into Caroline's head was that Amanda was about to confess that she'd had some sort of affair with Elliot.

"I'm pregnant," she said in a low voice.

"You're what?" Caroline asked stunned. "Is it Elliot's baby?"

Amanda laughed, a little louder than she wanted, and quickly put her hand over her own mouth. "Hell no! I told you Ron and I were talking about starting a family. That's the in-law problem… remember. When we told them our decision, they started making trouble. They said we were too young, that we hadn't been married long enough, that we should buy a house first. We are renting now," she added. "It was one thing after another. When Ron started to cave-in to his mom's nagging, I told him to choose—his mom or me. We decided it was best if he moved out until he made his decision. What I didn't know at the time and what Ron still doesn't know is that the bun was already in the oven." She proudly patted her tummy. In an almost inaudible tone she added, "If anything happens to this baby, I'll personally kill Elliot."

Caroline put her arms around Amanda and gave her a hug. "All the more reason we have to get you safely out of here. I was thinking that maybe we should split up as we head out. I'll leave now and you wait fifteen or twenty minutes. If—God forbid—Elliot shows up, one of us will be able to go for help."

"I'm not that anxious to go it alone." Amanda's voice was unsteady. "I have absolutely no idea where I'm going. At least you've seen the path; I know you'll be able to lead us out of here. Please stay with me. Let's hope Elliot is out like a light and not tramping the woods, but if he… Please Caroline let's stay together."

The frightened look in her eyes left Caroline no choice. "Okay, it's you and me together. Just keep your eyes and ears open. Even if he were to come out here, he is not expecting to see us. If we keep alert we can hide quickly and there's a good chance he'd walk right past us."

Amanda nodded her agreement. Just at that moment, Caroline heard Amanda's stomach growl. She took the candy out of her pocket and handed it to Amanda.

"Do you have one?"

"Of course." Caroline lied. She removed the foil wrapper that she had in her pocket from when she and Mickey had shared their candy yesterday and pretended to unwrap a second Werthers.

Amanda quickly removed the wrapper and popped the candy into her mouth. "I swear, I'm buying some of these and I'm not going anywhere unless I have a couple in my pocket." She savoured the sweet caramel candy.

The sun wasn't yet up, but the hint of early morning light was already making things look better. Before Caroline stepped out into the clearing, she scanned all around. "Come on Amanda, I want you to meet my Jason," she said matter-of-factly taking hold of Amanda's hand.

The ground was considerably drier than yesterday. There were still soggy patches, but it was a much easier walk.

When they reached the vicinity where Caroline remembered the path being, she said, "Let's hope we can find the path quickly."

"Be careful: this is the spot where Elliot showed up yesterday." Amanda's palms were sweating from her jangled nerves, not the warmth of the oncoming day.

"Just look for the opening," Caroline said as she pulled on boughs. "Elliot must have come out of here somewhere."

They'd searched about ten minutes when Amanda excitedly called out, "I think I found it."

There was about two body lengths distance between them and Caroline amazed herself at how swiftly she closed the gap.

They stepped from the clearing onto what was definitely a path. Caroline wasn't sure if it was the right path, but it was going in what she thought was the right direction. "Good work Sherlock."

Amanda literally glowed. "I hope your Jason has breakfast ready when we get there." Finding the path had put them both in an elated mood.

"We're one step closer to safety, but let's not hang around here."

"Let me fix my dancing shoe." Amanda tugged on her rope sandal.

Caroline was concerned that they were depleting their strength too quickly as they almost ran down the path. She took hold of Amanda's elbow and forced her to slow down. They were both thirsty. Their breath came in shallow pants. Caroline tried to visualize a guardian angel sitting on her shoulder and she allowed herself to think of Jason.

"I see it," Amanda said breathlessly.

For a moment, Caroline misunderstood. She thought Amanda meant Elliot. She could hear her heart pounding in her ears. Then she also saw *it* as well. The first morning rays of the sun sparkled and danced over the rippled surface of the lake. They hugged each other, and then hurried toward the shore.

"Wait," Caroline cautioned. "Let me check to be sure the coast is clear. I want you to move off the path; we can't screw up now. Stay hidden until I come back for you." Caroline was once again assuming a leadership role.

Amanda was about to protest, but instead she asked, "How long will you be? How will I know you are okay? What if you see Elliot?" The questions kept coming fast and furious.

"Whoa, calm down. I'm not going to expose myself; I'm just going to have a look around. Move in off the path and hide; I'll be back."

Amanda nodded and moved off the path. When she had manoeuvred far enough in, Caroline whispered, "Okay, stay there and be real quiet."

"Like I need to be told that," Amanda whispered back. "Hurry," she added as an afterthought.

The palms of Caroline's hands were also sweating. She approached the shore as silently as possible. She watched as a couple of seagulls flew unconcerned over the blue water. Other than the gulls, there was no sign of life. She waited, and watched. When she was certain that Elliot was nowhere nearby, she stepped away from the trees. The sun was peeking above the horizon. It appeared as an orange semi-globule. The day would be beautiful. Today, she and Amanda would be safe, or...

A large black crow swooped by her head and landed in a nearby tree. It squawked and kept up an ungodly racket. Caroline jumped and let out an unconscious yell. Her heart nearly came through her rib cage. The crow again swooped from the tree, narrowly missing her head, and continued its noisy tongue-lashing as it soared and landed nearby in another tree. She was probably somewhere close to its nesting area. The repeated cawing was grating on her nerves; she wanted to yell *shut up*, but held her tongue. She took a minute to compose herself. Her breathing had started to return to normal when the snapping of a branch underfoot made her whirl around toward the sound. She felt light-headed and might have fallen over if fear hadn't cemented her feet in place.

Amanda appeared at the base of the path. Her eyes darted up and down the beach. Seeing nobody, she nervously gasped, "Are you alright? I heard you cry out." Again, she checked the beach.

"Yes...yes, I'm alright," Caroline assured her. "That damn crow just scared the pants off me." She motioned toward the crow just as it made another swoop, this time skimming Amanda's head as it kept up its noisy ruckus. "What are you doing here? You should have stayed hidden."

"Yeah right," she said shrugging her shoulders. "Are you sure you would have stayed hidden if the situation were reversed?"

There was a long silence.

"Just as I figured," Amanda said coming to stand beside Caroline. "Do you have a sister?"

"No, I'm an only child. Why?"

She laughed, "I'm an only child myself, but if I could choose a sister, you'd be the one I'd choose."

They stood in the middle of the beach, fully out in the open and hugged each other. The crow finally fell silent and their vulnerability flooded back over them. "Let's get out of here," Amanda said.

Without another word, they headed out in opposite directions. Only a few steps apart, they stopped and faced each other.

"We have to go this way," Caroline said pointing toward the right.

"Are you sure? I thought I remembered hearing the water on my left side before Elliot dragged me into the woods." She hesitated. "I don't know. I was so disoriented. He may have taken me in circles just to further confuse me."

"I'm sure we have to go that way." Caroline again gestured to the right. "If we follow the shoreline we'll reach our dock." Caroline hadn't mentioned the north path or having seen Amanda's shoe on the path. If she did, Amanda might want her to search for the other path and Caroline's instinct told her that could be dangerous. Caroline knew that Elliot must have been on the north path when Amanda lost her shoe, but she was also sure that if they followed the shore to the right it would come out, as she said, at the cabin dock. She would just have to hope that Elliot wouldn't show up before they passed the concealed entrance to the north path just in case that was his usual way to reach the shed.

"So which way will we go?" Amanda asked hopelessly.

After a moments thought Caroline said, "My way. If you even think that the water was on your left side then that could mean Elliot might be that way—so we go to the right. If Elliot does come from the other direction, he'll turn up the path and it will be ages before he discovers we are missing and comes after us."

"So it appears that I would have chosen not only a kind, compassionate sister, but a pretty smart one as well," she smiled. "To the right it is."

They started out, hand in hand, picking their way along the rocky shore. Caroline kept her eye open for the north path, but saw nothing. It was slow going over the rough terrain.

After awhile Amanda stopped. "I can't look at the water any longer without a drink."

"Just a little bit further and if my direction is right we should come to a waterfall. We can chance having a drink there."

"If—did you say *if?*"

"When!" Caroline corrected herself. She kept moving down the beach. As they travelled over and around the jagged rocks, Caroline began thinking about her taking the wrong path in the first place. When she had discovered the lovely little waterfall yesterday, it was the sound of the water falling that first made her aware of its location as it was hidden by trees and brush. After her discovery, she had proceeded even further down the beach. When she finally turned back to return to the north path she didn't remember passing the falls. By that time, the wind had picked up considerably and she told herself that she hadn't noticed the waterfall because she hadn't been able to hear the water rushing over the rocks. It was necessary for her to keep her eyes on where she was going so she didn't fall on the uneven ground. A feeling of panic swept over her; what if she was confused about the direction and they ran head-on into Elliot? She didn't share her uncertain feelings with Amanda. Before long, they were out of sight of the path that led from the clearing. Caroline felt as though a heavy weight had been lifted from her shoulders. As they rounded a bend she heard the sound of the waterfall, and relief flooded over her.

They hurried toward the welcome sound. They waded into the shallow water and approached the small cascade of crystal clear water.

Caroline removed the two remaining clamshells from her pocket and washed them in the cool water. "Here Amanda," she said offering her a shell. "My best Mother of Pearl...nothing is too good for us." At that moment, the cold water tasted better than either of them could imagine. Caroline knew that she would never drink untreated water in New York, but here the water was so pristine... and this was certainly an extreme situation. They drank until they were no longer thirsty.

Chapter
EIGHTEEN

J ason stood on the porch in the early morning light waiting for
Officer Bruce to arrive. He'd waited about fifteen minutes,
which to him seemed like forever, when he saw the lights of the
first car coming up the road. Several others trailed Officer Bruce's
vehicle. Within minutes, the scene had changed from dead silence
to a number of people, both uniformed officers and a few others in
civilian clothing receiving orders from the OPP.

Jason noticed that several of the men had GPS units.

As the men moved off in different directions, Jason approached
Officer Bruce. "What can I do to help?"

Before he could answer Jason, two men pulled up in a pickup
truck. "Come with me; I want you to meet someone," Officer Bruce
said heading toward the new comers. "Hi Ron."

"Hi Bruce, you know Steven, my neighbour. He offered to
come along—brought the beagles too." The dogs were barking and
racing from side to side in the back of the pickup. They were no
doubt anxious to get out of the truck and start the hunt.

"Thanks Steven. We can use all the help we can get."

Jason was a little confused when the fellow named Ron called Officer Bruce – *Bruce*, but when he later asked one of the other men he was told that most of the OPP were friends, neighbours, cousins, brothers, or fathers and most went by their first names. Officer Bruce was in fact Officer Bruce Wilson.

Officer Bruce turned back to Jason. "Mr. White, this is Ron Harrison."

Ron extended his hand. "Call me Ron."

"Hi Ron; I'm Jason, Jason White. Thanks for helping search for my wife."

Now it was Ron's turn to look confused. "I guess Bruce didn't explain who I am. When I say I understand how you feel—I really do—you see my wife is the other missing woman."

For a second Jason was stunned. "Sorry Ron, you must be going out of your mind."

"Damn close to it, but I have to keep believing that we'll find my Amanda and your..." He hesitated.

"Caroline," Jason supplied.

"Yeah, my Amanda and your Caroline and the sooner the better."

Steven had the three beagles on leashes. They were impatiently waiting to be set free.

"Mr. White, Steven needs a piece of Mrs. White's clothing; something with her scent."

"Sure, I'll get you her sweater; she had it on last night." After he said it, he realized that it had actually been the night before last when she had worn the sweater while they were sitting out on the porch. He hurried inside and found the sweater draped over the arm of a chair near the door. It was soft and he wanted to hug it to him, but didn't want to add his own scent to the fabric. Taking the porch steps in one stride, he handed Caroline's sweater to Steven.

"These dogs are good," Ron said to Jason. "I've seen them track before. We think my Amanda either got into a car, or was put in a car, otherwise they would have been able to track her," he said lowering his head. "Maybe searching for Caroline will turn up something positive for my Amanda." He clapped his hand on Jason shoulder and squeezed. There was no need for him to say more.

"Thanks Ron, believe me when I say I'm praying for them both." Jason watched as Ron and Steven readied the dogs.

Officer Bruce was instructing some of the other men on his search plan. Jason couldn't hear every word he was saying, but as he approached, he heard one of the men say *"the longer she's missing the less chance she'll be found alive."*

Jason hadn't allowed his thoughts to go that far, now he felt sick to his stomach. Officer Bruce was talking, but Jason couldn't concentrate on what he was saying.

Last night, after his visit to the cottage, Officer Bruce had gone directly to Elliot's place to question him about the second missing woman; Elliot wasn't home. Officer Bruce finally located him in the pool hall. Henry was behind the bar. He confirmed that Elliot had been there for several hours. Elliot was drunk and when Officer Bruce approached him, he'd said he was on his way home. He adamantly denied knowing anything about either women and after several minutes of questioning, Officer Bruce, reluctantly told him to head for home.

Elliot's car was out back in the parking lot. He knew he'd be watched so he asked Henry to call him a cab. He staggered to the door and waited for his cab to arrive.

Being questioned by the cops had not only succeeded in frightening him, but had also made him mad as a hornet. "Those broads are making my life hell, but I'll get even," he cussed under his breath, dragging his body into the backseat of the waiting cab. When he reached home, he fumbled for some cash to pay the fare. It pissed him off to have to pay good money for a ride home when he had his own car parked behind the bar. He pulled himself from the backseat of the cab and teetered on the curb until the driver pulled away. "Well now ladies, that settles that; you broads ain't giving me a hell of a choice," he slurred aloud. "I guess tonight will be my last visit to you my pretty little angels. Tonight I'm goin to put an end to all my problems." He reached into his pocket and pulled out his car keys. "Oh shit," he cursed, "I'll have to walk all the f---ing way back to town to get my car." Instead, he groped for his house key and went inside; he poured himself a large glass of whiskey. When it was gone, he poured another. The second glass wasn't yet empty before he topped it up. His trip to the shed would have to wait until tomorrow. And his pretty little angels would have one more night to live. He thought Gloria would be happy to have their company.

"We'll find her," Officer Bruce was saying as Jason tuned in the words. "Okay Mr. White, I know you are anxious to help and you aren't going to be too happy with what I'm going to ask of you." He appeared to stand taller as he asserted his authority. Officer Bruce glanced around to be sure there was nobody else within earshot before he continued. "I want you to show me where you found the knife and then I want you to come back here to the cottage." Again, with authority he said, "It's necessary for you to stay here."

Jason was about to protest, but Officer Bruce held up his hand to stop him.

"If someone is holding Mrs. White they might try to contact you. We have plenty of people out there searching. You need to stay here by the phone."

"Both Caroline and I have cell phones; I can take them with me."

"Sure you can," he was humouring Jason. "But everyone in these parts knows the cottage is listed under the Millers' name. They could easily find that number, but your cells wouldn't be where they would call."

"I never thought of that," Jason said a little embarrassed.

"It's hard to think when something like this happens. Don't worry about it, just stay close to that phone. I'll give you my pager number, and if you hear anything you call me right away."

What he did not say was that if they were to find Mrs. White's disappearance was a homicide, it would be better if Jason weren't present at the scene.

Jason reluctantly agreed to do as Officer Bruce instructed.

Officer Bruce called out to Ron. "Ron, before you and Steven set out will you stay here by the phone in case anyone calls. Mr. White is going to show me something, and then he'll be back. Shouldn't take long."

"Sure thing. Steven will want to water the dogs before we leave here anyway."

Jason led Officer Bruce to the bushes on the north path; then he returned to the cabin. He watched as Steven had the dogs smell Caroline's sweater. Once they had the scent, Ron helped Steven release them. They ran haphazardly in every direction in what appeared to be total chaos, all the while wagging their tails and barking. Soon, all three dogs were barking their way down the path toward the shore. Jason wasn't encouraged by this since he and Caroline had taken that path on numerous occasions; it didn't take a beagle's nose to realize Caroline's scent would naturally be evident there.

Jason went back inside feeling useless. He flipped the lid on his cell and dialed Doug and Tabitha's number. Doug answered on the first ring. "Doug—Jason here. Sorry if I woke you so early, but I thought you'd want to know they just started the search for Caroline. I'm beside myself. They didn't want me to go along. There's a land line here at the cabin and they want me to stay here in case the abductor calls."

"No problem buddy; do the police think she's been kidnapped?"

"I guess they have to cover every angle. Anyway, I'm stuck by this phone and I feel useless. There's a huge wrinkle in the picture… something I didn't mention yesterday."

"What do you mean *wrinkle*?"

"There's another woman missing as well."

"Another woman?"

"Yeah, I don't know where to start. Last night when I talked to you, I didn't want to frighten you."

"You knew about another woman last night? Does Caroline know her?"

"No, the other woman went missing the day before we arrived; she's been missing for several days already. I read about it in the local papers, but I didn't connect the two. I still don't know if there is a connection or not. But…"

"Jason, don't jump to conclusions. Keep it together. Caroline may have sprained or even broken an ankle and is just waiting to be helped back home. The cops know the area and they know what's best. I can't imagine how you must be feeling, but you have to do as they say."

"Sure," Jason said without conviction. "Just pray that they find her soon. I'll call you later and keep you up-to-date."

"Okay buddy. Our prayers are with you, and of course with Caroline."

Jason snapped the little phone shut and slipped it back into his pocket. He could still hear the dogs in the distance. What he didn't see as the dogs travelled down toward the shore was that all three of them turned, without hesitation, onto the north path. As far as he knew, Caroline had never explored that path, at least not with him; besides, he had already searched that path all the way to the cliffs at the shoreline.

It wasn't easy for Steven and Ron to contain the dogs' excitement. They gathered around the bushes where Jason had found the knife, but soon lost interest in whatever scent they had picked up there. When Ron and Steven examined the area, they saw nothing out of the ordinary. Bruce knew what they smelt, but didn't mention the knife; that was police business. The dogs continued down the path, noses to the ground, tails wagging and keeping up a cross between a bark and a howl. Several times Steven found it necessary to call them back when they would get too far ahead of the men.

Ron's excitement was increasing and Steven had to tamper down his bubbling optimism.

"Yes, it's a good sign that they are on a trail," he confirmed to Ron as he offered the dogs a fresh sniff of Caroline's sweater, "but they're dogs, they could be following a rabbit just as easily."

"I know," Ron agreed, "but after days, it's all I have to hold onto right now."

Back at the cottage, Jason paced between the living room and the kitchen. He poured water in the back of the coffee maker and measured out the coffee. He opened one of the upper cabinets and took down two cups. Without thinking, he placed a tea bag into one of the cups. When he realized what he had done, tears filled his eyes. "Please God—bring her back to me safely," he whispered.

The telephone assaulted his thoughts and he raced through to the living room and snatched up the ringing phone. "Hello," he said not recognizing his own voice.

"Hey guy—are we going fishing on Saturday?" The voice at the other end of the line asked.

"Who is this?" Jason snapped.

"Hey Bob…is that you?"

Jason didn't answer immediately. "No, this isn't Bob you idiot… you've got the wrong number; get off this phone I'm waiting for a call." Jason sounded frantic.

"Sorry guy, I guess I dialed the wrong number—don't get your shorts in a knot!"

Jason listened as the caller slammed down the phone; the line went silent and Jason stood transfixed, almost as if he were wishing the call had been from or about Caroline. He couldn't handle not knowing where or how she was much longer. He lowered the phone from his ear and returned it to the end table. His mouth was dry and his hands were shaking.

Further down the path the dogs started a combination of howls and yappy little barks. Breathlessly Steven said, "They've found something!"

Steven rushed to catch up to where the dogs stood their ground. Ron slowed down, both wanting to know what the dogs had found and at the same time not wanting to know.

Two of the dogs excitedly barked at the bushes at the side of the path, the third sat with its tail wagging across the ground and waited patiently for Steven. They were good trackers and had been trained not to touch their find. Steven had witnessed other dogs seize and destroy their quarry before the human part of the team arrived at the scene.

Before investigating the bushes, Steven tethered the dogs and paid appropriate attention to them. He praised each in turn, patted them, and rubbed their ears. He removed treats from his pocket to offer as a reward. The barking stopped and they calmly sat back and enjoyed their chewy treats.

"What have we here?" Steven asked. "These sticks appear to have been planted purposely here on the path. See how these marks indicate that this stick was rocked back and forth to dig the end into the earth."

The dogs had partially knocked over one of the sticks, but its end was still embedded in the ground. A second stick lay close beside the first.

"Why would anyone want to mark this particular location?" Ron stood a short distance back. He held the dog leashes while Steven and Bruce investigated their find.

At first sight, there was nothing out of the ordinary about this part of the path. Steven poked about in the bushes; he lifted a few of the low boughs and let out a soft whistle. I think I found the answer to your question," he said to Ron.

When Ron caught a glimpse of the shoe, his heart sank, and blood drained from his extremities.

Steven used one of the sticks to pull the sneaker from beneath the bush. He stood and turned toward Ron. "It's a woman's running shoe."

"I can see that," Ron choked out. "Amanda has shoes like that."

"So do hundreds of other women, probably even Mrs. White," Bruce said. He produced a plastic bag from his pocket. He held it open and Steven let the shoe fall into the bag. Bruce slid the zipper lock across the top. He examined the shoe through the clear plastic. "There appears to be stains here on the side and here on the toe," he said pointing out the areas.

"It looks like blood," Ron said quietly.

"It's possible that it is blood, but we can only be certain after we've checked it at the lab."

Steven nodded. "Ron, maybe you should go back and stay with Mr. White? Bruce and I will keep going with the dogs."

Ron couldn't take his eyes off the shoe in the bag. "I'm going with you."

The dogs were each given another small treat; they practically swallowed it whole. They were anxious to go on with, what to them was a game of hide-and-seek. Steven removed Caroline's sweater from the bag he carried it in and the three dogs enthusiastically sniffed, seemingly to drink in her scent.

Ron bent to assist with the removal of the taunt leashes. Again, the dogs performed a dizzying little ritual, sniffing, wagging, and barking, and then they were off down the path. Before long, they reached the shore. Steven called to the dogs. They wiggled about at his feet as he attached a leash to each of their collars. He led them to the water's edge for a cool drink; they lapped noisily at the water. The three men also drank greedily from their water flasks. The morning had warmed quickly. Bruce had large wet rings under the arms of his light blue uniform. Ron peeled off his shirt and tied it loosely about his waist. Steven had a sleeveless Tee underneath his unbuttoned shirt. He also removed his shirt and fastened it loosely around his hips. It was going to be a hot, humid day.

They had travelled close to five kilometers, almost three miles to the shore. The dogs had probably covered twice that with their continuing crisscrossing pattern. The search team, both human and canine, needed to rest. After a short time, Steven gave the *find* command and the dogs followed the scent that led them close to the waters edge along the rugged shoreline. They didn't hesitate for a minute as they followed the trail with their keen noses. They had travelled quite some distance before for some unknown reason they stopped advancing and continued to cover the same ground. Their little howls and yappy barks stopped and silently they sniffed the ground, and then they doubled back on their own trail.

"Why are we turning back?" Ron asked.

"It looks as if Mrs. White only went this far and then she must have changed directions."

Officer Bruce surveyed the area, but saw nothing out of the ordinary—nothing in particular to make anyone change direction.

The trail now led away from the shore and up closer to the tree line. The dogs ran haphazardly back and forth, and seemed to be following different trails. Steven whistled for them to return to him.

Chapter
NINETEEN

Back at the cabin Jason continued his worried pacing, as Caroline and Amanda slowly picked their way along the rocky shoreline praying they would reach safety before Elliot reached them.

"I'm sorry Caroline, but I have to take a breather." Beads of perspiration stood out on Amanda's forehead and her damp hair clung to her neck.

"Let's see if we can get into some shade."

"Okay."

They moved even closer to the tree line and found a couple of large boulders on which to sit. Caroline had suggested they could make better time by traveling closer to the edge of the water, but had explained to Amanda that they would also be easily seen out in the open. They had opted to stay closer to the upper portion of the beach where they could duck into the trees if necessary.

"We can catch our breath here and cool down a bit." Caroline studied Amanda's face. Amanda had fine features, huge blue eyes, an up-tilted nose, and a beautiful mouth with slightly pouty lips.

Her hair was a warm, sandy-blond colour and she wore it long and straight. When the sun shone on it, there was just a hint of a red pigment. After so many days of stress, Amanda had small dark circles under her eyes, but she was still beautiful. Caroline envisioned her all cleaned up with just a touch of makeup and a little lipstick. She would be a stunner, but Caroline was more concerned about the way she looked right now. "You are feeling okay?" Caroline asked.

"I guess so. Nothing that a thick, medium rare steak, baked potato with sour cream and chives and a quarter pound of golden brown mushrooms couldn't fix." She forced a smile. "And last but certainly not least, about three days in my own bed… with Ron," she added.

Caroline put her arm around Amanda's shoulder. Although Amanda's face was red and hot, her body felt cold and clammy. "I'd suggest we take a dip, but with you being so hot it might be a shock; we have to think about your little passenger," Caroline said. "So next best thing…" Caroline whipped her cotton Tee over her head. Be right back." She scanned the length of the beach in both directions before picking her way from rock to rock down to the water's edge. She was surprised by how cold the water felt. She scooped handfuls of water and splashed her face and arms; she didn't drink, but wet her lips. She picked up her Tee, which now floated around her ankles and headed back to Amanda. She did not attempt to wring out any excess water from the fabric. As she made her way back, the sopping wet Tee slapped against her bare leg.

"Couldn't find a thick, juicy steak, but you're going to love the latest fad at Spa Caroline." She tossed the cold Tee to Amanda.

Amanda giggled as the cold material plopped into her hands. She buried her face in the shirt. "This feels wonderful," she mumbled into the cool fabric.

When she raised her head, Caroline was glad to see the redness in her face had almost disappeared; she looked much cooler now.

"Want me to wring this out for you? I have the strength of a wrestler in my hands." She made a menacing face and a choking sign with her hands.

"No, I'll wear it like that…I'm entered in a wet T-shirt contest later today."

"And…you could win!"

They both laughed.

"Sit down and rest a moment then we'll be on our way," Amanda said.

Caroline sank down onto the rock and pulled on the still very wet shirt. It twisted and clung to all the wrong places, but it felt great.

They passed the next few minutes in absolute silence. The sun reflecting off the water was hypnotic and made them both very sleepy.

"I don't know if I have the strength to go on just yet," Amanda whispered as though she didn't have the strength to push the words from her mouth.

"It's okay, we can rest awhile longer. If Elliot has discovered us missing, he wouldn't come this way. He'd hightail it back to his car and get as far away from here as possible. Surely, Elliot has the brains to know we would go straight to the police," Caroline said.

"I'm not sure you can use *brains* and *Elliot* in the same sentence."

Caroline moved aside a few small rocks at the base of the larger rock to expose a sandy patch on which to sit. She slid down the side of the boulder and leaned back against its hard warmth. "Almost a chaise lounge, come on down," Caroline said flinging a couple more pebbles away from where Amanda would sit.

Before Amanda joined Caroline, she reached into her pocket and pulled out the gold wrapped candy. "I saved this," she said, "you know—just in case we had to dine again before the BBQ gets hot."

"But…I thought…"

"Yeah, I know. I do have a confession though, I gave it a good suck and even bit off a little piece; I was just so hungry. I don't have cooties," she laughed. "We can split it now. Don't tell my dentist I did this," she said placing the candy between her teeth and biting down.

"I seeeee nothin…I knooow nothin," Caroline said in a true Hogan's Heroes German accent.

This time, both women enjoyed the sweet taste of the little pieces of heaven.

No conversation passed between them. Caroline glanced over at Amanda. She had her eyes closed. Caroline felt her own eyes closing and was helpless to stop herself from falling asleep.

Chapter
TWENTY

The dogs rested for maybe ten or fifteen minutes and were showing signs of being anxious to get going again. Steven walked them back down to the water's edge. They lapped a couple of times, but they weren't interested in another drink.

"Well gentlemen, I guess the girls are ready to go." Out came the sweater for the fourth time. The beagles poked at the sweater with their noses to acquired Caroline's scent.

Steven unclipped the leashes. As expected, the dogs performed their little ritual again. Two dogs turned and headed toward what looked like another path into the woods while one darted off to the east back down the beach. Steven looked a little bewildered. He whistled and all three promptly returned to sit by his feet. He patted each head as they adoringly looked up at him. Again, he offered them the sweater to sniff. He gave the command, *find*, and they were off without hesitation. One headed toward the path and two went east along the beach. This time one of the younger dogs had changed direction joining Julie. Julie, Steven's eldest and most experienced dog insisted on going back towards the east.

Steven gave another whistle and the dogs stopped on the spot. He motioned one back. The other two didn't move.

"We go east."

Now it was much slower going for both dogs and men. This was a difficult stretch of shoreline to travel as it was strewn with jagged boulders and the hot sun wasn't making them any more comfortable. After more than an hour, Steven estimated that they probably had not travelled much more than a mile or two. The dogs were showing signs of fatigue. Julie, as the lead dog would periodically lead the other two into the shallows to drink, and then they would have to find the trail again. Steven never underestimated the wonder of how they could pick up an individual scent. He was sure there was an abundance of wonderful and not so wonderful smells along a beach; fish, birds, coons, and other animals came here to drink. To pick out one particular scent and that of a human being to boot was truly a bit of a miracle. Julie was not much for swimming, but once she waded out until the water almost touched her underbelly. She plopped down allowing the water to wash up around her sides. It was not yet eleven o'clock, but the temperature had soared. "I know how much you want to press on gentlemen, but I have to give these girls a rest."

When they had first reached the beach and followed the trail in a westerly direction, it had been much easier going as it travelled closer to the edge of the water where the rough boulders were far less abundant, but now, as they appeared to be backtracking along a different scent trail the dogs stayed closer to the tree line.

"I think we can all use a rest. We can cool off in the shade." Bruce mopped the sweat off his brow. The formality of the uniform had long gone. He had opened the top three buttons of his shirt and the back clung to his body like wet toilet paper.

Ron considered himself in pretty good shape, but even he was feeling the strain.

They found a shady spot and sat down.

"How did you know which way to go?" Ron asked.

"I didn't, but I'd be willing to bet that Mrs. White, at some point went in both directions. Julie was following the freshest trail; something the younger dogs are still learning. He leaned down and gave Julie a gentle rub. "She's teaching these other two girls more than they could ever learn from me."

As tired as the dogs were, they didn't easily settle down for a rest. Steven had to hold a tight rein on them at first.

Twenty minutes later, they set out again. As they worked their way along the rocky beach the excitement of the dogs increased; only Steven could comprehend this change. He felt confident that they would find Mrs. White today. He didn't want to theorize about what condition she would be in when they found her; at least it appeared that she was still moving. He had confidence in his dogs. The dogs continued fairly close to the tree line, but never further out than the middle portion of the rocky shoreline. Now they turned in a different direction and headed straight into the woods. Even Bruce who had been in the area all his life was surprised when he heard the falling water and came upon the enchanting waterfall. The three men stood in awe at its sheer beauty.

"I had no idea there was a waterfall around here," Steven said.

"I didn't either," Ron intoned.

"I knew about the waterfall, but I've never seen it. I remember—well, this goes back many years—when someone told me about a falls and underground lake somewhere up in these parts, but I never knew exactly where," Bruce said. "It's called *The Crying Falls*. Nobody really knows where the water comes from. Folklore tells that a beautiful Indian Princess fell to her death here while trying to sneak down to the shore to meet her lover—a young Indian Brave from an opposing tribe. Sort of a story of unfulfilled love. The story, as I remember it, tells that she now cries in heaven and it's her tears that continue to spill over the rocks. That is supposed to be what makes the falls."

Ron and Steven listened with interest as Bruce recounted the tale.

Leaving the falls behind, they returned to the beach and continued toward the east.

Chapter TWENTY-ONE

Caroline was jolted awake when she felt something touch her outstretched leg. A small snake had slithered alongside her calf. She suppressed the instinct to cry out. Caroline couldn't imagine how Amanda might react to a snake after seeing her response to just the mention of a mouse. She didn't need a hysterical woman on her hands. She could feel the sun burning down. The area where they had settled in the shade was now in full sun as the huge yellow ball had advanced its way beyond the tree line and was now almost directly overhead.

Amanda was still asleep. Her cheeks were flushed from the heat.

Caroline checked her watch; it was just after 1:00 p.m. She had no idea how much further they had to travel, but from here on there was no question that it was going to be hot. It would be slow going, but there was no way she wanted to spend another dark, hungry night out here. She reached over and gently took hold of Amanda's hand.

"Amanda," she spoke softly. "Amanda, wake up Honey, we have to go."

Amanda's eyes fluttered open. For a second she didn't know where she was. She was slouched down against the rock. "Sure," she said groggily, "but first I have to pee." She groaned as she got to her feet. "Not the most comfortable chaise lounge," she said as she stepped into the trees for privacy.

Caroline had to agree. She stood and massaged her neck. She prayed Elliot wouldn't come this way, but by now, he had very likely discovered that they had escaped. She tried to think logically that he'd be out of this area faster than seventeen ways to Sunday, but then would he be thinking logically?"

Caroline looked back down the beach. It was vacant except for the many rocks. The area of the cliff and waterfall was out of sight and sound. Caroline wondered how far they still had to go before reaching the dock and Jason.

As Amanda stepped back through the trees into the open Caroline's stomach growled loudly.

"I heard that way over here."

"I guess talking about the steak didn't quite cut it," Caroline laughed. She was surprised that she and Amanda could still laugh; it was part of what kept them going. They had to keep thinking that the next bend would reveal the dock, Jason, or a search party.

"What was that?" Amanda snapped her head in the direction of an unfamiliar sound.

Caroline also turned to stare down the beach. "It sounds like a dog barking—it sure as hell isn't the seagulls. Elliot doesn't have a dog—does he?"

"Not that I know of," Amanda answered nervously.

"Then it's got to be someone searching for us," Caroline said excitedly.

"This may sound crazy, but what if Elliot somehow got his hands on a dog? If we reach safety and turn him in, he has a lot to lose. He just might be crazy enough to get his hands on a dog to track us down. He mentioned that he does a lot of hunting around here. I didn't see a dog at his place, but that doesn't mean he didn't have one."

Caroline considered what Amanda was saying. "There is a slight chance that you could be right—I hope not, but we have to err on the cautious side. We have to get moving; we have to reach Jason before the dog catches up. I think we have to risk being in the open. Let's see if we can make better time and put some distance between us and that dog by wading in the water close to shore."

Amanda's rope sandal was not doing well. There were still numerous rocks in the shallow water, some of them quite slippery, but they seemed to make better headway. Caroline kept her shoes on, but Amanda removed her sneaker and her rope sandal, which by this time had come somewhat undone.

"Are you sure you can walk barefoot?"

"I've been walking barefoot most of my life—I'll be okay. Just keep moving." Fright had returned to her voice.

Caroline's T-shirt was bone dry now and she removed it and dunked it into the water. Pulling it back on she sighed, "That feels better."

Amanda followed her example.

The bottom was less rocky, but wading through the knee-deep water was tiring. The distant sound of the dog barking kept them moving forward.

This time Caroline had to stop. "I have a cramp in my side," she said, "I have to rest a minute."

Reluctantly, Amanda agreed to stop. "Okay, but only for a minute."

Caroline stretched and felt the cramp easing. She splashed water on her face. "Let's go." She was amazed at Amanda's fortitude. She was like the energizer bunny. The lack of sufficient food and water would take its toll, but right now she showed the necessary determination to reach safety at any cost. Caroline thought about the baby. Amanda was strong and the baby was probably doing just fine, maybe even enjoying the bumpy journey. She forced herself to think positively.

The barking seemed to be getting closer, possibly because they were so obviously aware of the disturbing sound. The cliffs and the water distorted sound. Caroline continuously searched the shore for any sign of the dock. The inlet was behind them now.

"I think I see it," Caroline called out minutes later. Disappointment flooded over them both as they got closer and discovered it wasn't the dock but a logjam jutting out into the lake. Thinking they had reached safety and then discovering their error took both a physically and mental toll on them both.

Hunger was making Caroline feel woozy, but there was no way she could give up, not when she marvelled at the way Amanda pushed on. Caroline again saw what she thought was a dock. This time she didn't say anything. She knew Amanda was keeping her eyes on the bottom as she picked her way between some of the jagged rocks as they continued to move forward. Her rope sandal dangled from her pocket.

"Hey Cinderella, don't lose your glass slipper," Caroline said pointing to the rope hanging from her pocket.

"No, I may need this rope to personally strangle Elliot," she said as she shoved the rope deep into her pocket.

The dock became more recognizable as they got closer. Caroline still didn't say anything until she could make out the dock locker. Tears flowed uncontrolled down her cheeks as she grabbed Amanda. "We made it—we're safe."

The women collapsed in each other's arms. Now with safety mere steps away, their last stores of energy drained from their bodies.

Before they reached the bottom of the path leading to the cabin, Jason appeared. Caroline couldn't call out; she used the last of her strength to hurry toward him.

Amanda stood back and watched as Jason ran down the beach to embrace Caroline. The tears that slid from Amanda's eyes felt cool in comparison to her scalding hot cheeks.

Jason grabbed Caroline and swung her off her feet in a wide circle. Tears poured from his eyes unchecked. He held her close. "Are you alright?" He sobbed into the top of her head.

"I am now," she whispered back.

Caroline moved away from Jason and motioned for Amanda to join them.

Jason engulfed Amanda in his arms. "Ron is so worried about you." He held her at arms length and examining her tear stained face.

"How do you know Ron?" Amanda asked.

"It's a long story." Jason took both Caroline and Amanda back into the protection of his arms. "Let's get you two up to the cabin. I left one of the cops watching the phone. He can notify the searchers that you are both okay. You are okay—aren't you?" He asked with a pained look.

"Yes, we need food and a rest, but we're okay," Caroline answered for them both.

The barking was closer now as the water carried the sound. Amanda paled and moved closer to Caroline and Jason. She thought about the shotgun that Elliot carried.

Jason examined Amanda's frightened face. The barking of the dogs was terrifying her. "The dogs are searching for you," he reassured her, "they are with Steven, Ron, and Officer Bruce."

Amanda collapsed to the ground at the mention of Ron's name. Caroline knelt beside her.

"We are safe," were the only words Amanda could get out of her mouth. "We are safe!"

Less than a mile back the dogs had come to the place where Caroline and Amanda stopped to rest and had fallen asleep.

Steven and Bruce closely examined the area at the base of the large boulders. "It's possible Mrs. White isn't alone," Bruce said.

"How would you know that?" Ron asked.

"The rocks here have been cleared away to allow someone to sit down on the sand. It looks like two areas were cleared."

The dogs sniffed and pawed at the sandy ground.

Steven gave the commend *find* once again and immediately Julie turned and headed back down to the beach. A short distance up the beach all three dogs went to the water's edge. They didn't drink; they sniffed the edge of the shore, moving back and forth over the same general area.

"I'm afraid our trail has gone cold," Steven said.

Bruce could see the disappointment on Ron's face. "We'll keep going along this way. It probably means the person or persons we are following decided to walk in the water to cool off. That's all!"

The three men and the dogs continued to pick their way over and around the large boulders along the beach.

Minutes later, the beagles rounded the bend and bounded toward Caroline and Amanda. They stopped dead in their tracks several feet away, but they didn't quiet down. Their barks and howls became more persistent. Julie, sensing that one of the women was extremely upset, corralled the other two dogs, nipping at them and changing her barks to small whimpers. Soon the other two dogs also quieted down. All three tails wagged victoriously.

Steven turned the bend and spotted the two women with Jason. He whistled for the dogs.

Ron was a few feet behind Steven. When he caught up and saw Amanda, he raced towards her. He felt Steven pat him on the back as he passed.

"God bless them," Steven called after Ron.

Reluctantly, the dogs left Caroline and Amanda and returned to sit proudly at Steven's feet. He praised them lavishly and offered them pocketed treats. For them, the game of hide-and-seek was over.

For the two couples embracing on the beach—life had once again begun.

Chapter
TWENTY-TWO

Back safely in the cabin, Jason and Ron saw to it that Caroline and Amanda got something to eat and drink. Jason insisted that they eat light. "Tomorrow, Caroline and I would be honoured if you'd join us here—I'll cook up those thick juicy steaks you two have been babbling about," he said hardly daring to take his eyes off Caroline. "That is if you agree Honey. Tonight, you both need your rest then we'll play it however you want…we can go home if that's what you decide, whatever you want." He was the one babbling now.

Caroline reached over and took Amanda's hand. "Amanda, if you and Ron want you are welcome to stay over tonight—we have plenty of room."

Amanda didn't answer right away; she looked towards Ron.

"Thanks Caroline, but I think Amanda and I will be sleeping in our own bed tonight—together," he answered seeking Amanda's approval.

Amanda nodded; her cheeks were flushed. "But if that steak offer still stands I'd really enjoy spending time together under different circumstances."

"You bet it does." Caroline buttered another slice of toast. "Jason is a whiz with the barbecue."

Officer Bruce and Steven joined them on the porch. "I've got the dogs all settled in the truck," Steven said. "I'm going to head on back to town. Bruce has offered to take you and Amanda back home," he said to Ron.

"Yeah, that's right. You take your time though. I'll wait in the cruiser; I've got a couple of calls I have to make."

"You guys are welcome to join us for steaks tomorrow if you'd like," Jason said.

"Thanks, but I'll have to take a rain check," Officer Bruce answered Jason.

"A rain check for me too," Steven said.

They went out to the porch as Jason thanked Officer Bruce and Steven. Ron walked Steven to the pickup where the dogs were patiently waiting. Somehow, they knew the game was over for them.

Ron returned to the porch. He took Amanda's hand and gave it a gentle squeeze. "I guess we'd better go too."

"Ron, can you give me a few minutes, I'd like to speak to Caroline—in private?" Amanda asked quietly.

Jason stood. "You two stay here, where you're comfortable. Come on Ron, I'll get us a cold beer in the kitchen."

Before they left Jason turned and kissed Caroline on the top of her head. "Don't leave the porch," he said protectively.

"You don't have to worry about that," Caroline whispered.

Ron released Amanda's hand; he placed it daintily in her lap. Before he could leave, she held out her hand to him and asked, "Can you help me up? I don't think I have the strength to move on my own. I'd like to sit over there beside Caroline." She pointed to the other large chair.

Ron helped her to her feet and watched as she settled into the other padded chair beside Caroline.

"Jason, when we were in town I bought some new slip-ons, will you bring them out for Amanda?"

"Sure, only one—no two questions. First, describe said slip-ons and second, where would I find them?

Both Caroline and Amanda smiled. In unison they said, "It's a man thing!"

"Look on the floor beside my night stand and bring whatever you find there. After Jason went inside she said, "I don't know where you're getting your second wind. Must be your age. I'm exhausted."

"Sure Granny. You must be all of what…a few years older than I am?"

They laughed and Amanda stretched her hand between the two chairs and took hold of Caroline's hand. "Let's get serious for a moment."

Caroline was about to make an off-the-cuff remark about the seriousness of the past days, but she bit her tongue when she saw the look on Amanda's face.

"What is it?"

"Ron doesn't know about the baby," she whispered. "I want to see my Doctor before I say anything to him. He's already been through so much."

Caroline was silent for a moment as she thought about what Amanda had said. "You are something else," she whispered back. "After all you've been through you're concerned about Ron?"

"There's no reason to get him all worried, unless he has to be." She lowered her voice as Jason pushed open the screen door.

"Found the *slip-ons*," he said all knowing, "and this." He held out a Werther's candy. "You asked me to bring whatever I found."

Both women burst out laughing and a happy tear slid down Caroline's cheek. "Thanks, but we're not hungry. I never thought I would ever utter those words again." Caroline wiped the tear from her cheek. "Here, try these on Cinderella."

Amanda took the shoes and the candy. She slipped the Werthers into her pocket and patted it protectively. "I swear I'll never leave home again without a couple of these in my pocket or purse."

Jason didn't get the obviously private joke shared between the two women about the Werthers.

Amanda slipped her feet into the shoes. "I'll get these back to you tomorrow," she said adding, "They fit perfectly."

Ron joined the others on the porch. "Honey," Ron said, "We should be heading home," he emphasized the word *home*.

"I'm so happy to be safe; I'm not even sure what I've told you."

"You and Caroline told us enough to put that Elliot fellow behind bars for a very long time. Steven and Bruce are filing reports. By now, the OPP are out looking for Elliot and before long he will be locked behind bars. He won't be hurting anyone anymore," Ron stated. "It's a good thing that Jason has a level head on his shoulders, because my first reaction was to go after the creep myself," Ron added in a serious tone. "To think, I actually played pool with him. He seemed like a regular guy. I would have never suspected him of being capable of anything so horrible. I hope they hang him by his balls."

Jason didn't say anything, but he thought about the last twenty-four plus hours and he had to admit to himself that he had been anything but levelheaded. He had acted like any other husband. He would have a different understanding in the future for what a stressful situation can do to a person's mind-set. Right now, he could only feel relief. Caroline was safe and that was all that mattered.

Chapter
TWENTY-THREE

If anyone had passed the car at the side of the road and caught a glimpse of Elliot in the front seat, they would have probably thought he was dead, but rarely did anyone come this way. Elliot was slumped back against the driver's seat. He slowly opened his eyes. At first, he didn't know why he was in his car. He ran his hands over his eyes trying to clear his vision. He had the mouth of someone who had swallowed a nice plump pillow. He raised his hand again and wiped it across his mouth. His breath was so foul it even turned him off. He slumped behind the wheel trying to get his bearings. He wasn't sure exactly where he was, or why. In time, reality came flooding back. How long had it been since he went to Amanda? Then he remembered Amanda's friend. It's too bad she had to show up; she would be an additional problem for him to deal with down the road. He lowered his head to the steering wheel and tried to sort things out.

His car was sitting at a precarious angle; he'd had a lot to drink and thought he must have run off the road. He straightened his body behind the wheel. The keys still hung in the ignition. He pressed the clutch to the floor and turned the key. The motor grudgingly cranked over several times before it finally responded; he shifted into first gear. He released the clutch too quickly and the car leaped forward and stalled out. Elliot was surprised by the unexpected forward lurch. The bottle he had stashed under the passenger seat slid out onto the floor of the backseat. Before he attempted to restart the engine, he twisted his body back and leaned between the two front seats to retrieve his Scotch. He could barely reach it and finally wound up pushing it back under the front passenger seat to its original hiding place. His head pounded and when he leaned over, he thought he was going to puke. He pulled himself back upright and closed his eyes for a moment. Slowly his equilibrium returned and again he pressed down on the clutch and turned the key. This time he slowly released the clutch while giving the engine gas, almost too much gas; the engine roared unnecessarily. Slowly the car crept back onto the road. He drove on to the place where he usually parked when he visited his unwilling captive. How long had it been—two, three, maybe four days now? He tried to reconstruct the past few days without much success. The last week or so had been nothing more than a blur— one long binge. He pulled the car as far off the road as possible. He reached for the large bottle of booze under the passenger seat and took a long swig. The strong Scotch trickled down his unshaven chin and he used the back of his hand to wipe it away. Almost immediately, his body reacted and he retched. He replaced the screw cap on the bottle and tossed it on the passenger seat.

When he pushed open the driver's door, he almost fell out onto the road. It was somewhere around noon. The sun was almost directly overhead. It was hot, really hot. His mind was foggy; he decided that if she didn't love him today, he would have to put a stop to this. She would have sealed her own fate. He wondered about Amanda's new friend, maybe she'd be able to love him. He'd see what developed there, but for now, he dismissed her as nothing more than excess baggage, an extra hole to dig. Thinking about digging a second grave in this heat made him angry. He made his way around to the passenger side of the car and opened the front door. He removed a flask from his small knapsack and filled it from the Scotch bottle. He held the large, nearly empty bottle up to the light. After tucking the flask back into a pocket on the knapsack, he drained the large bottle of its remaining contents. His body gave an involuntary shiver, but he didn't retch. He recapped it and tossed the now empty bottle back onto the passenger seat. He slammed the door shut and steadied himself against the car frame. The sun had turned the car into an oven; he couldn't keep his hands on the hot surface for long. He retrieved his shotgun from the back seat and pocketed the shells before he staggered toward the path leading to the clearing.

Elliot thought back to the day he had watched Caroline in her cute little bikini. He remembered how she had picked the flower and daintily pulled off each petal. He bent down and ripped a daisy from the ground, roots and all. Unlike Caroline, he grabbed several of the petals between his large thumb and trigger finger and ripped them from the flower head. "Love me, love me not, love me, love me not," he chanted as he flung the petals. They fell to the ground to be followed by the next clump of discarded petals. He stared at the last petal remaining. "Love me—or else," he slurred as he crushed the remaining petal and flower head in his clenched fist. "I'll teach you it's better to love me than not—you'll be sorry." He stared at the destroyed flower that now lay at his feet. Again, he picked a nearby flower. This time he placed it in his shirt pocket; he'd give it to Amanda.

He was sweating profusely by the time he reached the clearing. Once out of the shelter of the trees, it got hotter. Again, he cursed at the thought of having to dig two graves. Halfway across the clearing he remembered that he hadn't brought Amanda a sandwich. He almost turned back, but decided his captive ladies would certainly need a potty break even more than food. He couldn't remember when he had last paid them a visit. In his brain fog, he hadn't given any thought to bringing a shovel. He cursed loudly. He'd return later with food and a shovel, or maybe just the shovel. He couldn't go on like this; it was hard to think straight. Maybe he'd just stash the bodies in the root cellar until this heat wave broke. Amanda would proclaim her love for him or he'd have her join Gloria—it was as simple as that. After all, what was there about him that was not to love? "Gloria," he groaned, "I gave you every possible chance and you turned me down. You humilitated me." He had pronounced *humiliated* wrong and laughed at his error. "Oh devil liquor, release my tongue. Hu-mil-i-at-ed," he sounded out. "Humiliated me, you bitch, you humiliated me," he repeated.

He remembered the day he had dug the shallow grave for Gloria. She had looked so beautiful. It was a shame that she had shunned him and had chosen instead an early grave. He remembered the hardest part of all. After placing her in the shallow grave he had covered her entire body with earth and when some of the dirt landed on her face he had carefully and gently brushed it away saying, "Sorry Sweetheart, you could have stopped me, but you refused to love me the way I loved you." When nothing other than her face remained visible, he'd walked away. Later and very drunk, he had returned and asked the dead face if she was sorry she hadn't loved him. Gloria's unseeing eyes stared up into the sky. He blew his top. He'd shouted, "I'll show you—you bitch, nobody treats me like that." Then he had finished covering Gloria's grave. After that, he'd cried; his body had convulsed in sobs. He'd begged her to come back. He'd professed his love.

Back in those days, he didn't live anywhere near here; he was a drifter. Nobody suspected him in the disappearance of Gloria Ganyou. He suspected that nobody even knew he existed.

Gloria had also been a drifter. She'd been in town a day or two. Elliot picked her up hitchhiking. He had an RV at the time and they had gone there for a few drinks.

Elliot let his thoughts drift back to that day. She'd been nice to him. She'd kissed him and allowed the front of her blouse to gap open so he could see her sexy black bra. She'd been quite a tease. They fooled around a little and he fell asleep. When he opened his eyes, she was gone—so were his wallet and his Scotch. He jumped into the car and within fifteen minutes caught up to her. The little bitch was trying to hitchhike her way out of town with his wallet. He'd showed her. After that he stayed away—far away from this area for a good year. His mind wandered, was that four years ago, or maybe five?

The shed was quiet, but that's how he expected it. He entered through the sagging doorway. It took a minute for his eyes to adjust to the darkness inside the shed after being out in the bright sun. Before he could focus properly he called out, "Good day Angels—Charlie's here." He laughed at his own joke. *Charlie's Angels* was one of his favourite retro TV shows. On the show there were three gorgeous women. He wasn't doing so bad… he had two beauties of his own. Counting Gloria, he would have had three. When he approached the root cellar door and found it more than half-open, he freaked. "You bitch," he roared, "You took my Amanda." He reached into the pocket for the flask of Scotch. It wasn't there; somewhere it had fallen from his knapsack. Again, he yelled, "I'll get you. I'll get you both." He stepped back and stared at the open hole of the root cellar. Just then, a mouse showed itself on top of one of the hay bales. "Oh shit," he groaned, "maybe they got scared off by you." Even through his fog he knew how outrageous this was; he fell to the floor in uncontrolled laughter.

The mouse watched, unconcerned. It wet its paws and washed its whiskers.

Elliot sank down to the floor. He leaned against one of the hay bales and passed out.

Chapter
TWENTY-FOUR

Caroline and Jason stood on the porch and waved goodbye as Amanda and Ron got into Officer Bruce's cruiser. "Don't forget—steaks will be on around four tomorrow," Jason called after them.

After the cruiser left the driveway, Jason pulled Caroline toward him. "Honey, you must be exhausted, let's tuck you into bed."

"In a minute, first I want to sit as close to you as I can physically get."

He took her in his arms and held her tightly. "After we get you settled, I'll call Doug and Tabitha. They are almost as worried as I was."

"Call them now. I'll have a quick word with Tabitha."

Jason examined Caroline closely. She was running solely on relief and adrenaline. He attempted to talk her out of it, but quickly gave in to her wishes. As he dialed the number he said, "Tomorrow we'll talk about going home if that's what you decide. It's ringing," he said handing her the phone.

Tabitha grabbed it up on the second ring. "Jason," she said, "have you found Caroline?"

Caroline felt tears stinging her eyes. "Tabitha, it's me," she said into the phone. "I'm home."

"Oh my God, where have you been? We've all been worried sick. Thank God you're home. Are you alright?" Tabitha didn't give her a chance to squeeze in a word sideways.

"It's a long story; I'll let Jason explain—briefly," she said. "What's important is that I'm home safe and sound."

"Caroline, we were so worried." Tabitha choked on her words. "Are you sure, you're okay? Have you spoken to your parents?"

"My parents...I haven't had time..." Jason heard Caroline mention her parents. He took the phone from her hand. She didn't have a chance to say goodbye to Tabitha.

"Hi Tabitha," Jason said. "Caroline is exhausted, but she'll be fine. I have to make sure she gets some rest. I promise I'll get her to call you tomorrow." Jason was blunt, but polite. "By the way, please don't call her parents. I didn't tell them she was missing. It would have been awful for them and until I had something...well, you can understand where I'm coming from. I didn't want them worried."

"Sure Jason, we understand. As long as you're sure she's okay, that's our only concern. Tell her we love her, and I'll talk to you both tomorrow."

Jason snapped the little cover of the phone shut and Caroline jumped at the unexpected sound.

"Let's get you into bed," he said softly.

"I want to take a shower first."

Jason hesitated before asking the necessary question. He didn't want to upset Caroline, but he had to know. He held her close and cautiously asked, "He didn't touch you...did he?"

"No Jason, thank God, he didn't touch either of us that way. He thinks he's in love—in his own sick way with Amanda."

Jason wanted every detail of what Caroline and Amanda had been through, but he would let her tell him—in her own good time. "Come on, let's get you settled down." Jason placed an aromatherapy candle beside the bathroom sink. The scent was mild and relaxing; it was one of Caroline's favourites.

Caroline returned from the bedroom with her nightgown over her arm. "Jason, I know I haven't had much time to think about the past hours, but what I do know is that I have choices to make... I could flip out, and that would be no good for anyone, especially me, or I can thank the good Lord that I'm home safe again. I choose the latter. I also want to take a page from Amanda; you can't believe how strong she was. I'm so thankful to be here with you. I only pray they catch that..." She sighed deeply, "Man before he hurts someone. I'm going to shower now, and then I'm going to sleep like a baby."

Caroline closed the bathroom door. She smiled when she saw the candle flickering. She thought how lucky she was to be safely back with Jason. She imagined how it could have turned out. She pushed the negative thoughts away and let the pleasant ones engulf her the way the scent from the candle engulfed the bathroom.

The hot water felt good as it washed over her tired body. The familiar smell of her shower gel was comforting. She noticed a good size bruise on her hip from where she'd been lying on the clamshells. She stepped out of the shower and towelled herself off. She wrapped a second smaller towel around her wet hair. She tried unsuccessfully to stifle a yawn. While brushing her teeth another yawn overtook her. "Guess I'll skip the 'Late, Late Show' tonight," she said to her reflection in the mirror. Other than the dark circles under her eyes and the bruise on her hip, she looked none the worse for wear.

Jason rapped lightly on the door. "Are you okay? I thought I heard you talking."

"I'm just talking to myself, but yes, I'm fine; I'll be out in a minute." When she emerged from the bathroom she said, "I'm ready to hit the sack. I know it's early for you, but will you stay beside me until I fall asleep?"

"You don't have to be afraid anymore. I'm not letting you out of my sight until that…criminal is locked behind bars." Jason was kind with his choice of names.

"I just want you right here beside me tonight." She crawled into the big bed and pulled the soft covers up around her. Caroline hadn't yet told Jason about their being spied upon. Now, she wondered if Jason was the only one not letting her out of his sight.

"Try to keep me away," Jason said as he kissed her cheek and lay down beside her.

The thought of Elliot spying on them gave her the creeps and she suppressed a cold chill running through her body.

"Are you cold?" Jason asked.

"I'll be fine," Caroline said pulling the covers even closer to her. She reached over and took Jason's hand, "Did you lock the door?"

"It's all taken care of. Get some rest; we'll talk in the morning."

Within minutes, Caroline's slow, rhythmic breathing confirmed that she was asleep. He studied her face as darkness settling in around them. Carefully, so as not to disturb her, he eased his way off the bed. He turned on the nightlight in the bathroom. As he returned to the bedroom, Caroline opened her eyes.

"Can you run me into town in the morning?" She asked sleepily.

"Sure, any special reason?"

"A very special reason. I'll tell you about it later," she whispered.

Chapter
TWENTY-FIVE

"A re you sure you're up to this? I spoke to Ron earlier this morning and he assured me that Amanda would understand if you decided to cancel our dinner date. He mentioned that she had an earache and that they were going to see the doctor."

"Yes Jason—I told you last night. I have so much to be thankful for, I can't let this rob me of my life. I have wonderful parents and by the way, we won't ever have to tell them about this. When I spoke with Tabitha earlier she agreed with me that it wouldn't serve any purpose."

"You're right about that."

"I have a wonderful, beautiful, precious little son, fantastic friends in Tabitha and Doug and of course our beautiful little Goddaughter. I think we'll both be calling Amanda and Ron *friends*, and last but certainly not least—I have you."

"I was wondering if I'd fit in there somewhere."

"You—my love—are my reason for being." She planted a big mushy smooch on his cheek. "But, if you think holding such an exalted position around here is going to get you out of cooking—

you're wrong. Our newest friends will be here soon and I don't see you firing up the grill." She laughed as she pushed him toward the side doors.

"I married such a slave driver," he said rolling his eyes as he left.

Caroline returned to her job of putting the finishing touches on the salad and other dishes. She was putting on a good front, but there was no way she could put Elliot or his shotgun out of her mind. She knew that as long as he was on the loose, she and Amanda were in danger. Hell, everyone was in danger with that lunatic running free.

Earlier she and Jason had driven into town so she could purchase something she referred to as "a little something for Amanda," but she wouldn't tell Jason what was in the little box. Carefully she wrapped the box and put it on the counter for later.

As she worked, she stood with her back toward the large double doors. From out of nowhere, a feeling of being watched flooded over her. She reeled around to stare out the door. The open grill was in full sight, but there was no sign of Jason. Cautiously she approached the door and peered out. Their car was gone. Cold shivers ran up Caroline's back and she couldn't move; she was afraid to open the door to look for Jason. Cautiously, she reached out and locked the door. Almost at that same second, Jason came around from the other side of the cabin and tried to open the porch door. Caroline nearly jumped out of her skin at his sudden appearance.

"Hey, who locked the door?" Jason asked as he nearly walked though the glass when it didn't yield as he had expected.

It took a second for Caroline to respond. She unlocked and opened the door; she threw herself into Jason's arms. "Where were you?" She asked nervously.

"I went up front to move the car over so Ron would have room to park in the shade," he answered. "Are you alright?"

"Yeah, I think I am," she said weakly. "I guess I'm suffering a little aftermath of the past couple of days."

"It will take you time to get over this," Jason said tenderly, taking her in his arms.

"I'll be fine. I'm going to go freshen up; you'd better get the fire going," she said changing the subject. She was being paranoid; just a case of jumbled nerves, she thought.

"Okay, call me if you need anything." Jason watched as she headed toward the bathroom.

"They're here" Jason called out a few minutes later as he watched the car make its way up the drive.

Caroline tossed her apron over the back of one of the kitchen chairs.

"Hi Sis," Amanda called, before she got out of the car.

Ron and Jason exchanged curious glances and hearty handshakes.

"What's that all about?" Ron asked.

Jason laughed. "Take some advice from an old married man—don't ask. If they want you to know, they'll tell you; if not, you're probably better off not knowing."

"Now that sounds like good advice. Hey… something smells good."

"If we don't want our dinner burnt, I'd better get back to the barbecue." The two men headed for the side porch, leaving Amanda and Caroline chatting amicably. "Caroline filled me in on some of what they went through and thick juicy steaks were mentioned, so this part will be a breeze." Jason shifted the steaks.

"Maybe you can give me some pointers. I'm not much of a cook. Actually, I'm not a cook at all, and the BBQ terrifies me. So far, I've mastered burnt hot dogs, burnt hamburgers, and burnt pork chops," he laughed. "At the price of steak, I thought I'd better perfect my technique on the cheaper cuts."

"I can teach you everything I know about barbecuing in about two minutes. Caroline's the cook in this family."

Caroline and Amanda had made themselves comfortable on the front porch where Caroline had a huge pitcher of ice-cold lemonade waiting. "How's your earache?" Caroline asked smirking.

"Better—much better," she said looking around to see if Ron was within earshot. "But I'm jumpier than a cat in a room full of rocking chairs." Amanda laughed. "I've always wanted to say that. My old Grandpappy used to say that all the time."

"You guys want some lemonade?" Caroline called to Jason.

Jason looked toward Ron and mouthed the word *beer?*

His affirmative nod confirmed the beer order.

"Thanks honey, but we'll be looking for a nice cold beer. You keep Amanda company; I'll get the beer."

From the kitchen, he could see Caroline and Amanda through the window as they chatted like old friends.

Jason returned to the porch and handed Ron a cold beer. "Amanda," Jason called, "How do you like your steak?"

"Medium rare, almost anyway but burnt."

Ron shrugged his shoulders. "Does my wife know me—or what?"

"Ah, but once I've taught you all my secrets you can dazzle her with your finesse."

"Is finesse spelt *b-u-r-n-t?*" He faked a groan, "Now we'll have to travel all the way to New York to get a decent steak." The air was filled with the delicious aroma of steaks sizzling on the grill.

"Okay, prepare yourself, you're about to learn all my secrets. Jason explained the technique of grilling. "A good hot grill and making that ninety degree turn is the only real secret. You want to get those great looking crisscross patterns. Keep practising you'll get the knack."

Caroline came around to the side porch and asked, "Are we eating soon?"

"Give me a few minutes longer," Jason said as he turned the steaks over.

The table off the kitchen was set with colourful plates and napkins and a bouquet of wild flowers. A few of the flowers Jason had purchased for Caroline in town had somehow managed to survive, even without the benefit of water, and she had placed them in amongst the wild variety.

"It's so beautiful here; I hope you don't mind eating outside."

"We love eating outside and we do until the cool weather chases us indoors," Amanda said. "We don't BBQ that often though. Can't chance burning the rental house to the ground," she laughed.

Jason rounded the corner of the porch with the steaks on a large wooden board. "Dinner is served," he said with a flourish.

"Look at that—they look even better than they smell and— they smell wonderful. So these four are for Caroline and I, what are you guys going to eat?"

"Enough pampering—you gals are going to have to share."

Amanda selected the smallest steak.

"I thought you'd want this one," Caroline said pointing to the largest of the four steaks.

"I want it alright, but I do know my limits."

"Well Ron, I guess we'll have to pick up Amanda's slack." Jason moved the huge steak to Ron's plate and selected one that was almost identical in size for himself.

"That's a tough job, but somebody's got to do it," Ron agreed.

Caroline passed the other dishes she had prepared.

"This is a feast," Amanda said. "I'm just leaning how to cook, but I'm not very good yet."

"Well, you won't have to worry about that, at least in summer," Jason said. "I just taught Ron all of my BBQ secrets."

Caroline laughed. "Well you do know your way around a BBQ, but there's more to cooking than tossing a slab of protein on a hot grill. Hey, I have a great idea. Do you two have a computer?"

"Sure, doesn't everyone nowadays?"

"If you'd be interested; I could periodically send you some of my tried and true recipes with detailed instructions. In a year's time you'll be a pro," Caroline said.

"Then we'll have to come back and have Amanda cook us a meal," Jason said between bites of steak.

"If it's not too much work for you; I think it's a great idea," Amanda confirmed.

"It would be my pleasure."

"It's a deal Sis."

Jason looked toward Ron, and Ron shrugged his shoulders. "Sounds to me like no matter what, I'm going to be the winner."

They all laughed, unaware of the danger lurking a short distance away, or that they were being watched.

Chapter
TWENTY-SIX

After dinner, Jason offered to clear the table while Caroline showed Amanda and Ron photos. Caroline proudly showed off the photos of Michael Jay.

"He's adorable," Amanda cooed.

Ron held the photo and studied the little boy. As Amanda and Caroline went through several other pictures, Ron continued to be transfixed by the angelic face of the child. Amanda passed him another photo and was surprised to catch him secretly wipe a tear from his eye. "Are you okay?" She whispered.

"Uh-huh. I hope someday we'll have a son or daughter."

"I'm sure we will…someday."

Shortly Jason returned from the kitchen. "I've done what I could. I wasn't sure where to put some of the dishes, so I left them on the counter."

"Thanks Jason, that's great. I'm sure it will take me less time to put them away than it would take me to find them later."

Amanda nodded her head in agreement.

"Now, who wants coffee?" Caroline asked stacking the photos and slipping them back into the photo envelope.

"I'll pass. But I'm sure Ron would enjoy one, he's a coffee fiend."

"Good, I won't be long."

"Hey Ron, do you like to fish?" Jason asked.

"Sure do."

"Why don't we take our coffee down to the dock and try our luck?"

"Sounds perfect—if that's okay with you Honey?" Ron asked Amanda.

"You two go ahead, enjoy yourselves. Caroline and I can chat right here on the porch. Safety in numbers," she said.

Caroline soon returned with a steaming pot of coffee and two insulated mugs.

"How did you know we'd want *take out?*" Ron asked

"I could tell you I read your minds, but the truth is I overheard Jason mention fishing and the dock; I put two and two together. But watch out, because I really can read minds and predict futures." She winked at Amanda. "Back in a minute," she said disappearing inside.

Jason filled the two mugs and asked Ron to carry them. "Wait until you see the size of these worms," he said retrieving the large can from under the corner of the porch. "I'll bring the rods and when we get to the dock you can pick your weapon."

Amanda watched as they headed down the path towards the dock. They looked like Sheriff Andy Taylor and his loveable Deputy, Barney Fife of the old Andy Griffith show. She thought about her *safety in numbers* comment and remembered there had been the two of them when Elliot showed up in the field. She didn't think he'd be brazen enough to come here—not with both Ron and Jason close by. She tried, without success to put the thought out of her mind.

A few minutes later, Caroline appeared with a tray and two tall glasses of cranberry juice accompanied by the beautifully wrapped little box. "I took a chance that you might like cranberry juice. I've been a bit off coffee lately."

"Maybe you can read minds," Amanda told her. "One of my favourite drinks is cranberry juice. I sometimes like to add a touch of nutmeg and a squirt of lime or lemon."

Amanda took a sip from one of the glasses. "Did you put lime in here—and nutmeg?" She asked in total surprise.

"That just happens to be one of my favourite drinks as well," Caroline confirmed with a little laugh. "I also added a little orange juice."

"It's great!" Amanda said.

As they sat and sipped their cool juice, they could hear faint voices and laughter coming up from the dock.

"It's nice that Jason and Ron seem to have hit it off so quickly," Caroline said.

"I'm glad that we have the chance to get to know each other better. I can't wait any longer though…aren't you even curious about the baby?" Amanda asked.

"One of my virtues is patience. I learned that as soon as I became a Mother."

"I went to see my Doctor earlier this afternoon. Ron insisted on going with me; he has hardly let me out of his sight. I told a little white lie and said I had an earache that needed to be checked out."

"So you didn't have an earache?" Caroline questioned already knowing the answer.

"No, but I had to make up something since Ron insisted on coming with me to the Doctor's office."

"Don't keep me waiting too long, my virtuous patience does wear thin," Caroline said leaning closer to Amanda. The smile on Amanda's face told her more than words could ever express.

"Ron and I are going to start out the New Year as Mommy and Daddy. We're due January 2nd. The baby is fine; it has a good strong heartbeat and Dr. Sachis says things couldn't be going better.

"Did you tell Ron yet?"

"No, if he knew he'd be strutting around here like a peacock," she laughed. "I'm not sure how I'm going to break the news; I'd like it to be special."

"I'm so happy for you both. I knew everything was going to be okay, in fact, I have a little baby gift."

"Is that what that lovely little box is all about?" Amanda asked indicating the beautifully wrapped gift on the tray.

"Actually no, that's something else. Something I want you to have. It's a memento of how we met."

"I can't think of a single thing that I might want that even remotely reminds me of the past days." She looked questioningly at Caroline.

Caroline ignored the comment and changed the subject. "Do you want to be alone when you tell Ron the happy news?"

"I was thinking of slipping it into the conversation here tonight. He'll burst if he can't share the news with anyone. Did you see his face when he was looking at your little Michael Jay?"

"What if I give you this little gift and I give Ron the baby gift? It might take him a few seconds to figure it out, or he may just think I had too much sun? Of course, then he would know you told me first; maybe he wouldn't be so happy about that."

"I don't think he'd mind that I confided in you under the circumstances. That sounds like a fun way of letting him in on my little secret. It will be one of those stories we can tell our kids when they are older. Let's do it."

Caroline excused herself to get the baby gift. I'll just be a minute; I have to re-wrap the other box. We don't want the paper to give any clues as to the contents. Will you be okay here alone for a couple of minutes?"

"Oh sure, I'll just enjoy my drink and the last rays of sun…you won't be long."

Caroline rose and headed indoors.

Amanda picked up her glass and leaned back comfortably. Suddenly, for God only knows what reason, the hair on her arms bristled and a chill ran up the back of her head. She stood and quickly looked in all directions. She could faintly hear Ron and Jason's voices in the distance, but everything else was quiet. She couldn't shake the feeling that something wasn't right. Again, she thought about how Elliot had appeared out of nowhere yesterday. She and Caroline were no match for a madman with a gun.

A cracking sound coming from somewhere in the nearby woods threatened to push her over the threshold and back into panic mode. Being careful to keep her back to the cottage, she nervously scanned the trees for any sign of Elliot. Although she saw nothing out of the ordinary, she couldn't shake the uneasy feeling knowing Elliot was still out there. She was about to go inside when Caroline met her at the door.

"Is everything alright?" Caroline asked noticing how pale Amanda was.

"Yes...yes, I'm still a little jumpy... that's all. It's going to take some time before I really feel safe; probably not before they have Elliot behind bars."

"I think we both feel that way," Caroline said taking Amanda's hand. "Would you rather sit inside?"

"No, I'll be fine out here with you. After being in the dark for so long, I don't want to miss a minute of this glorious late sun."

Caroline placed the second beautifully wrapped box on the table. The paper, with its pictures of saws, drills, screwdrivers and other manly tools would give no clues as to the contents. "Will you open yours now? That way, all the attention will be on Ron when he discovers what the other package holds. I also brought out the camera. You'll need photos to go with the story."

"I thought you'd never ask," Amanda said taking the smaller box from Caroline.

"It's almost too pretty to open," she said as she removed the fancy bow and picked daintily at the tape.

"Oh, just go for it; I can't wait for your reaction."

"Reaction?" The paper came off quickly now. Amanda struggled to open the box. Inside she found layers of carefully tucked and folded tissue paper. "Whatever it is, I'm guessing it's breakable." She used more caution when she got to the last layer of tissue paper covering the little porcelain figurine.

"Well—hello Mickey. He's beautiful," Amanda said examining the cute little mouse figurine. "You're right; if it hadn't been for you talking to Mickey I would have never known you were in the shed up above me. This Mickey doesn't freak me out one little bit." She gave him a little kiss on his shiny black nose. "Thank you Caroline; he will be cherished." She stood and hugged her new best friend. "I have to confess though…if we had been in reverse places and Mickey showed himself, I would have run like a rabbit, regardless of the storm. If that mouse had showed up in the root cellar with me, I wouldn't need rescuing; I'd have died on the spot."

Caroline laughed. "Then it's a good thing it worked out the way it did."

"Listen to this…the city girl saying she isn't afraid of mice and the country girl screaming eek, like a sissy. So what's in the other box?" She asked giving it a shake and placing it back on the table.

"You'll have to wait until Daddy opens it, and shows us what's inside."

"Daddy! That's the first time I've heard Ron referred to as Daddy; I like the way it sounds."

Chapter
TWENTY-SEVEN

The exhilaration spread quickly amongst the police officers when Bruce called in that both Caroline and Amanda had been located—safe and sound. Elliot had never been stricken from the suspects list as he was seen with Amanda on the night of her disappearance, but at that time, they had nothing concrete to go on. He had been in the pool hall that night, so were a dozen other people, including some of the construction crew from up the highway. Nobody remembered seeing Amanda leave that night. Now the police had the evidence they needed. They were going to pounce on the man like a jungle cat. There would be a list of charges longer than your arm.

An All Points Bulletin was issued and cars were out looking for the accused.

"We'll make sure that son of a bitch pays his dues," Bruce had told Jason.

Bruce pressed the interoffice intercom button. "Randy, will you come to my office?" He spoke into the little black box on the corner of his desk. The office was equipped with the latest up-to-the-minute gadgets, but Bruce liked his old-fashioned intercom; it had been a gift from his wife on his first day at the station, more years ago than he liked to admit.

"Sure thing, be right there," Randy responded.

Bruce's door was open. Randy entered the office and took a seat in front of Bruce's large desk.

"Randy, I'm concerned about the Harrisons' and the Whites'. By now it's almost certain that Elliot has discovered the ladies have escaped, he could run for the hills, or he might get ugly. Either way, we've got a problem on our hands until we can lock him up"

Randy agreed with Bruce. "I've been thinking we should assign someone to keep an eye on them."

"Good work Randy; my thoughts exactly," Bruce said. "Until we pick up that creep, I'd like you to stake out the White's cottage. Leave the cruiser here and take one of the unmarked cars. It might be better if you stayed invisible; we don't want to get them upset, they've been through enough already."

"What about the Harrisons'?"

"I'm going to send one of the guys out to keep an eye on their place as well."

"Okay then, if there's nothing else, I'm out of here," Randy said.

"We'd better find him soon. With a loose cannon like that on the street…well, we can't be too careful. Use caution if you have to deal with him," Bruce added.

"I'll be careful."

"I'll get someone to relieve you for the night. If we don't arrest him before morning…head out there again tomorrow.

"What about the old shed?"

"We've checked that out and the surrounding area, but there was no sign of Elliot. He's out there somewhere; it's just a matter of time before we apprehend him. In the meantime, we'll all feel better keeping an eye on the Whites' and Harrisons.'"

Early the next day, Randy came across Elliot's car on one of the back country roads not far from the cottage. There was no sign of Elliot. The keys hung in the ignition. Randy checked out the vehicle. He lifted the Scotch bottle from the front seat; it was empty except for the strong smell of booze. He again read the detailed report of the kidnapping. "That drunken pervert is probably going to walk out of the woods right into my hands," he told the station over his radio. "I'm going to hang in here and wait for him."

"That's a *roger*," the police radio operator responded. "Be careful, the report says that he was carrying a shotgun."

"I'll be careful. I read about the shotgun in the initial report taken from Mrs. White and Amanda."

"Do you want me to send out backup?"

"No. I'll be able to handle him. In any event, I'll check in on the half hour just to keep you posted." Randy confirmed his location and the location of Elliot's car.

"Okay Randy. Be careful," the woman said before she disconnected the call.

Randy returned to Elliot's parked car and removed the keys. Once back inside his own vehicle, he relocated it further down the road. He was able to pull it far enough off the road that unless you were specifically looking for it, it wouldn't have been noticed. Randy moved his seat back as far as it would go and stretched his legs. He opened all the windows. As hot as it was, he didn't want to keep the air conditioner running. The environment would someday belong to his future grandkids and he knew how important it was for everyone to do their part. His OPP detachment stressed environmental protection. He figured he might as well get comfortable while he waited for Elliot to, hopefully, make an appearance.

At one time this had been a logging road. It had also been the back way into the Miller's cottage. The same cottage the Whites' were renting. Nowadays, hardly anybody used it except maybe the occasional hunters, or lovers. The Whites' probably had no idea that this old road even existed. It was now a dead end.

The hours on a stakeout were long. Randy scouted around a little and was just returning to his car to settled in and wait for Elliot's arrival when the cell phone in his pocket vibrated. Randy was surprised to hear Bruce's voice.

"How's it going?"

"There's still no sign of our accused, but I feel sure he'll show up here sooner or later since he left his car here."

"You're probably right. Listen Randy; there's been a little change in plans. With Elliot's car out there and you with an unmarked vehicle, I've decided we should let the Whites' know you're there keeping an eye on things. It could be more frightening for them if they discover you or the cars on their own."

"Okay, I'll let them know we're watching over the place. I can inform the Harrisons' as well; they arrived here about four o'clock this afternoon."

"Be careful Randy. Elliot's a big man and you can't predict how he might react. Henry, over at the bar, said he's seen him get pretty aggressive. With that shotgun of his you can't be too cautious."

"I can handle the son of a bitch," Randy replied. "That creep can't escape me."

Bruce wasn't too happy with Randy's over confidence. "Just be careful," he warned again. "Okay Randy, I'll leave it in your hands. Call in if you think you need assistance. Talk to you later."

Randy glanced at the ashtray where he'd thrown Elliot's keys. It was clear Elliot wasn't going anywhere in his car. He left the keys in the ashtray and locked up his car before he started up the road towards the cottage.

As Randy approached the cottage, he called out to Ron so as not to startle them. Ron introduced him to Caroline and Jason.

"I won't keep you folks; I just wanted you to know I was around."

"Would you like some dessert, there's plenty?" Caroline asked.

"No thanks, my wife makes sure I'm well fed." He patted the little bulge in his tummy. "I'll be around until about 11:00 tonight, then my relief will take over for the night. Brenda, that's my wife, packed me enough food to last two days." He took the porch steps in one stride.

Amanda and Caroline looked at each other and in unison said, "It's a man thing."

"Caroline, where is your bathroom?" Amanda asked.

"Go through the living room and it's the only door at the back past the bedrooms. You can't miss it."

Amanda excused herself and left the men discussing fishing.

Caroline listened silently to their tall tales before placing a couple of empty glasses on the tray and heading for the kitchen. Just as she opened the door, Amanda let out a blood-curdling scream. Caroline almost threw the tray to the table as she raced toward the bathroom with Ron and Jason hot on her heels.

Amanda flung open the door and bolted from the room, all the while tugging on her shorts. "He's in the bathroom," she gasped racing into Ron's arms.

Jason flew past Caroline and burst through the bathroom door. He stopped dead in his tracks. He backed out of the bathroom and turned toward Caroline. Shrugging his shoulders, he said, "There's nobody in there."

Amanda stood in the protection of Ron's arms; she was pale as a ghost. "I'm sorry," she apologized. "He scared the hell out of me."

"It's okay Amanda," Caroline tried to console her. Caroline thought back to the way she had felt just before the arrival of their guests when she thought she was being watched. "There's nothing to be afraid of now." She hoped she was right.

"I saw him," she said. He ran behind the laundry hamper."

Ron, Jason, and Caroline all stared at Amanda in animated disbelief.

"What did you see?" Ron patiently questioned.

"The mouse!"

Jason and Caroline didn't quite know how to react or what to say. They stood staring at Amanda.

Ron was the first to start laughing and before long they were all laughing, even Amanda through her tears.

Chapter
TWENTY-EIGHT

Elliot opened his eyes and was puzzled to find himself lying on the shed floor. The reality of the situation slowly seeped over him. The root cellar was empty. He wondered how long he had been asleep. He didn't think of fleeing, he only thought of getting even with the bitches for trying to get him into f---ing trouble. Getting even with Amanda would have to wait; he couldn't show his face in town, but he knew where to find Amanda's little friend. She'd take her cute little fanny back to the cottage she was sharing with her friend, or her husband, or whoever the dickhead was. He'd show her...he'd find her a nice spot close to Gloria. He figured he'd have to take out the dickhead, but that would work out better. With him out of the way, there wouldn't be anybody to report the little cutie missing. He'd wait awhile then he'd make Amanda pay for not loving him. He struggled to get to his feet. The daisy he had placed in his shirt pocket slipped to the floor. He picked up the wilted flower and flung it on top of one of the hay bales. His vision blurred. He reached into his knapsack and removed the bloodied butcher knife. Angrily he ran his fingers along the sharp blade. Bright red blood rose to the surface of the deep cuts across all four fingers and mixed with the dried blood on the blade. He felt no pain. "Soon my pretty little angels I'll have your blood on my hands," he laughed aloud. He blinked several times trying to clear his vision. The wilted daisy caught his eye; he turned and plunged the knife through the centre of the flower. The blade penetrated deep into the soft hay. "I warned you, I warned you both; now it's too late." A tear slipped from his eye. He grabbed the handle of the sharp knife and pulled it from the hay. The flower head stayed impaled on the blade. He threw the knife across the shed; it hit the old tractor with a loud clanging sound before falling to the earthen floor.

To retrieve the knife he'd have to crawl beneath the tractor; his head pounded and he decided he'd leave it where it landed. He remembered seeing the mouse on the hay bale before he passed out. As he left the shed he called back to the little mouse, "So long you scary little bastard." He farted. "That's for you," he said laughing.

The sun was sinking lower in the western sky. Elliot wasn't sure what day it was. He had a horrendous headache. Elliot wondered when the hell it was going to cool down. This was your typical summer heat wave with no relief for well over a week. He reached for his flask and cursed when he remembered he had lost it on route to the shed. He was now sober enough to realize that if his girls reached safety this place would be swarming with cops in no time. He knew of another place to hide out for a little while. He crossed the clearing and returned to the path that led to the shore. "Well glory be," he said when he stumbled across his lost flask. Two hundred feet into the path, he changed direction. Elliot had made sure this new path was well hidden. The new path took him deeper into the woods where he had established a small hunting blind. This would have to do until the heat was off. He'd stashed a box of crackers and some beef jerky sealed in zip-lock bags. He'd be okay. The crackers and jerky were welcome, but the full bottle of Scotch was what he applauded. A precaution just in case he was hunting and didn't make it back to town.

He drained the flask of its contents. Once he reached the blind, he ate a few of the crackers and some of the beef jerky. He carefully refilled his flask from the large bottle and tucked it back into his knapsack. He took a long drink from the other bottle and then he lay down. He closed his eyes and tried to imagine what it would be like if Amanda had loved him. He could have showed her what a real man was capable of. He was angry that he hadn't had sex with her when he had the chance. Finally, he slept.

When he awoke, the sun was almost directly overhead; he had slept, or more likely passed out through the night and most of the morning. He wasn't feeling well, but didn't want to wait any longer before finding *his girls* and showing them he meant business. He ate a couple of the crackers and washed them down with the remains of his stashed bottle. Before leaving the blind he patted the pocket on his knapsack to be sure he still had his flask. "Damn it's hot," he cursed, wiping the sweat from his forehead with his arm. He checked to be sure he had loaded the two shells into the gun. "Now my little angel… it's school time… time to teach you a lesson." He started out toward the cottage. Several times he stopped to rest and each time he took a good swig from his flask. With the alcohol still in his system it hadn't taken much to take him back to a drunken state. Although he was still a good distance from the cottage, he could smell the aroma of steaks cooking.

Elliot heard voices before he could get close enough to see anyone. He carried his shotgun tucked under his arm. As he got closer to the cottage the smell of the steaks cooking got stronger. He couldn't remember the last time he had a good meal—probably when he stewed up his rabbit. The booze was making his body and mind react weirdly. He wasn't sure whether the smell of the steaks was making him drool, or making him feel sick to his stomach. It pissed him off that his angel was cooking for another man. "If they'd loved me, I'd have let them cook for me too," he said aloud. Again, he farted. He chuckled and fanned the air around him.

Ugh, that's ugly, she wouldn't be happy with that foul smell around her food he thought to himself.

He left the overgrown path at the back of the cottage and crept closer. He would have to be careful; he didn't want anyone to catch him before he had his chance to get even. Back at the shed he'd loaded the twelve-gauge shotgun with two shells and put the third shell in his pocket. He fingered the bump it made in his tight jeans.

Still well camouflaged by the surrounding foliage he stood still and listened. The first voice he recognized was that of Amanda. "She should have talked to me like that," he whispered, his words being barely audible to his own ears. "Now Sweetheart it's too late; you'll have to pay for humiliating me." He patted himself on the back for saying *humiliating* correctly.

Elliot was pleased that Amanda was here, now he wouldn't have to chance going into town. Again, he felt the shotgun shell in his pocket. With four people and only three shells, this could still work out for me, he thought. "I'll take care of the two dickheads and then one of the broads. Sex is still on the menu," he spoke in a whisper. "But with which of my girls?"

He listened awhile and then crept forward so he could get a peek at the diners. They were busy talking and eating. He was sure he'd be able to get right up behind the cottage without alerting them of his presence.

Either there was an underground spring close by, or the rain hadn't yet seeped into the ground. The back of the cottage was high and the ground sloped quite steeply away from the back wall into a water-filled ditch. Elliot cursed when he got his feet wet crossing the ditch. There was a small window about five feet off the ground on the back wall. Directly below the window sat the remains of an old woodpile box. He gingerly climbed up onto the box where he teetered for a second until he was able to steady his footing. The top of the box was covered with patchy clumps of slippery green moss. He pressed his face against the glass to peer into what turned out to be the bathroom. He could see a shower and sink. Before he could climb back down, the bathroom door opened and Amanda walked in. Beads of perspiration stood out on Elliot's forehead. He watched as Amanda pulled down her shorts and her bikini undies. God she was gorgeous, he thought. It made him angry that once she sat down she was out of sight. He tried to imagine how she would look sitting on the porcelain throne. The last time he'd watched her pee had been in the woods. He wished he could see better. The jeans around his privates tightened. He rubbed his hand over his erection. You'll get your chance to show one of these broads what kind of a man you are, he told himself. When the erection subsided, anger took its place. "I'll show you!" He said under his breath.

He waited until she stood and then he raised the gun and took aim at the back of her head. "Sorry Sweetheart; I warned you," he whispered as he began to squeeze the trigger.

Chapter
TWENTY-NINE

E lliot had her directly in the line of fire. He could already feel the pressure on his finger as he slowly began to squeeze the cold metal trigger. Beads of perspiration stood out on his forehead. With Amanda out of the way he could have sex with her little friend without making Amanda jealous. Not such a bad deal he thought to himself. Again, he felt the crotch of his pants tighten. Just then Amanda let out a scream. The unexpected scream and the speed with which Amanda fled from the bathroom took Elliot by surprise. He thought she had seen him through the window. He lost his balance on the slippery wood and went ass over teakettle off his wooden platform. He stumbled, fumbled, and did some fancy footwork in an attempt to recover his balance but wound up face down on the wet ground. He half expected the two men from inside to come racing around the corner and grab him. Hell, he fully expected them to come after him. When they didn't appear, he was relieved and damn surprised. He regained his footing and as quickly as he could he took cover in the nearest clump of bushes. "Oh shit!" He said. His shotgun had slipped from his hands during his free-fall and slid down the slope quite away from where he had landed. He crouched behind the bush and waited. When nobody showed, he decided to take a chance getting his gun. He realized he'd have to move out into the open area to retrieve the shotgun. With all the commotion inside he didn't think anyone would notice him. Cautiously, he moved from the bushes into the open area and grabbing the gun, he hightailed it for cover. Once back into the protection of the trees he stopped to regain his composure. "Shit," he said knocking mud off the knees of his jeans, "My little sweetie, you don't know how lucky you were; I almost got you," he whispered. "I can't handle much more of this shit. What I need is a drink." Elliot continued to brush mud from his jeans as he moved back further into the woods. He entered another path that led to his parked car. He knew these woods like the back of his hand.

Unbeknownst to Elliot, he and the four people inside weren't the only ones to hear Amanda. Randy was a piece down the road when he heard the woman's scream. He pulled his revolver and raced back toward the cottage. He approached the cottage cautiously, and quickly worked his way around to the double doors on the kitchen side. He thought he heard laughter, but was prepared to handle whatever he came across. He raised the revolver to chest level and with both hands outstretched burst through the door.

When Jason saw Randy enter by the kitchen door, revolver drawn, he stopped laughing and rushed toward Randy. "It's okay," he quickly assured Randy. Jason explained about the mouse. Randy used all his restraint to hold his laughter. He returned his revolver to the safety of its holster and left shaking his head. Although Randy found the whole thing humorous, he did understand because his own wife was terrified of mice.

Chapter
THIRTY

Back at the car, Randy barely had time to get settled before he caught sight of Elliot making his way through the trees. He was hammered. Fortunately or unfortunately for Randy, this could go either way. Perhaps Elliot would be easier for Randy to deal with in his present condition, or he could become much more difficult. Randy would have to stay sharp. He noted that Elliot still had the shotgun slung under one arm. Randy had no way of telling if it was loaded or not. Elliot's keys were still in the ashtray. Randy put them in his shirt pocket. He hoped Elliot would put the gun in the car.

Elliot stopped and scanned the area before leaving the protection of the woods. Convinced everything was okay he approached his car and leaned against the passenger door. He reached in the open window and retrieved the bottle from the front seat. After removing the cap, he tried to take a swig. "Those bitches drank my Scotch," he bellowed holding the bottle up to glare through its emptiness. He flung the empty bottle back into the car.

Randy held his ground. He'd wait to see what Elliot's next move would be. He didn't want to approach the man while he was still in possession of the weapon.

Elliot, still clutching the gun, walked behind the car to the trunk. He found it locked and searched his pockets. Not finding the keys, he moved toward the driver's side. He opened the door and reached in expecting to find the keys in the ignition. In his drunken state, he almost fell into the car. "Damn those broads took my keys too," he shouted. He raised the barrel of the gun into the air as if to shoot, but he didn't pull the trigger. Elliot swore again and lowered the gun. He leaned back against the car and lowered his head.

A couple of minutes went by without Elliot moving. Randy wondered if he had fallen asleep standing up. Just as Randy was about to move in Elliot pulled himself away from the car and propped the gun against the back door of the vehicle. He again checked the ignition for his keys.

Randy would have liked Elliot to stow the gun in the car before he approached, but it was hot and he didn't want to wait around all day. Randy made his move.

When Elliot heard Randy's voice, he tried to keep his cool.

"Hi there Randy. What you doin way out here?" He asked trying to form his words clearly without much success.

"Well now Elliot, I was going to ask you that. Why are you carrying a gun? What have you been shooting at?" Randy didn't want to spook him. He wanted the chance to cuff him without a struggle.

"Not a damn thing," Elliot replied trying not to slur his words. "Randy, you and I both know it ain't huntin season. My old shotgun's been a little off lately… just thought I'd come way out here and sight it…you know, before huntin season begins."

"Is that gun loaded?"

"Hell no; I don't carry a loaded gun."

Randy knew better than to trust him. Once he got cuffs on Elliot, he'd check out the shotgun himself.

Elliot was a tall man, well over six feet; he was a good head taller than Randy. Randy watched as Elliot tried to steady himself against the car; he quickly retracted his hand after it touched the burning hot surface.

Randy was now in a good position. "Actually Elliot, I'm doing a little hunting myself today."

Elliot looked puzzled and nervous. "How's that?" He asked.

"I'm hunting for a guy who abducted two women."

Elliot's mouth was dry and he had a hard time swallowing. "Don't know nothin bout that," he said. Now he was leaning his full weight against the car door. He could feel the heat of the metal coming through his clothes. He shoved one hand deep into his pocket. Beads of perspiration stood out on his forehead and sweat soaked his shirt.

Randy wasn't concerned about any concealed weapons as Elliot's jeans were so tight he was amazed he was able to get his hand into his pocket.

"You sure Elliot you don't have any information about those missing women?"

"No, I don't know nothin. I told you guys, the last time I spoke to that Amanda broad was at the pool hall."

"Who were you shouting at just now?" Elliot didn't answer. Randy continued. "Didn't you tell us she went home with you that night?" Actually, Elliot had said no such thing. Randy was just baiting the conversation.

Elliot hesitated before answering. "I might have, but I was pretty drunk; I don't member that."

"Convenient. You know Elliot; it's too damn hot out here to stand around talking."

"Yeah," he agreed. "Can I hitch a ride in with you Randy? I somehow lost my keys."

"Hell Elliot, that was my plan too." Randy dangled Elliot's keys in front of him.

"Hey, where'd you get my keys?"

"I took them out of the ignition after I checked out your bottle. Didn't figure you'd want to be driving anywhere."

"Oh that." He kept his eyes lowered. "That's been empty for days."

"Has it now? Is that a flask in your knapsack pocket... a different flask than the one you offered Mrs. White at the old shed in the woods?"

Elliot jerked himself to an upright stance. "What are you talkin bout?" He asked.

"You know Elliot, the woman you were—holding with Amanda." Randy chose his words carefully.

"I don't know what the hell you're talkin bout." Elliot was getting more nervous by the second.

"Hand over that knapsack." Randy could make out the shape of the shotgun shell in Elliot's pocket. "Give me whatever that is in your pocket as well."

"Why do you want my knapsack? What are you saying?

"What I'm saying is that you're in big shit pal."

Elliot cursed, but he didn't attempt to move. Randy was glad that Elliot wasn't putting up any resistance. It looked like this arrest was going to be a piece of cake.

"Let's have that flask too," Randy said.

Elliot removed the knapsack from his shoulder and tossed it to Randy. Randy caught the bag and removed the flask from the side pocket. He shook the flask and could feel the remaining liquid sloshing around. He slipped it from its worn leather cover and held it up to the light to check the contents. In a flash, Elliot grabbed the shotgun by the barrel and smashed it hard over Randy's skull. Randy hit the ground like a sack of potatoes. The butt of the gun had opened a long gash on the side of Randy's head. Blood seeped from the opening and ran down over his ear and down the side of his neck. Randy struggled to get to his feet.

"You bastard," Randy shouted.

Elliot raised his foot and kicked Randy in the groin with his heavy work boot. He scooped up his flask, grabbed his knapsack, and ran toward the woods. Randy regained his footing and chased after Elliot. Randy managed to catch hold of Elliot's arm. They struggled, but again Elliot used the butt of the shotgun to give Randy a nasty blow. Randy fell back against a nearby tree. He felt as though he was going to blackout. Elliot snatched the car keys from Randy's shirt pocket and ran. Randy tried to follow but his vision blurred and he was forced to grab hold of a tree to steady himself. By the time Randy had regained control Elliot had disappeared into the dense woods.

Randy returned to his vehicle and radioed the station. "I lost the bastard," he reported to the operator. "Put me through to Bruce."

"Sorry Randy, but he left the office."

"That bastard is still out there in the woods somewhere. He has his gun and his car keys. He's armed and dangerous." Randy could attest to that by the bump on his head and the blood on his shirt, but he hadn't mentioned either when he spoke to the station. He'd checked it out in the car's rear view mirror. He had a huge bump developing but the cut appeared to be mostly surface damage. His vision was still a little off.

Elliot was a good piece into the woods before he stopped to rest. He pulled his car keys from his pocket and examined them. Randy's shirt pocket dangled from one of the keys. He laughed. "Nobody messes with me," he sneered. He took a long swallow from his recovered flask. He didn't dare go back to his car, at least not yet. His mind wasn't clear but he thought maybe he could sneak back for his car after dark. For now, he'd return to his hunting blind and kill a few hours. No longer worried about Randy he walked down the centre of the winding path with contemptuous boldness.

"Going somewhere?" A voice behind Elliot asked.

Elliot whirled around so quickly he almost lost his balance. "Holy shit!" He whispered.

Bruce stood only feet away with his revolver drawn. He had come from nowhere. Elliot wasn't the only one that knew these woods like the back of his hand.

"It would appear that you weren't too cooperative with one of my law enforcers," he stated. "Now Elliot, that makes me angry. Almost anyone around these parts can tell you it's not a good idea to make me angry."

Elliot stood motionless. He couldn't take his eyes off the end of the gun pointed directly at him.

When Bruce had spoken to Randy earlier, he hadn't been able to shake a nagging feeling that Randy might need backup. After disconnecting the call he'd loaded his service revolver and headed out. When he came upon Randy and saw the head wound he had ordered Randy to return to town and have it checked out. Randy protested, but Bruce wasn't taking no for an answer. "I'll go after the son of a bitch."

"He's a big bastard and high as a kite," Randy had told him. "You've got twenty years on him so be careful."

"You know I will," Bruce had responded. "Take care of that head. I'll bring in the bastard. We'll wrap him up tighter than an Egyptian mummy." Bruce had watched as Randy got into his vehicle and drove away. Bruce checked his revolver and placed it back into the holster before entering the woods.

"So Elliot my boy... I wonder how long it would take someone to find you if I took you back to that old shed and tied you up in the root cellar. Gee... I wonder if anyone would even come looking. Who would report you missing? Sure as hell not me." It was Officer Bruce's turn to laugh.

Elliot felt the sweat run down his back.

"I didn't do anything and you can't prove I did," Elliot said after regaining some of his composure.

"We'll see about that. Put the gun down real gentle like and toss that knapsack over there," he said pointing off to the side of the path.

Elliot knew, at least for now that he was beaten and did as Officer Bruce ordered.

"You are under arrest for...let's see... abduction, forceful confinement, aggravated assault, failure to provide, threats against a life, breaking and entering, stalking, and last but not least, impaired driving. Oh yes... anything else we can come up with. Maybe even murder."

Elliot cursed, but he didn't attempt to move.

Bruce was glad of that. Not that Elliot had a chance of getting away, but it was just too damn hot for a chase or a struggle "Okay Elliot, let's get those hands behind your back." Bruce removed the cuffs from somewhere in the back of his uniform belt and cautiously moved behind Elliot. Bruce knew that anything Elliot said now wouldn't be admissible in a Court of Law unless he'd been informed that he was being recorded so he said, "Elliot, you don't mind if I have my tape recorder running—do you?"

"I don't give a f--- what you do. But you could give me back my flask," he added.

Bruce checked to see that the little recorder was running. "Now listen up, I'm going to read you your rights." He proceeded to obey every letter of the law; he didn't want this slime bag to slip through any loopholes. He walked Elliot back to his police car. He opened the back door and placed his hand protectively on the top of Elliot's head as he guided him into the backseat of the car.

"Hey, what about my car?"

"Oh yeah—your car. Maybe I should just let you drive on back to town and then you can turn yourself in later." Bruce was having a little fun. He was so disgusted by the likes of Elliot that if he didn't try to keep it light he'd just as soon stuff the animal in the trunk of his car and let him rot right here in the hot sun.

"Sure Brucey, I'll drive real careful."

"First, don't call me Brucey. Remember what I said about making me angry."

"Sure Bruce, but what about my car? He repeated with more respect.

"Oops, I forgot—you're already under arrest. It just wouldn't be right if I let you drive back on your own."

Elliot knew he was screwed. His nervousness turned to anger. He cussed as they drove towards town.

Bruce radioed the station. "Get the guest room ready," he said to the operator, "I'm bringing home a visitor. By the way, he'll be staying a long, long time."

"Good work Bruce. Want me to call the Harrisons' and the Whites'? They'll be relieved to hear that Elliot's been picked up."

"No, I'll call them myself when I get to the station. Has anyone checked on Randy yet?"

"Yeah, he'll be fine. It was just a surface wound, but he'll probably have a really big headache for a couple of days."

"I'm about ten minutes out… see you soon." Bruce ended the call.

"So Elliot, what ever possessed you to do something like that?" Bruce asked.

"It was Gloria's fault," Elliot volunteered immediately.

Bruce wasn't sure Elliot had understood the question. His recollection was that Mrs. White's name was Caroline. He had no idea who Gloria was. "So Gloria told you to abduct Amanda?"

Elliot laughed an evil laugh.

Bruce looked at his passenger in the rear view mirror. The accused had his eyes closed and his head tilted back against the back of the seat. He was not asleep but he certainly wasn't very coherent.

"All I ever wanted was for her to love me but she wouldn't. She was spitefully cold to me. I warned her," he slurred. "All she had to do was love me. Now it's too late. She can't come back now," he mumbled without opening his eyes.

"Where did she go?" Bruce wondered who *she* was.

When Elliot didn't answer, Bruce thought he'd passed out. They rode the next couple of miles in stony silence.

After Bruce had secured Elliot in the back of his cruiser, he had confiscated the empty Scotch bottle from Elliot's car and removed the shells from the firing chambers of the shotgun. He had also taken the extra shell from Elliot's pocket. The flask from the knapsack was less than half-full. As they drove in silence he got to thinking about the shotgun. "Why did you shoot her?" Bruce asked in a loud voice. It was a stab in the dark, but he hoped Elliot would hear and would start talking again.

Startled, Elliot's eyes flew open. "I didn't want to—she made me; she was a bitch!"

Now it was Bruce's turn to be startled. "Why don't you tell me about it, you know, get it off your chest." Bruce tried to maintain as friendly a tone as possible. He reached over and picked up the little recorder. The REC light indicated that the recorder was still capturing the conversation. He placed it back on the passenger seat. "Hey Elliot, we've known each other for awhile... you can talk to me."

"Amanda was no better than Gloria." Elliot groaned and closed his eyes again. "Ever have a bitch like that turn you down? Humiliating you?" He opened his eyes just a slit. "Hey Bruce, I've got a hell of a headache; can I have my flask back?"

Bruce didn't answer.

It didn't matter because Elliot didn't wait for an answer anyway. He continued to ramble on. "I coulda fixed those broads too, but no, I had to be the nice guy. Now they wanna get me in f---ing trouble."

"What did you want with Mrs. White?"

"Uh! Who the hell is Mrs. White?"

"You know—the other woman with Amanda."

"Oh her. She should have kept her nose out of my business." He fell silent for a minute. "You should have seen that broad in a bikini—va-va-voom." He laughed again, this time it was a cynical laugh.

Bruce checked his rear view mirror. Elliot hadn't moved, but he'd closed his eyes again.

"She could drink too. If that old man of hers was out of the picture, I'll bet she woulda enjoyed being with me. I'm quite a ladies man—you know."

"So you knew the Whites'?"

"Who the hell are the Whites'?"

"You know…the woman with Amanda," Bruce prompted him again.

"No, I didn't know him. I partied a little with the broad—that's all," he lied to impress Bruce. "That broad really liked me. We did some serious drinking together."

Elliot's speech was so slurred now that Bruce hoped the recorder was able to pick up the conversation.

"So tell me more about Gloria?" He pressed.

"Not much to tell. If she'd played her cards right, I wouldn't hada teach her a lesson."

"What kind of lesson?"

"It don't matter now. She's gone, and I'm not telling you nothin."

"Sure pal just thought you might want to get it off your chest." Bruce was driving slowly hoping Elliot might get chatty.

"Hey, Bruce my boy, you wanna stop at my place? I've got me some fine Scotch left."

"Maybe another time," Bruce said still trying to maintain a friendly tone.

It was obvious that Elliot didn't realize what kind of trouble he was in and now there were new questions about Gloria to be answered.

When they reached the station, Bruce clicked off the recorder.

Elliot hadn't said a word during the last few minutes.

"Come on Elliot." Bruce opened the back door of the cruiser.

"Hey, you can't keep me here." Elliot swore and spit on the ground.

"We'll see about that!" This time Bruce didn't attempt to protect his passenger's head as he dragged him from the backseat.

Chapter
THIRTY-ONE

The phone rang and Caroline excused herself. "Let me get that; it might be Michael Jay. He calls us every third night before he gets ready for bed. I hope you'll get to meet him someday—he's quite the little guy," Caroline said swelling with pride.

Amanda stretched her legs out and enjoyed the late rays of sun. She was not for one second unmindful of her surroundings.

Minutes later Caroline reappeared on the porch. "I've got news."

Amanda looked toward Caroline. It wasn't necessary to ask what the news was. The excitement and relief on Caroline's face told the whole story.

"They got him—didn't they?" Amanda rose and moved swiftly to Caroline.

Caroline didn't answer. She wiped away the tear that slipped down her cheek and shook her head. "He's been charged and is safely locked up," Caroline said.

They held each other and truly felt safe for the first time since their escape.

"Let's walk down to the dock and share the wonderful news," Caroline whispered. The words were barely out of her mouth before she heard Jason and Ron's laughter as they made their way up the path.

"Here come our hunters and gatherers, or maybe I should say our fishermen and fibbers," Amanda said with a laugh.

"You're back early; I thought you'd be down there until after dark. Were the fish not biting?" Caroline asked.

Ron kissed Amanda on the forehead. He started to tell them about the fishing when he caught the look on Amanda's face. "Did something happen while we were down at the dock?"

Jason returned the can of worms to their corner under the porch. He came back around the corner just in time to hear Ron ask if something had happened. His eyes fixed on Caroline. He was relieved to see that she was smiling. "I think our girls have a secret," Jason said taking the two steps as one. Leaning the rods against the wall, he said, "Okay, spill the beans." He put his arm around Caroline's shoulder.

"No secret. We just got a call from the police station. They got him."

The two couples cast long shadows across the porch as they hugged each other.

"Thank God," Jason finally managed to get out. "We'll all sleep better tonight."

"Yes...yes and now we can put this behind us," Caroline affirmed giving Amanda's hand a squeeze.

Amanda was glad the men had come back early from their fishing expedition. She was anxious to let Ron in on *her* secret.

"You still haven't told us why you are back so early...what no fish?" Caroline asked again.

Amanda was glad that Caroline was taking the initiative to change the subject.

"Sure, they were biting, we got—what would you say Ron—a dozen or so, but we released them to grow bigger for another day," Jason said with a wink.

"Good thing we have food in the freezer."

Ron eyed the wrapped box and the smaller box with the pile of tissue paper beside the little mouse. "Did someone have a birthday?"

"No, not yet," Caroline said with a little smile.

"This is Mickey." Amanda held the mouse out to Ron. "After Caroline and Jason of course, this is my best new friend."

Ron laughed. "I would have thought you'd had enough of mice for one evening. I can't even image that you—you, of all people, have a mouse as a friend, and he's got a name and everything." Ron truly looked puzzled. "Now I've heard everything," he shook his head as he examined the little figurine. "There must be one hell of a story behind this one."

"It's quite a story alright; tell you all about it later. In the meantime, Caroline, in all her wisdom, thought you might want, or need what's in the other box."

"Me, I don't want or need anything now that I've got you back home safely."

"Maybe you should open it and see what's inside." Caroline passed the gift to Ron.

"What is it Amanda?" He asked turning to look at her.

"I can honestly say I have no idea what's in that box."

Ron looked toward Jason. Jason made it clear that he had no idea what was in the box, or what the girls were up to, but it was obvious they had something up their sleeves as they exchanged knowing glances.

"I guess there's nothing left for me to do but say *thank you* and open the gift." Ron unceremoniously ripped away the wrapping paper. It was another one of those man things—no picking away at the tape or trying to salvage the beautiful paper. He used his pocketknife to break the tape holding the lid of the box closed. He folded the lid back and removed the layer of tissue. Inside he discovered a pale green and yellow crocheted blanket. Attached to one corner with multicoloured ribbons was a small rattle shaped like a baby bottle, a pacifier, and a bib that read *"Daddy's newest project."*

It took Ron a few seconds to clue into what he was looking at. He tore his eyes away from the gift and studied Amanda.

She gazed lovingly at his puzzled face and nodded her head.

Ron flew out of his chair and swept Amanda into his arms. "Are you sure…how…?"

Amanda laughed. "Well, if you don't know *how* maybe we should have a long talk."

Jason and Caroline joined hands and delighted in the love they watched pass between their two friends. Jason leaned over and whispered in Caroline's ear; "I'm jealous."

When Amanda and Ron parted, Jason and Ron shook hands and the congratulations went around the circle they had formed.

Chapter THIRTY-TWO

"Okay Elliot, we'll be back in a minute." Officers Bruce and Randy pushed their chairs away from the table.

"Can I have another coffee?" Elliot asked meekly. He was not the same angry and very drunk man that Bruce had brought in yesterday. Now that he was sober, the situation he was in was making itself more evident every minute. The table was strewn with empty and half-empty Styrofoam cups.

"Sure, help yourself."

The two officers left the interrogation room closing the door behind them.

Elliot poured another coffee. His hand shook as he added sugar and powdered milk. He would have given his right hand for a drink. He looked around the windowless room. A large table, several wooden chairs, and a small side table, barely large enough to hold the coffee maker, cream, sugar and a few cups was all the room contained. There was a large mirror on one wall with a sticker that read *unbreakable glass*. Elliot had watched enough TV to assume it was probably two-way glass and that he was being watched. Who knows why, he certainly couldn't escape from here even if he tried.

The two officers had played good cop, bad cop. Randy badgered Elliot, and Bruce pretended to be the more understanding of the two.

Elliot admitted nothing. He was right about one thing. The mirror was indeed two-way glass.

Bruce, Randy and a third OPP officer watched as he got his coffee. His hands were shaking noticeably.

"What do you think Randy? If I play the recording, he might break down and confess. It could save us and the two ladies a lot of hard work and heartache that a trial would mean."

"Sure Bruce let's see if we can trigger him into talking. We'll put him away for abducting Amanda and Mrs. White, but I'd like him to spill the beans about Gloria. Our guys are trying to track down the info on anyone named Gloria who went missing."

"Let me go take a leak and then we'll see if we can get him to talk," Bruce said already heading down the hall to the restroom.

"Okay Elliot," Bruce began when they returned to the interrogation room. "I wasn't going to let you hear this, but once you do… it will be all over my friend." Calling Elliot a friend gave Bruce a bad taste in his mouth.

Elliot looked puzzled. He swallowed the last of his lukewarm coffee.

"Now, if you cooperate we'll see if we can cut you a break on the abduction charges. We'll even throw out the impaired charges for good measure." What he didn't say was…"If we can make a murder wrap stick, we'll hang you by your balls, you little shit face." Bruce fell silent. He wanted Elliot to have a minute to wonder what he was about to hear.

"This is a waste of our time. Throw the book at the lowlife and save us all time and trouble," Randy bellowed. He stood up so quickly that his chair went flying across the room.

"Now calm down Randy," Bruce said moving between Randy and Elliot. "If it were your friend, you'd want to cut him a break."

Elliot's eyes bulged as he looked from one man to the other.

Bruce let him squirm. "Now Randy, if you'll take a seat, we can do this real friendly like." He pulled the recorder from his pocket and placed it on the table in front of him. "The quality's not great, but you know what you did. Remember what I said about cooperating." He fingered the play button. "I want to make this easier on you," Bruce said placing his hand on Elliot's shoulder.

Bruce pressed the play button. Strains of Shania Twain filled the room.

Elliot looked surprised and Randy again feigned a blow up at Bruce's supposed error.

"Sorry fellows... wrong place on the tape." Bruce pressed another button and then the play button once again.

Elliot had moved all the way forward on his chair and rested his arms on the large table. At first, there was only a rustling sound and then he heard his own voice. He listened in silence to his conversation with Bruce. He became increasingly agitated.

When Bruce knew he was at the end of the recording, he pressed the stop button. "There's more," he lied, "but what's the point? You told me all about the bloodied knife." Bruce was speculating again. "You also said you'd tell me where Gloria is."

Elliot was sweating, although the room was quite cool. He ran the back of his hand over his top lip.

Randy and Bruce remained silent. They gave Elliot time to sweat.

After an appropriate lapse of time, Randy said, "This guy has taken enough of our time." Randy spoke in a normal tone of voice as he pushed his chair away and suggested Elliot be return to his cell.

"Wait..." Elliot said. "What kind of deal?"

"Forget it," Randy said heading for the door.

"Give him a minute Randy," Bruce pleaded. "He's not stupid; he knows what's best."

Randy turned and pretended he was reluctant to return to the table. "I don't have any patience left," he said showing agitation.

"Are you going to give us a statement, or are you going back to your cell to rot?"

Elliot looked back and forth between the two cops. He let his eyes rest on the silent recorder.

Randy sighed and began to push back from the table as if to leave.

"Okay, I'll tell you what happened, but it wasn't my fault."

Bruce pressed a button under the table and almost instantaneously the station steno appeared.

"Go ahead Elliot, let's hear what happened. Start at the beginning and don't leave out anything."

"What kind of a deal are we talking about here?" Elliot asked again.

"That depends on how cooperative you are," Bruce said leaning over the table to look him square in the eye. "Or—we can forget it."

The next hour was a busy one for the steno.

Elliot sang like a canary. He got caught up in the telling and at times was actually bragging about the horrific things he had done. He told them where the butcher knife was and he described where they would find Gloria. He swore the blood on the knife was his own and that of a rabbit and surprisingly this later proved to be the truth. Once he got going, he didn't stop. He told how he'd imprisoned Gloria Ganyou and how and where he had buried her lifeless body. He described watching the women pee in the woods and what a turn on it was for him. He bragged about how close he'd come to shooting Amanda in the head when she was in the bathroom at the cottage. When speaking of Caroline, he said, "I should have put a bullet in that friend of hers; she would have been happier with me. You should have seen that broad in her little string bikini. It wouldn't have taken me long to get past that. I'd have showed her what a real man is all about." He was getting aroused just talking about *his girls*.

"Sure Elliot, we know what kind of man you are," Randy said. "Just go on."

"I didn't want to give Amanda any reason to be jealous though," he added. "I wanted her to love me, was that too much to ask?" Suddenly he stopped talking. He mumbled that he regretted killing Gloria so soon. He should have given her more time to fall in love with him. They listened to his horrendous confession. This was one hideously sick puppy. By the time he had finished his statement both Randy and Bruce had sick stomachs.

"I guess that's all," he said almost proudly.

Bruce and Randy would have loved to punch in his ugly mug, or worse, but instead, Bruce said, "Elliot, we're going to take you back to your cell now. We'll check some of this out. When the steno has your statement ready, we'll ask you to read it and sign your name—okay?"

"Yeah okay," Elliot said. "Tell Amanda and the other broad that I'm sorry they didn't cooperate with me."

Bruce mulled over Elliot's comment. This sleaze bag wasn't showing any sign of remorse. Randy cuffed Elliot and returned him to his cell. He then returned to the main office and met with Bruce.

"That was a rough one," Bruce said.

"If that was the only aspect of police work I'd have taken my dad's advice and become a plumber," Randy lamented.

"But it's not. You're a damn good cop Randy; the people around here like you. More importantly, they respect you. Someday, when I retire, it will be your town." Bruce was proud of Randy. "In the meantime, life goes on. Amanda and Mrs. White will sign the necessary paperwork tomorrow. We'll have to drop the impaired charges—couldn't make them stick anyway, but if they find he was telling the truth about Gloria, that's all we'll need to keep him from ever committing another crime. We'll put this one through a psychiatric examination as well. You'd almost have to be a few bricks short of a load to do what he says he did. In any case, he's going away. One way or another he'll be a burden to the honest taxpayers—probably for life."

Chapter
THIRTY-THREE

"With that degenerate behind bars, I see no reason for us to shorten our vacation; as a matter of fact, I feel we owe ourselves the remaining time together," Caroline assured Jason.

"Officer Bruce is coming out later this morning; he's bringing the official papers out for you to sign."

"Good, the quicker they're signed the further I can put this ordeal behind us all. Do you know if Amanda has signed her statement yet?"

Bruce told me he'd be stopping at her place before coming here."

"Bruce?"

"Did I say Bruce—you know, Officer Bruce. After all that's happened around here, I feel like I've been part of this community forever. It's a good community. When I saw all the people that showed up to help find you...a complete stranger; I felt like I wanted to be a part of them." Jason shrugged his shoulders. "He's officially Officer Bruce Wilson, but he told me I could call him Bruce."

Caroline began clearing the breakfast table. "I'm glad you weren't alone. I knew how worried you would be. I wished I could have done something about that, but I couldn't."

Jason took Caroline gently by the shoulders and turned her to face him. He placed his finger under her chin and tilted her face up so they were looking into each other's eyes. "Once those papers are signed, this will be over. Your fright, my worry…they will all fade. This cabin and this vacation will remain only a pleasant memory." Jason bent and kissed her softly.

She gave him an affirmative nod.

"How about if I run the vacuum over the rug while you finish up these dishes?" Jason said slowly releasing her and turning the conversation onto a new subject.

Before either could begin their tasks, the sound of gravel crunching and a couple of small toots of a horn announced Bruce's arrival.

"Beautiful morning—isn't it?" Bruce said as he unfolded himself from the front seat of the cruiser. He grabbed Jason's hand and enthusiastically pumped it up and down. He then turned to Caroline. She thought he was going to shake her hand as well, but instead he leaned and placed a small kiss on her cheek. "How is the prettiest lady on the Peninsula this morning?"

Caroline laughed. "I'm just fine Officer Bruce… none the worse for wear."

"Since you two are going to be around these parts, you might as well start calling me Bruce," he said more to Caroline than to Jason.

Jason and Caroline glanced at each other and again Jason shrugged his shoulders.

"Let me grab the papers and we'll wrap this up."

Jason and Caroline waited while Bruce retrieved the papers from the cruiser.

"There's still coffee, if you'd like a cup."

"No thanks, I'll just get you to sign on the dotted line and then I'll be out of here."

As Caroline signed in the numerous places Bruce indicated, Bruce chatted.

"Will Amanda and I have to testify at a later date?"

Bruce patted the back of her hand. "Now don't you give it another thought. We have enough on Elliot to put him away for good. Yours and Amanda's charges are just icing on the cake—a formality.

Bruce rose and scooped up the small pile of documents. Again, he shook hands with Jason and placed a fatherly peck on Caroline's cheek. "It will be nice seeing you both around these parts. Enjoy the rest of your vacation." He bounded down the porch steps with the energy of a man half his age.

Jason and Caroline escorted him to where he'd parked the cruiser.

As he pulled away, he called out..."Welcome to the community and hurry back."

Jason took Caroline's hand and they watched as Bruce turned the cruiser around and headed back down the drive, waving goodbye.

"I feel like we've been adopted," Caroline said with a little laugh.

"He's a nice guy—isn't he?"

Caroline laughed. "Yeah, he's a nice guy!"

"What's so funny?"

"You are," she replied. "Not even two weeks here and you're already talking like a true Canadian."

"You'll have to explain that."

With a giggle, she explained. "Canadians often make a statement then finish the thought with a question. It's like they are asking for your agreement or approval."

"I don't get it...give me an example."

"Well—you said, "*He's a nice guy,*" and then you questioned your statement by adding, "*isn't he?*" Bruce greeted us with "*Beautiful day—isn't it?*" See what I mean?"

Jason thought about what she said.

"I guess it's contagious—eh? Jason said turning his puzzled look into a smile.

"Yeah—eh!" Caroline chuckled.

Holding hands, they took the porch steps in one stride. This was much easier for Jason than for Caroline.

"Let's do our chores and then do something fun," Caroline suggested.

"Your idea and my idea of fun might be somewhat different," Jason said giving her a mischievous grin.

"Oh no…we are definitely thinking along the same lines, but first lets go swimming then afterwards we'll explore our mutual idea of fun."

The next week and a half passed quickly. Jason and Caroline learned more about the area. They visited many beautiful and interesting sites including a visit to Wiarton Willie, the albino weather prognosticating groundhog. They checked out an Indian Reserve, some local ruins, took a scenic flight over the Bruce Peninsula, hiked on the Bruce Trail, and discovered Sauble Beach, one of the most beautiful stretches of white sand either of them had ever seen. They visited with Ron and Amanda at their home. "Amanda may claim she's not much of a cook, but she certainly has a flare for interior decorating," Caroline commented to Ron.

"She has an eye for all that kind of stuff," he agreed.

"Maybe if I send her some pictures she can give me some suggestions. I'd like to change Michael Jay's room so it's more little boy and less baby."

"Speaking of baby, and that's all I seem to think of lately, you should see the sketches she's made for *our* baby's room. We're losing a junk room and gaining a dream nursery. She's got talent alright."

Caroline thought it was nice the way he emphasized the 'our' baby.

They grew closer each time they met and discovered how much they had in common. This was becoming a friendship that would easily span the long-distance.

Chapter
THIRTY-FOUR

C aroline had mixed feelings as she packed their belongings for the trip back home. She hated to leave what she had come to call "our cabin," but she was ecstatic about going home to Michael Jay. If she hadn't known how much he was enjoying his stay with his Grandparents, she would have been unable to stay the full three weeks.

"I think that's about it," she said placing the last bag by the front door.

"Let's take a walk down to the shore one more time before we go." Jason led her out onto the porch.

"It's nice here—eh!"

"For a home away from home, it can't get much better." Jason smiled at how Caroline had said—"eh!"

They stood hand in hand looking out over the water. Each time they admired the view, the water itself seemed to reveal a brand-new shade of blue. Seagulls soared overhead while the waves lapped up onto the shore and a large green bullfrog croaked his song as he sunned himself at the side of the dock. The morning sun caressed their faces.

"This place will probably be sold by next summer. If we come back, we'll have to find someplace else," Caroline said downheartedly.

"Ron and I were talking and rumour has it that there is already a buyer on board." Quickly he added, "There are lots of places around here. We'll find a place that's perfect." He noticed the disappointed look on Caroline's face.

"I think we already found the perfect place." She leaned her head against his shoulder.

Jason let the silence of the lake surround them. "I guess we should get going."

It was more than a fifteen-hour drive to their home in New York and they planned to split the drive into two days. They would cover the first six or seven hours today and then get an early start on the home stretch the next day.

"Yeah, I guess we'd better go." Caroline started up the incline to the cabin.

Jason took hold of her hand as they navigated the rocky path. When they reached the cabin, Jason placed the last couple of bags into the car. The huge fire truck was the last thing in so it could be the first thing out. Jason handed Caroline the keys and asked her to lock up.

Caroline opened the screen door and took a last look around. She did a walk through to be sure she had everything. On one of her town excursions, she'd bought a small white birch plaque that read: "Welcome to God's Country." She'd hung it on the living room wall. She smiled and thought how it really was God's Country. She went through to the kitchen where she ran her fingers over the petals of the daisies in the small silk flower arrangement she'd brought back from a trip to a local farmer's market. At the last moment, she decided to leave it on the table for whom ever got to enjoy the kitchen next. Normally she didn't form such strong ties to a place, but something about this cabin was special. In some, inexplicable way, the beauty of the place and the time spent with Jason had miraculously erased the hours of terror. This was a happy place. Returning to the porch, she closed the door behind her and turned the key. She took another look around before she slid into the passenger seat. Jason had the air conditioner on and the interior of the car felt cool. "Okay," she said, "I guess we do have to go." She held out the keys to Jason. "It's hot out there," she said. "Can we pick up a cold soda when we drop the keys into the realtors?" The keys dangled from her hand. "Here, take these," she said giving the keys a little shake as she reached for her seat belt.

"Why would I take the keys?"

"To give to Chris at the real estate office."

"What's Chris going to do with our keys?"

It took a few seconds before his words registered. "Our keys," she squeaked out.

"That's what I heard myself say." Jason's grin would have wrapped all the way around his head if it weren't for the placement of his ears.

"Stop the car," she said excitedly.

"Just in case you hadn't noticed… we haven't moved an inch. I knew you would want one last look at our place."

She flung herself across the seat to embrace him. "Are you sure?"

"Oh I'm sure alright," he said. "We might have to give up our habit of eating, but we are now the owners of a summer place in Canada. Actually, it was a good deal; we'll still be able to send all our kids to college."

"All our kids?"

Jason looked over at Caroline and laughed. "Yeah—all our kids, as long as we stop at two, three tops," he kissed her soft lips.

"I have to take one more look—from an owner's point of view," she said as she flung opened the car door and stepped out.

"This was one of the hardest things I've ever done." Jason also stepped from the car.

Caroline waited for him to continue.

"The day I went to town alone..." He began. "Well, I had already signed the deal with the real estate office when you suddenly disappeared. After that, I wasn't sure either of us would ever want to be in this place again. I was..." Jason searched unsuccessfully for the right words. "I was uncertain if..."

Caroline remained silent for a moment. "Oh Jason," she said, "Please let me assure you that I love it here and we have to look on the bright side." She collected her thoughts before going on. "If we hadn't been here, I may not have been able to help Amanda. God only knows what might have happened to her. That in itself is enough reason to love being here. We can count our blessings. If I recall, not that long ago, you told me that God sometimes makes things happen that we may never understand. I think my stumbling upon Amanda was one of those things."

Jason nodded his head.

Caroline moved away from the car and surveyed her new *"home away from home."*

"So, this was a good decision on my part?"

"A perfectly wonderful decision," she said deliriously. "My only problem is leaving it here when we have to go home... but I guess that's part of the charm; we'll get to come back," she said wrapping her arms around him.

"One final look and then we will have to go," Jason said leading her toward the porch. For the last time, this vacation, they took the porch steps in one stride.

Caroline turned the key in the front door and they did one more walkabout together. This time she looked at the beautiful rustic log walls and the efficient kitchen through the eyes of a proud and excited owner. "On our next visit I'm going to rearrange all the kitchen cupboards," she giggled.

Jason smiled. "It must be a woman thing," he said and they both laughed.

Caroline squeezed his hand and whispered, "Thank you."

They returned to the car. They drove in silence for a few minutes as Caroline mulled over her surprise. Then practicality flooded over her. "What about winter maintenance? The water should be shut off and I'm sure there must be a hundred other things we should be doing?" Caroline felt an anxiety attack wash over her as they drove down the road.

"It's okay Honey. You're not the only one that can keep a secret. Ron is going to take care of everything while we aren't here."

Caroline calmed herself and then she asked, "Does Amanda know all about this?"

"Sure, but she was sworn to secrecy. She said she owed you a secret. She can't wait until next summer when we come again; she asked me to tell you that we're invited to dinner and she's cooking. Ron is going to send us some pamphlets about Groundhog Day. He thinks we should come for the festivities; you know—see how beautiful it is in the winter. He'll arrange to have the snow ploughed and the heat turned on before we arrive."

"Wow that sounds like a great idea, if you think you can take the time off. Michael Jay will love the snow; maybe we can even get in a little ice fishing."

They found a good radio station and sang along as the miles clicked away. When the 1:00 o'clock news came on, Caroline and Jason half listened, not really paying attention to the newscaster until the story about Elliot Johnson made them both reach for the volume knob. They just caught the last few words. "The accused has been remanded to custody without bail. A psychiatric evaluation has been ordered." The newscaster went on to say, "A multiple alarm fire is now under control in the ..." Jason reached over and turned off the radio. "Justice will be done," he said.

Just then the Canada/US Bridge came into view. Caroline dug into her purse for their passports. They had been driving for several hours. She looked out over the water from the top of the bridge. It was always a nice feeling to return home, but she was going to miss the cabin and their new friends Amanda and Ron.

Jason paid close attention to the heavy traffic on the bridge crossing the border.

"Good afternoon folks. Where are you heading today?" The border guard asked.

"We're on our way home to New York." Jason handed the two passports through the window.

"How long have you been in Canada?"

"Three weeks—a much needed vacation."

"Do you have anything to declare?" The guard questioned as she opened each passport and placed a little stamp inside.

"We bought a few souvenirs and a fire truck for our son." Jason pointed to the back of the car.

"Hope you had a pleasant holiday," the young woman said.

"Now that's an understatement."

"Pardon me?" The guard asked.

"Nothing," Jason said glancing knowingly toward Caroline.

"You have a safe drive," the border guard said as she returned the passports and motioned them through.

Chapter
THIRTY-FIVE

"I can't wait to go back there," Caroline said. "The cabin itself is great, but what actually won me over was the beautiful scenery. The water, the trees, the fishing; I can't wait until Michael Jay catches his first fish. He'll definitely want to bring home a raccoon—you'll have to handle that." Caroline tucked the two passports back into her purse. The traffic was heavy but moving nicely. The miles slipped away as they drove through Buffalo and got on the New York Thruway. Caroline couldn't stop talking about the cabin. "You know, now that we own property in Canada we'll have to say we have a *cottage*."

"*Cottage* it is," Jason said with a slight English accent.

Caroline wrinkled her nose. "What's with the accent? We bought a place in Canada not England. If anything, you have to say *Cottage eh!*" She said with a giggle.

Jason's stomach growled.

"You must be hungry," Caroline said. "I've got sandwiches and I picked up cold sodas at the last gas station."

"That sounds great. Let's stop at the next rest area. We can have a picnic."

Caroline nodded her head in agreement.

Sandwiches and sodas gone, Jason helped clear the picnic table. "Having a picnic was fun, but I think we'd better get back on the road. In a couple of hours we'll start looking for a place to spend the night," Jason said.

It was a beautiful day. Two hours sped by before Jason suggested they start looking for a hotel.

"That sign we just passed advertised a Marriott six miles ahead. Do you want to stop there? Caroline asked.

They chatted as they watched for the appropriate exit sign. Jason slowed down as they approached the ramp. "Oh shit," Jason shouted as a car came careening across the entrance to the ramp and smashed into the front fender of their car. Both airbags exploded in their faces. Jason pulled hard on the steering wheel in an attempt to avoid the crash. Their car spun out of control and left the road. The grinding sound of metal on metal was heard as a sturdy guardrail kept them from going down a steep embankment. The car swerved back into moving traffic and was struck again. Caroline opened her mouth to scream, but the screech of brakes as the car slid further along the road swallowed all other sounds.

When the car came to a stop Jason sobbed "Are you okay?" Jason reached for Caroline with shaking hands. "Caroline... are you okay?"

Her head was against the back of the seat at an odd angle and her eyes were closed. She didn't answer him.

Jason was frantic with worry. "Caroline," he called as he reached to feel her pulse.

She opened her eyes and blinked several times before she whispered, "I think so."

The car had stalled and come to rest protruding part way into the right hand lane of traffic. Brakes squealed as cars avoided the crash scene. Quickly, Jason restarted the motor and shoved his now deflated air bag out of his way as he manoeuvred the crippled vehicle to the shoulder of the road. Once safely out of moving traffic he attempted to open his door. He couldn't budge it due to the extensive damaged. He reached across Caroline and pushed open Caroline's door. "Do you think you can get out by yourself?" Concern showed in his shaking voice. He helped Caroline to unbuckle her seat belt.

Caroline swung her legs around and pulled herself from the car by holding onto the door. She cried out in pain. A gasping moan escaped her lips as she used the open door to support her weight.

"You're hurt!" Jason was beside himself. He scrambled over the middle console and exited through the open passenger door.

"It's my ankle," Caroline told him.

Three crumpled cars sat haphazardly on the side of the road. Jason lifted Caroline and carried her well back from the road where she would be safer. Sirens could be heard in the distance.

"Do you think it's broken?" He asked as he tenderly examined the already swollen ankle.

"It really hurts but I don't think it's broken." Caroline noticed that Jason was holding his left shoulder. "You've hurt your arm," she said anxiously.

"Don't worry about me; I just banged my shoulder...I'll be fine."

An ambulance, followed closely by a highway patrol car, lights flashing came to a stop directly behind their vehicle. The other drivers involved in the crash had come to inquire about Caroline and Jason's condition. Two paramedics had also joined the accident victims.

"Is anyone hurt?" One paramedic asked. The other medic had already kneeled down beside Caroline.

"We're okay," both drivers from the other vehicles assured the medics. "Help the young lady," one said.

"I'm sorry," the other said. "I missed the exit and when I pulled over at the last second... well I guess you were in my blind spot," he said to Jason. "I didn't see you at all. I'm so sorry." He also knelt beside Caroline showing genuine concern.

The highway patrol officer questioned the driver of the third car involved in the accident. One medic examined Caroline's ankle while the other checked on Jason's shoulder.

"We don't appear to have a break here," the medic assured Caroline as he carefully placed the ankle in a balloon splint. "It's a bad sprain and there's always the chance there might be a fracture. We're gong to take you to the hospital for medical attention and an x-ray just to be on the safe side. The hospital is just up the road; they'll look after you there."

While Jason spoke with the highway patrol officer Caroline was helped into the waiting ambulance. Jason rode in back with Caroline. He held her hand on the way to the hospital.

The x-ray department was bustling. Nurses, doctors, and patients shuffled in and out. Caroline waited with Jason at her side. After some time Caroline was taken to another area to have her x-ray taken. A long time passed and Jason grew impatient. "Can you please check on my wife?" He asked a nurse behind a large busy desk.

Without moving from behind the desk, she tapped a few keys and the computer beside her came to life. Moments later she said, "Mrs. White is in ultrasound," she reported.

"No, she's here for an x-ray," Jason said.

The nurse gave Jason a funny look, then she said, "You can go in with her if you'd like. She's down the hall on the left. Her chart will be in the bin at the side of the door."

Jason hurried down the corridor. He passed several charts before he came to the one that read "White, Mrs. C."

He knocked on the door and a voice told him to come in. The room was very dark. The only light came from the ultrasound screen. A woman lay on the bed in the dark.

"Oh, I'm sorry; I thought this was the room where my wife was waiting to have an x-ray. White is such a common name." Jason stammered as he turned to leave.

Caroline voice came through the darkness. "Jason, you have the right room,"

Jason was confused. "Oh God, does she have internal injuries?" he asked the technician with great concern.

"No, nothing like that," the technician replied. "Come see for yourself."

Jason didn't move from the door.

"Well, don't just stand there; come see your little son or daughter," Caroline said beaming as she beckoned him to her side.

Happy tears spilled from Jason's eyes. "Did you know?" He asked. "Is everything alright?"

"Yes, I was waiting for the perfect time to tell you the great news. I gave away something that was yours."

Jason looked puzzled.

"The baby gift I gave to Ron was actually meant for you! Under the circumstances I didn't think you'd mind if I gave it to…"

Jason interrupted her words by giving her a tender kiss. He watched the screen as the technician pointed out little arms and legs and the face of his child came into view. "Is it a boy or a girl?" He asked.

"We'll have to wait until later to answer that question," Caroline said.

"I swear," the technician said with a little laugh, "that baby is smiling. Congratulations Mr. and Mrs. White. You stay off that ankle for awhile and you'll be right as rain."

"How…?" Jason began. He was going to ask Caroline how she had kept the baby a secret, but this time Caroline interrupted his words.

"How?" She laughed. "We'd better get you and Ron in a room together and have the birds and bees talk. I guess I'll have to start crocheting again… this time for our new baby."

He held her so close he could feel her heart beating. "I love you," he whispered into her ear.

EPILOGUE

E-mails and photos were exchanged over the next few months.

The agency has been busy, but Jason has managed to cut back his hours. He's been so helpful with Michael Jay and other chores around the house.

Michael Jay is excited about becoming a big brother. Usually he judges time by the number of sleeps, but now we're trying to use winter to spring.

I hope March comes soon before my swollen feet explode.

Good news! Our doctor says there's no reason why we can't spend Groundhog Day in Canada, We look forward to seeing you.

Love to you both and to baby Kimberly or Kevin
Write soon.
Love Caroline, Jason, Michael Jay and baby?

*   *   *

Hi Sis:

We won't go into the area of swollen feet. Ron and I are settled in our new house; it's so exciting. Wait until you see the nursery. Ron's parents have been very supportive. I can already see little Kimberly or Kevin is going to be spoiled.

Last night we invited them for dinner and I made your recipe for *Cider Beef Stew with Potato Dumplings*. Ron was so proud of me. (So was I). His mom is a great cook; she asked me if I would give her the recipe. I can't wait to cook for you.

I'm learning to crotchet; I'll need a few pointers there as well.

Today is my last day at work. I'd love to try some baking now that I'll be home. What yummy goodies do you have that a beginner can pull off? I'd like to bake my baby his or her first birthday cake—from scratch. I can't wait to cook for you. Opps, I think I already told you that.

I also gave up my part-time job at Henrys. The girls here at the insurance office are taking me out for Chinese food tonight, and then there's a baby shower at a friends place. I wish you could be here.

Till later—kisses for everyone, especially Michael Jay.

Love Amanda, Ron (and baby)

*   *   *

Amanda gave birth to Kimberly Ann on the fourth of January. Ron was ecstatic when he phoned with the news. "If you hear Ron tell the story, "*they*" gave birth to their baby daughter.

Amanda, God bless her wonderful sense of humour, tells it a little differently. "When I was in labour, Ron was whiter than the sheets; he broke out in a cold sweat and one of the nurses had to sit him down and put a cold cloth on his forehead. It wasn't that bad…" She laughs… "To give you an idea of what I went through," she tells, "take hold of your bottom lip and stretch it up over the top of your head until it's even with the top of your ears on the back of your head, then nail it in place with a few big, rusty railway spikes." As she tells the story, she laughs so hard tears spill out of her eyes. "Meanwhile, my poor Ron is ready to hit the floor. More nurses were looking after him than me; I think that was his plan all along." It is usually around this time she gives Ron a big mushy kiss. "The nurses told me that daddies that react like Ron often make the best fathers—and you know, they were right—he's the greatest."

Ron nods and laughs right along with her as she relates the story.

*   *   *

On Groundhog Day they arose early and dressed warmly for the ride into town. Michael Jay was excited about taking his first horse drawn sleigh ride. Ron's friend Steven insisted they use his sleigh and team of horses for the day. Ron's parents were thrilled to look after Kimberly.

Ron and Amanda arrived early with the sleigh to chauffeur the Whites' to their first Wiarton Willie Festival. The air was cold and clean and the snow crunched underfoot. Michael Jay had a hard time containing his excitement when he saw the sleigh coming up the drive. The horses' bridals were adorned with silver bells and bows. The bright red sleigh was decorated with fragrant green boughs and shiny ornaments. Thick seat cushions were covered in dark green velvet, and there were plenty of faux fur throws to snuggle under. On the way to town, Ron explained that this was the very sleigh Santa rode in during the Santa Claus Parade. Michael Jay's eyes were as big as saucers when Ron allowed him to take hold of the reins.

Wiarton Willie, the albino groundhog predicted an early spring and Michael Jay was delighted…he thought it meant he'd be getting his new baby sooner.

Michael Jay and Jason built several snowmen with Caroline as their official photographer.

Jason and Ron stayed out half of one night making a sleigh run down to the shore. When they came in they were soaked to the skin and half frozen, but elated. The sleigh run was definitely the hit of the week. The votes haven't yet been counted as to whether Michael Jay, the little boy, or Jason and Ron, the adult boys had the most fun. The lake wasn't frozen solid enough to ice fish, but Jason promised to take Michael Jay fishing in the summer.

Amanda and Caroline watched TV and played Scrabble (Amanda beat Caroline two out of three games). They talked about everything under the sun. There's a good chance if Amanda and Caroline were put in charge, they would be able to solve quite a few of the world's problems.

Phenomenal drifts and wind swept sculptures turned the whole area into an artist's canvas.

Michael Jay spent a lot of time checking out Kimberly. Once, while he was holding her, she spit up on him. As Amanda quickly cleaned him off, he had assured her "Don't worry Aunty Amanda, she'll grow out of that."

When it was time to return home, Caroline again had a hard time packing up to leave.

*   *   *

After reading a chapter of Charlotte's Web one night, Michael Jay suddenly became very serious. "Mommy and Daddy, I want to tell you something," he began. As adorable as he looked in his Wiarton Willie pyjamas, the serious look on his face told us both that this was something he'd given considerable thought. "I want to tell you something about our baby."

Jason and Caroline looked at each other wondering what was about to come from his little mind.

"What about our baby?" Caroline asked just as the little one stretched out a leg creating a gigantic bulge in the side of her tummy.

"Before, I only wanted a brother, but after seeing Kimberly, I guess it's okay if you get me a baby sister," he said throwing his arms around Jason's neck. "She's cute—eh?"

Caroline blinked back tears as she tickled their baby's big brother. "That's good to know Michael Jay. We'll just have to wait and see which one God has chosen for us. What we already know is that whether we get a boy or a girl, the baby already has a super big brother."

Several weeks later Jason stood at Caroline's bedside with a large bouquet of daisies nestled in baby's breath. Jason lifted Michael Jay so he could get a good look at his new sibling. Jason and Caroline gazed at their newborn. They fondly remembered the day at their cottage in Canada when they had tenderly removed each petal from the beautiful flower Caroline had picked. Jason removed one snow white daisy from the bouquet and handed it to Caroline. "He loves you," he said softly.

"She loves him too!" She replied.

The beautiful flowers couldn't compare to their beautiful gift from God. They laughed as Michael Jay put both hands over his ears when the room filled with the sound of a new baby's cry.

IT'S A GIRL!

WHITE, Daisy Lynn—Caroline and Jason White are delighted to announce the safe and happy arrival of Michael Jay's baby sister. Daisy Lynn was born March 10th and weighed 7 lbs. 14 oz. She is lovingly welcomed by her Grandparents Darlene and Patrick Steel of New York City and her Godparents Amanda and Ron Harrison of Ontario, Canada.

Printed in the United States
141265LV00002B/2/P